I've stopped listening entirely. I've also stopped breathing. I'm thinking about a letter my mother once wrote me about the beaked sea snake, and how she barely escaped its jaws. Commonly found off the coast of Madagascar, the beaked sea snake has enough venom to kill five people with one bite and can paralyze a victim with just one strike. But you don't die right away. So you just have to lie there, knowing the end is near, unable to move. That's exactly how I feel right now— totally and completely paralyzed, with the exception of my heart thwacking against my ribcage.

Because standing in the doorway of the classroom, looking directly at me, is Max.

My Max.

My Max of my dreams.

My Max who does not exist.

Also by Lucy Keating

Literally

Lucy Keating

DREAMOLOGY

HARPER TEEN
An Imprint of HarperCollinsPublishers

HarperTeen is an imprint of HarperCollins Publishers.

Dreamology
Copyright © 2016 by Alloy Entertainment
All rights reserved. Printed in the United States of America.
No part of this book may be used or reproduced in any manner whatsoever without written permission except in the case of brief quotations embodied in critical articles and reviews.
For information address HarperCollins Children's Books,
a division of HarperCollins Publishers, 195 Broadway,
New York, NY 10007.
www.epicreads.com

Produced by Alloy Entertainment
1700 Broadway
New York, NY 10019
www.alloyentertainment.com

Library of Congress Control Number: 2015943566
ISBN 978-0-06-238002-9

Design by Natalie C. Sousa

17 18 19 20 21   CG/LSCH   10 9 8 7 6 5 4 3 2 1
❖
First paperback edition, 2017

To my family,
and to our late summer dinners
where I learned to tell a story

AUGUST 28th

I am smack-dab in the middle of the Great Hall at the Metropolitan Museum of Art, exactly three feet from the spot where I barfed on my tenth birthday, just outside the Egyptian wing. But this time there are no fanny packs, no sounds of sneakers squeaking against well-polished floors. Pooling at my feet this time isn't bright pink vomit (raspberry gelato, if you're interested) flecked with Lucky Charms pieces ("Only on your birthday," my dad said—and never said again). It's a fifteen-pound gown, encrusted with crystals, just like the one Beyoncé wore to the Grammys. Tonight, the lights are bright and flashing and people are whispering and looking in my direction. Tonight, for some reason, I am someone. I sip champagne and glide from room to room, admiring the art. And that's where Max finds me, standing in front of the Degas ballerinas, in the Impressionist section.

"You know, I can dance, too." He slips an arm around my waist, and my whole body feels instantly warmer.

"Prove it," I say. I don't have to look away from the painting to feel his eyes on me, to know he is smiling. I have every inch of his face mapped in my brain, all of his mannerisms. I am constantly afraid of forgetting him.

He takes my arm and gives me a twirl, and I close my eyes. When I open them again, we're in the rooftop garden, swaying. The shrubs are covered in twinkle lights.

"You look good in a tux," I mumble into his neck.

"Thanks. It's the one Beyoncé wore to the Grammys," he says in a serious tone, and we both burst into laughter. Before I can even catch my breath, Max's arms grip me tighter and he kisses me, tipping me so far back I lose all balance and sense of self. I didn't realize there was a good kind of dizzy until this.

"I missed you," he says then, and twirls me again.

The delivery guy from Joe's Pizza on 110th appears, looking impatient.

"You hungry?" Max asks. "I ordered."

But inside the pizza box there's no pizza, just a giant Oreo cookie cut in eighths like a cake. We reach our hands in and each pick up a heavy slice. No sooner have I brought it to my mouth than I catch mischief reflected in Max's sea-gray eyes, and he swiftly smushes his cookie into my cheek. Whap. I throw mine right back at him.

We race through the galleries, ducking behind Roman statues and dodging mortified patrons as we hurl handfuls of Oreo cake at each other. I notice a museum security guard marching in our direction. When I look more closely, I see he's also my middle-school science teacher. I always hated that guy. We run faster.

When I'm finally cornered in the courtyard of Perneb's tomb, I stop and face Max. We're covered in cookie. Jewels from the European textiles exhibit dangle around my neck and arms, and Max has a medieval helmet on his head. We look like a royal couple gone horribly awry. A country under our rule would surely revolt.

Max says something, but I can't hear him through the helmet, so he flips the facepiece up, exposing flushed cheeks.

"Let's take a time-out," he says again. We lie on our backs in the courtyard of the tomb, listening to the symphony music and the low hum of chatter continuing outside. Above our heads, where the ceiling of the Met should be, there is instead a starry sky.

"You know when Egyptian royalty died, they often had loved ones buried with them," I say.

"I think it was just servants, actually, so they could be waited on in the afterlife," Max corrects me. Always such a know-it-all.

"Well, if I died, I'd have you buried with me." I turn over on my side to face him.

"Oh, babe, thanks," he exclaims. "That is by far the creepiest thing you have ever said to me."

A low snort echoes against the stone walls, and I notice a small African warthog lying beside Max, staring at him fondly.

"Who is this?" I ask.

"This is Agnes." Max nods to the pig. "She's been following me since the Oceania wing. I think she's in love."

"Well, get in line, Agnes," I say, resting my head on his chest and breathing deeply. As always, he smells like laundry detergent and something woody. The sound of his heartbeat lulls me.

"Don't fall asleep," he pleads. "We haven't had enough time."

But I disagree. This evening was perfect, all I could ask for.

"I'll see you soon," I say, praying I won't drift off until I hear him say it back. It's our thing, an almost superstitious habit, to make sure we find each other again.

"I'll see you soon," he finally says with a sigh.

My eyes float slowly closed, the sound of Agnes lightly snorting in my ear.

1

museums are for visiting, not for living in

JERRY IS SNORING directly into my mouth, his warm dog breath wafting at me with every exhale.

"Well, that explains Agnes," I mutter.

"Who's Agnes?" my dad calls from the driver's seat. Behind his voice comes the light clicking of a turn signal, back and forth like a metronome.

"Nobody," I say quickly, and he doesn't notice. My dad is a brain guy. A well-known neuroscientist—which doesn't mean much unless you also happen to be one—he understands things about the mind that are a mystery to most. But when it comes to the heart, he's clueless. I have no interest in telling him about Max, so at moments like this his shortcomings work in my favor.

I stretch and sit up. "I must have nodded off," I say, my voice a little hoarse.

"Motion has been knocking you out since you were a newborn," my dad explains, perpetually in professor mode. "Planes, trains, and automobiles . . . You and Jerry have been out for hours, but you picked the perfect time to wake up." He smiles in the rearview mirror. "Get a good look at your new city."

He makes an awkward Vanna White wave, as though Boston were a puzzle made out of giant block letters yet to be filled in. We are just easing off of I-90, and the historic downtown greets us politely from behind a picturesque Charles River. It makes New York, where we've lived for ten years, look like . . . well, New York. Does anything really compare?

The sounds of our wheels on the concrete off-ramp create a rhythm—one-two-three, one-two-three—and I nervously tap the three middle fingers on my right hand to the beat, like I'm playing piano keys. I was never any good at the piano. My teacher told my father I "lacked discipline" before quitting *me*, which must have been a first in the history of music lessons. But I still love music, particularly rhythm. Rhythm is a pattern, and patterns make sense of things. I find myself tapping one out whenever I'm nervous or unsure.

*

I lean against the passenger side door on bustling Beacon Street, clutching a box labeled KITCHEN SUPPLIES that almost certainly contains winter coats and dog food. I shield my eyes against the August sun with one hand and try to get a good look at the two-hundred-year-old townhouse in front of me. It's funny how everything seems so big when you are little, but when you revisit it at an older age, you realize in fact just how much smaller it is than you thought, and how tiny you were at the time. In the case of our house, which was my mother's before ours, and her mother's before that, this place is still gigantic. I wonder how I didn't go missing for days as a child.

"You did, a few times," my father calls from the front stoop when I voice these concerns out loud. "But we'd put Jerry on the case and he'd always find you." At the moment Jerry is slumped against the backseat, head resting in his usual apathy as he stares at me through the window.

"You must have been more virile in your youth," I say to him, raising an eyebrow.

The house is five stories of red brick, and the shutters and front door are painted jet-black, matching most of the other houses on the street. Lined up side by side, they remind me of the cliquey girls at my old school who all wore the same sunglasses. I can't help but wonder just how much of a New York City block it would cover if we flipped the building on its side.

"This is all ours?" I ask.

"Yup," my dad says with a grunt as he finally pushes the front door open, one suitcase tucked under his left arm. "Now that Nan is gone. Since your mom doesn't have any siblings, everything goes to us." He's trying to be breezy about it, to mention my mother without weight. But it can't be easy to come back to this house, where we all lived together before she moved to Africa and never came back.

I step into the circular, oxblood-painted foyer of the house, and gaze up the polished wood banister of a spiral staircase that seems to extend all the way to infinity. It smells old. Not *bad* old, just . . . dusty, as if the whole house is a box of antiques that has been left in a basement too long.

My father tours me through a formal dining room on the ground floor, decorated with landscape paintings and a heavy chandelier, and into the kitchen, which is spare but sizable, like it was designed solely to cater grand parties. Little things jolt my memory—eating cream puffs at the table with Nan, lying beneath the grand piano in the second floor living room while a dinner guest entertained a crowd, the mouse hole where I'd leave jelly beans at night that were always gone by morning, until my secret was discovered and the hole was sealed up. These are not the rooms of a modern family. There are simply too many to live in. And now there are just two of us. Well, two and a hairy half.

Eventually we find ourselves in a corner room on the fourth floor, with heavy blue brocade curtains and pale lavender walls.

"I thought this one could be yours." My dad shuffles his feet a bit, searching for the right words. "It was your mother's room when she was your age. It's a little more grown-up than the one you slept in before we left."

I look around, surveying the four-poster bed, photographs of faraway places, and the ornate fireplace strewn with little silver boxes and souvenirs shaped like hippos and giraffes. Now my mother lives in Madagascar on a research compound with real-life versions of these creatures.

"Okay," I say.

"Are you sure?" my dad asks.

"I think so . . ." I hesitate.

"Great," he says, and just like that he's gone, back out to the car to continue the business of uprooting our lives.

*

I have just pulled what feels like my millionth box from the U-Haul, while Jerry follows me to and from the house, staring. They say most dogs don't make eye contact out of respect and to show that they understand you are the alpha of the pack. Well, Jerry only ever looks me directly in the eye. What does that say about us?

Inside the foyer my eyes fall on a large manila envelope sitting on the hall table, with my name written in my grand-mother's scrawling cursive.

"I found that in Nan's sitting room," I hear my dad say, and look up to find him standing halfway up the staircase, struggling with a box labeled ALICE'S BOOKS. "Who knows what it is. She saved everything. She called it meticulous; I called it obsessive. You should go check out her closet. If I recall correctly, it's color coded."

I study the envelope, feeling a mix of confusion and an odd kind of relief. It's the first sign that I am actually meant to be here. Carefully, I spill its contents out on the marble surface of the table. Out fall a bunch of postcards printed on flimsy brown cardboard paper. I pick one up. On one side is a simple image of a trio of balloons, floating into the sky. On the other side, in thick typewriter font, is written:

HAPPY BIRTHDAY, ALICE!

FROM GUSTAVE L. PETERMANN AND ALL YOUR FRIENDS AT THE CENTER FOR DREAM DISCOVERY (CDD)

I frown at the card, drop it, and pick up another. It says the exact same thing. And so does the next. There are nine postcards, all with balloons on one side, all with the same strange birthday wishes on the back. I check the postmarks and realize one has been sent every year since I've been away, on the day of my birthday. I think of the appointment reminders my dentist's office always sent me in New York—a tooth with a face, wearing makeup. What kind of tooth wears blush?

At the bottom of the stack is a note, written on light turquoise paper, delicate between my fingertips:

Dear Alice—
Who knows if these will be of any use
to you, but I simply couldn't bear to
throw any of them away.
With Love,
Nan

I smile and shake my head. It's exactly Nan. Simple, elegant, to the point. At least in writing, which was mostly how I knew her. My father had never wanted to come back to Boston after we'd left, always coming up with an excuse. I'd seen Nan a handful of times over the years when she would pilgrimage to New York for the opening of a Broadway play or a show at the Guggenheim. Her hair was always perfectly done, her clothes freshly pressed. I wondered, did everyone just become immaculate in old age, or would I be eighty and still wearing sweaters with holes in the cuffs that I can stick my thumbs through?

Just then my phone buzzes.

"I thought you were dead," Sophie says when I answer. "Too busy pahking the cah in Hahvahd Yahd to answer any of my texts?"

I am already laughing. "So, do you miss me, or what?" I ask.

"Nope!" she quips.

"How come?" I whine.

"Because I have your clone, duh. I'm with her now. She's kind of pissed I'm talking to you, actually. She wants to know what you can offer that she can't." Sophie was my first friend in New York and my best friend ever since. We have an old inside joke that we secretly made clones of each other to keep us company when the other isn't around. Nobody gets it, and we prefer it that way.

"Well, I miss you," I say.

"What's wrong?" Sophie's tone is suddenly serious. She can always tell when something is up. It is totally annoying, for the most part.

"It's just weird here," I say. "You should see the house, Soph. It's like a museum."

"But you love museums!" Sophie exclaims. She wouldn't understand anyway, because she lives on Park Avenue in an apartment so spotless I was always afraid my mere presence would stain it. Sophie's parents sell art for a living. Big modern art, like giant spheres made of Astroturf, and videos of strangers swimming that they project onto the walls of their living room. "Really, Alice, if you went missing, the first place I'd tell the sexy NYPD detective who showed up at my door to look for you would be the Met or MoMA."

"I like to *visit* museums, not live in them," I say, rolling my eyes. "It's just not a home."

"It'll get there," she reassures me. "You're just tired from the drive.

"Actually, I slept most of the way . . ." I trail off, thinking about falling asleep on Max's chest. I tell Sophie about the night at the Met, and she says it sounds really romantic. But her tone says otherwise.

"I know I'm crazy to keep thinking about him like this," I say. "You don't have to tell me." We've had this conversation a million times before.

Sophie sighs. "It's just that you have a fresh start here, Al.

Maybe it would be smart to, you know . . . date a guy you can actually, like, be with?"

"It feels like we're together . . ." I say.

"You know what I mean, Alice," Sophie says, sounding ever so slightly impatient. "Someone you can actually *have*. And introduce to your friends. And make out with behind a bush on field trips. Someone who is . . . like . . . real."

Real. The last word hangs there between us, and I shake my head, embarrassed. She's right. No matter how I feel about Max, there is still one problem. The night at the Met was a dream. Every night with Max, for as long as I can remember, has been a dream. Because Max is the boy of my dreams . . . and only my dreams.

Because he doesn't actually exist.

2

venom of the beaked sea snake

I AM OBVIOUSLY entirely aware that it sounds one hundred percent nuts to be in love with someone I've never met, who isn't even real. But since I can't remember a time when I haven't dreamed about Max, it can be hard to tell the difference. The locations change and so do the stories, but Max is the constant, greeting me each dream with his mischievous grin and big heart. He is my soul mate.

I know it can't last forever, though. So just to be safe, I write it all down in my notebook. Sophie once called it my dream journal, which sounds like something you'd find next to the incense section in a gift shop. It goes with me everywhere, and right now it's riding in my I ❤ NEW YORK tote bag, in the wicker basket of a rusty old Schwinn I found in the garden behind Nan's house. I named the bike Frank, short for Frankenstein, since I essentially brought him back from the dead.

Currently Frank is standing between the two stone pillars marking off Bennett Academy from the rest of the world—pillars that seem to say, *Oh, no you don't. Not in here.* What they actually say, carved across their granite façade, is HE WHO FINDS SOLACE WITHIN THESE WALLS, FINDS SOLACE WITHIN HIMSELF. I am skeptical of this statement.

I survey the student parking lot, chock full of sparkling Volvos and Audi SUVs, and then glance down at Frank. The only reason I am even standing here is due to a reciprocity program Harvard has with Bennett for the children of its professors. The handbook claims it's because Marie Bennett, who started the school on her back porch in the 1800s, was the daughter of a Harvard president, and therefore a "relationship based on mutual respect" has existed ever since.

"Whatever that means," I'd said when my father read me the description out loud over dinner last night.

"It means having the child of the chair of the Neuroscience Department as a student makes Bennett look good," my dad explained. "And in return you get a top-notch high school education for free."

"Are you sure?" I said, tilting my head to the side and twirling some angel hair pasta on my fork. "Because I'm pretty sure I got the scholarship for my athletic prowess."

"Ah, yes." My dad nodded, playing along. "It's probably that trophy you won in the fourth grade. What was it for again?"

"Longest hula-hooper," I reminded him, taking a big bite of pasta. "The highlight of my sports career."

"That's the one." He wiped his mouth with his napkin and winked at me.

Now I chain my bike outside the main administrative building, which looks more like the White House than a high school, and all but tiptoe down the sparkling marble hallway, because no other way seems appropriate. I rap on the door of the dean of students' office for my nine a.m. "meet and greet," a term that made me wrinkle my nose when I read it in my info packet last night.

"Come iii-iiinnnn." The singsong reply surprises me, but I find nobody in the waiting area, so I wander into Dean Hammer's office, avoiding the serious gaze of old portraits. It looks like the New York Public Library has been condensed into one little room—dark wood, brass lamps, and rows upon rows of books.

"So, what did you do?"

I whirl around so quickly at the sound of someone's voice that I trip over the coffee table, landing flat on my back atop the cranberry carpet. I squint up at the figure now peering over me, grateful that I chose a pair of shorts instead of the tangerine sundress I'd thought about wearing this morning. All I can make out is hair. Lots of it, blond and unruly.

"N-nothing," I finally answer, blinking a few times. "I'm just... new."

"Well, my advice, run like hell," the hair says, holding out a hand and pulling me off the ground. The face that comes into view bares a bemused look due mostly to large dark eyebrows that contrast strongly against his bleached surfer curls and bright blue eyes.

"So what did *you* do?" I ask, eyeing him warily.

"Me?" he says, placing a hand over his heart as though I had stabbed him. "What makes you think I did anything?" But something about the way his eyes sparkle tells me not to believe him. "Can't a guy just take a nap in the dean's office in peace? I like the smell of his leather-bound books." The corner of his mouth rises in an almost undetectable smirk.

"Oh good, Oliver, you're here," Dean Hammer says as he shuffles in, removing his blazer and hanging it on the door hook. He's stocky, probably midforties, but looks older, no doubt due to dealing with students like Oliver. He wears delicate wire-rimmed spectacles and perfectly pressed pants.

"Yes, sir," Oliver-with-the-hair says, sitting down on the sofa and resting one arm casually along its back. "I missed you so much, Rupert, I couldn't wait to see you."

"Yes, you could," Dean Hammer says, taking a seat at a library table–sized desk piled high with papers. "You're actually here because, by some amazing circumstance I have yet to comprehend, you are already in trouble, before the school year has even begun."

"It's a minor offense, really." Oliver rolls his eyes.

"Paying another student for their on-campus car registration and sticking it on your vehicle because your own privileges were revoked at the end of last semester does not seem minor to me," the dean says.

"Can you blame me?" Oliver pleads. "How am I supposed to get my lunch? Do you want me to starve?"

"Here's a wild idea: How about the cafeteria," Dean Hammer deadpans.

"Rupert, if I have to spend days—actual full school days—at this claustrophobic hellhole for my entire senior year, I won't be paying for someone's registration, I'll be paying them to run me over."

At the word *hellhole*, Dean Hammer bristles, suddenly aware of my presence.

"And who are you?" he asks.

"Alice Baxter-Rowe," I say. "Though I'd prefer just to go by Alice Rowe, if that's okay. I can wait outside . . ."

"Don't move, Alice," Dean Hammer orders. "You're the one with the appointment. Welcome to Bennett, by the way. As for you, Oliver, I can't suspend you because I know that's exactly what you're hoping for. Do not leave this campus for the rest of the day, or so help me God I will find a way to make you sleep here, too. I'll be in touch about disciplinary measures once I've spoken with your parents."

Oliver's light eyes have gone nearly black. "Good luck with that," is all he whispers, and stalks out of the room.

"Miss Rowe," Dean Hammer says after the door slams. "Take a seat. I have to apologize for Oliver. I promise it's rare to find a student here so disillusioned."

"That's okay." I shrug, sitting. "He was actually pretty entertaining."

The dean frowns. "Not too entertaining, I hope. You've only been here about ten minutes, I wouldn't want you falling in with the wrong crowd. Speaking of . . ." He is unmistakably serious. Not necessarily sullen, but clearly interested in minimal bullshit.

Here we go, I think to myself. It's a tone I've grown accustomed to. Forewarning. "You have a great opportunity ahead of you, Alice."

"You sound just like my dad." My voice comes out a little strained.

But Dean Hammer barely seems to hear me. "Your grades are superb," he goes on, skimming my file. "But it's your teacher recommendations I'm a little concerned about."

I bite the inside of my cheek. "I assume this is about my focus?"

"You assume correctly," he answers. "All your instructors

mention the same word. *Potential.* The consensus seems to be that you tend to sort of 'scoot' by." He makes little quotation marks with his hands at the mention of the word *scoot.* "If you were to home in on what you really want, there's no limit to what you might achieve."

I know what he wants me to say. That I am ready! That I know where I want to go to college and who I want to be and what I want etched on my gravestone. But I'm not, and I don't.

At my stubborn silence, Dean Hammer clears his throat. "So, what's first on the docket today?" he asks pleasantly.

"Social Psychology with Mr. Levy," I answer, double-checking my schedule.

"A solid choice. I'm sure you'll enjoy it." He gets up and opens the door, and I realize I have not seen him smile once. "And remember, Alice, we're here for you. We just want you to get everything you can from this experience."

"Thanks." I shake his hand. And then I promptly roll my eyes as soon as the door shuts behind me.

"That bad?" Oliver asks. He's sitting on top of the desk in the waiting room like it's a kitchen counter, next to an ancient-looking receptionist who is trying not to appear amused.

"What are you still doing here?" I ask.

He hops off the desk. "Chatting with Roberta, my one true love, of course." He winks at the woman behind the desk. "Don't worry, Roberta, our illicit affair is safe with Alice. She's new here, so she doesn't know anyone anyway." In response, Roberta just shakes her head.

"Let me walk you to your first class," he says. And it's not a question.

*

"Somebody looks happy for their first day at a new school," Mr. Levy observes when I walk through the door of Psych 201. "You must be Alice. I had the rest of these guys last spring for Intro to Psych, and you're the only one who I don't recognize. Well, except for Kevin MacIntire, who apparently spent the whole summer eating his Wheaties."

He says the last part in a lowered voice, leaning forward with his hands in his pockets, a secret between the two of us while the rest of the class is still settling in. Mr. Levy is obviously the "cool" teacher you "respect." Wearing jeans and an olive-colored buttondown, he's also young. Like just-out-of-college young. And he seems pretty pleased with himself about that.

"You know what this means, right?" Levy continues. "You're going to have to introduce yourself to the group. Alice? Did I lose you already?"

He has lost me. I've stopped listening entirely. I've also stopped breathing. I'm thinking about a letter my mother once wrote me about the beaked sea snake, and how she barely escaped its jaws. Commonly found off the coast of Madagascar, the beaked sea snake has enough venom to kill five people with one bite and can paralyze a victim with just one strike. But you don't die right away. So you just have to lie there, knowing the end is near, unable to move. That's exactly how I feel right now—totally and completely paralyzed, with the exception of my heart thwacking against my ribcage.

Because standing in the doorway of the classroom, looking directly at me, is Max.

My Max.

My Max of my dreams.

My Max who does not exist.

You've finally lost it, I think. *You've gone and imagined him.* But just then somebody bustles through the door, bumping Max's shoulder and sending his books spilling onto the floor. I lean down to help pick them up, but he quickly grabs them, avoiding my gaze and moving to find a seat.

Okay, so not a mirage, I think. But perhaps a doppelgänger. Because there's no way his name is actually–

"Max!" Mr. Levy calls out, teasing. "I hope to see better coordination on the soccer field this season. Welcome back, buddy."

Max only looks up to give Mr. Levy a grin, then sits, staring down at his textbook like it's a bomb that might explode at any moment.

"So, Alice, we ready for that intro or what?" Levy asks. The whole class is quiet now, staring at me. Including the boy of my dreams, who just became a reality.

3

noodly

I MADE HIM up. At least that's what I always told myself. The combination of all my childhood adorations, combined into one perfect guy. The trouble is, I was wrong. Because right now Max is sitting directly across the quad from me, reading our psych textbook and pausing every few minutes to type something on his phone. He's wearing a heather-gray T-shirt and I want to go over and sit on his lap.

"Pull it together," I whisper, tucking a piece of hair behind my ear and staring at the U.S. history handout. I have yet to register a single line on the page. What was that article I read over my father's shoulder a few days ago? How the internet has connected our world so completely that it took six degrees of separation down to four? I probably just saw him on Facebook . . . Except for the fact that I've been dreaming about him since way before I ever knew Facebook existed.

When I was little, I was absolutely terrified of blood, which was inconvenient, since I also suffered from chronic nosebleeds. My dad and I had a word we used to explain the feeling I got when I saw blood of any kind, in real life or in movies. *Noodly.* Because one minute I'd be fine and then the next, someone would scrape their knee or knick their finger on an X-Acto knife in art class, and I felt like all my bones had disappeared. Like I was just a sack of skin wiggling in the wind, or one of those weird balloon people they put outside of car dealerships. Sometimes in non-noodly moments, I'd act it out for my father, holding my arms above my head and moving my hips in a dolphin kick.

Noodly is how I feel right now, despite there being no blood in sight. And I am determined not to feel this way for the rest of the year.

Don't be creepy don't be creepy don't be creepy, I repeat to myself as I make what feels like an epic journey across the well-manicured lawn. I have a million introductions swirling around in my head. Phrases that will make me seem witty and cool, a femme fatale of someone's dreams, which technically, I am. *His.* Like, "Fancy meeting you in reality," or, "Have any good REM cycles lately?" He will smile and pull me to him and we will kiss and he will explain everything and he will never let me go again.

"Hi," is all I actually manage to say, staring down at Max and rocking on my heels a little. It feels like every nerve in my body is suddenly screaming, and I have the urge to run very fast and very far away.

Max takes his time before looking up, giving me the impression he's seen me quietly stalking him across the quad this whole time. He finishes highlighting a sentence with exaggerated diligence, then sets his book to the side.

"Hi," he says back, finally looking me square on and folding his hands in his lap. There is something behind his eyes I can't read that I've never seen before. There is a formality to them. It's almost . . . challenging.

Suddenly, the idea occurs to me that I may truly be unhinged, like the homeless lady who used to call our apartment every Saturday from a pay phone down the block and ask what the lunch specials were. If I was in a good mood, I'd humor her. "Baked ziti!" I'd proclaim. "Is it good today?" she'd ask, and I'd say, "Oh, absolutely, our chef is famous for it," as my dad gave me a skeptical look over the top of one of his medical journals. But now that I'm standing in front of Max, he's so familiar that it's almost overpowering. This isn't a face I Photoshopped from the web into my subconscious. This is the guy I know and love. My guy. He is mine and I am—

"Did you need something?" Max cocks his head to one side.

I swallow. "Do—do you remember me?" I finally ask. And as I search his face for recognition—something like what I thought I saw in the doorway to Levy's classroom—it feels like my heart has fallen into my stomach and the sides of my stomach are folding around it like caramel on a candy apple.

Just then a wash of shining black hair leans over the back of Max's bench, and a pair of tan, toned arms encircles his neck. The arms belong to a girl, and she's kissing him.

"Hello," the-girl-who-apparently-also-kisses-Max says. "Who are you?"

Who are YOU? I want to yell. I feel tears forming behind my eyes, and I am doing everything in my power to keep them there.

"She's new," Max cuts in. For a moment his face shows the smallest sign of sympathy, but it is immediately replaced with the same eerily calm look. "It's Alice, right?" he says. The-girl-who-apparently-also-kisses-Max is still hovering over the bench, her elbows on Max's shoulders, her pretty face next to his.

It's Alice, right?

"Yeah," I muster, and extend a hand. The girl takes it, smiling politely.

"New blood." She nods. "I'm Celeste."

Oh god. *Celeste?* Names like Celeste kick dirt on names like Alice on the playground. Names like Celeste steal names like Alice's prom dates. Names like Celeste are apparently dating names like Alice's imaginary dream boyfriends.

"That's a pretty name," is all I say.

"Thanks. How do you two know each other?" Celeste asks.

Neither Max nor I speak. I can't bear to look at them together any longer, so I just stare at the ground, waiting for his response. And when it comes, I just shut my eyes altogether.

"We don't," Max says quietly.

Now I don't just feel noodly. Now I'm a noodle that's been chewed up by a mother bird, regurgitated, and fed back to her babies in the nest. My brain knows it's completely idiotic, to feel rejected by someone you aren't sure you actually know . . . but my heart does not seem to have gotten the message yet.

Thankfully we are interrupted by what sounds like a broken AC unit coming toward us, and I turn to find Oliver speeding down the path on a lime-green Segway. All across the quad people are laughing or rolling their eyes. Oliver just grins.

"Alice!" he cries when he gets closer. He makes a circle around me as he asks, "Care for a ride?"

"I thought you had your vehicle privileges revoked," I say.

"Oh, that situation. Turns out under article seven, section two of the Bennett Academy rule book, students cannot be prohibited from using a personal transport vehicle if they can provide documentation of a disability requiring such vehicle, be it physical, mental, or cognitive."

"That shouldn't be a problem," Max snorts. Then without pausing he says, "How do you know Alice?"

"When did you get so mean?" I blurt out. As soon as I do, I realize how crazy it must sound. But Oliver is oblivious, and Celeste is scrolling through something on her phone.

"Max Wolfe, clever as always," Oliver says. "Reminds me of something my seven-year-old stepbrother would ask me. Don't be offended; he's mature for his age. I met the beautiful Alice Rowe in the dean's office this morning." He has stopped the Segway and is leaning on it, staring at me admiringly. "You look great, by the way. Is this your natural hair color?" He reaches out effortlessly and lets a piece of my dark blond waves glide through his fingers.

Despite knowing he is totally full of it, I still blush when I nod.

"What do you care?" Max interjects.

"Okay." Celeste jumps in, taking Max's hand and giving him a tug. "I know you guys can't stand each other, but you're particularly grouchy today. Let's go grab a bagel, you big baby."

Max relents, but he gets up slowly, still frowning at us.

"So how about that ride?" Oliver asks me again.

"I'd love to," I say emphatically. He offers his hand like he is escorting me onto a horse-drawn carriage, and hoists me onto the Segway. As we speed off into the metaphorical sunset, I glance past Oliver's flying blond curls to see Max walking away with Celeste, his face turned back and looking right at me.

September 13TH

"ARE you Ready?" Max asks. I am perched on a foam boogie board, surfer style, at the top of Nan's twirling staircase, while Max holds on to my arms to keep me upright. I look down ahead of me and notice that this time, the staircase actually does seem to extend all the way to infinity.

"This seems less than safe," I observe.

"It's gonna be great," Max says. "And I'll be right behind you, I promise. And what's the worst that can happen?"

"I don't know, that I go somersaulting down instead, thereby breaking every bone in my body?" I say.

"On what?" Max asks then, and when I go to point out the obvious liabilities, I notice the walls of the staircase, even the stairs themselves, are made of sofa cushions. All colors and fabrics, deep salmons and pea greens and midnight blues. The worst falling on this staircase would probably do is put me immediately to sleep.

"I see your point," I say.

"So?" Max asks again.

I break into a slow smile. "Well, what are you waiting for?"

Max grins, kisses me on the cheek, and gives me a big push. Down I go, swishing along the cushion steps like I'm snowboarding. It's bouncy and smooth and way too fun. I start to notice I'm passing photographs, and when I look more closely, the staircase has become the central gallery at the Guggenheim in New York, which swivels like a corkscrew.

"Max?" I cry out.

"WAAAAHOOOOOOOO!" I hear Max yell as he comes zipping along after me. He looks like he's about to pass me but instead sticks an arm out, pulling my board up to his. And then we're sharing one, his arms wrapped around me tightly, as priceless artwork whizzes by.

When we come zipping onto the bottom floor, Nan is sitting in a chair in a red Chanel suit and a large gardening hat, holding a racing flag. She swishes it down.

"You win," she says in her normal tempered enthusiasm.

"Against who?" I ask.

In response, Nan just points, and coming down behind us on their own boogie boards are Dean Hammer and Roberta. Roberta picks up speed, and just as she is about to pass Dean Hammer, she gives him a swift push with one arm and he topples over.

"Hey!" Dean Hammer calls out. Roberta just chuckles to herself.

Max puts a gold medal around my shoulders, smiling broadly. "Nice work," he says, his eyes twinkling. But something is off. When I look closer, I see they aren't his normal, indecipherable gray green. They're bright blue like Oliver's.

"Max?" I ask. "Are you okay?"

"Why wouldn't I be?" he asks.

"Your eyes—" I start to say. And when I look closely at them again, they are a deep purple this time. But then they flash to sea green again. "Never mind." I shake my head.

4

beep-beep-honk, toot-toot-whistle

THE CEILING OF my new bedroom is covered in maps. Subway routes, nautical charts, world geography. It's obvious that from a very young age, my mother was desperate to get out. By the time the nauseating tri-tone alarm of my iPhone erupts through my bedsheets, I'm already awake and staring at a patch of the solar system in the far right corner, thinking about last night's dream. I could swear it's actually twinkling, but it must be a trick of the light coming through the window. Mornings used to be my favorite time of day. Those spare moments when I was able to hold on to Max. I could close my eyes and actually imagine his face right next to mine. Exactly what he looked like, the way it felt to be near him. Because no matter what happened when I was awake, Max was always my constant when I slept. Until now. Because now his eyes were turning purple.

It's been two weeks since we arrived in Boston, and now seeing Max—in dreams or reality—is basically torture. Last night he may have been the carefree guy I loved, but I am pretty sure when I get to school today, it will be another story.

Max has always been the guy who takes care of me. Who puts me first. Last year I kept dreaming we were in Thailand, riding elephants, floating in long-tail boats on crystal-blue waves, watching sunsets from the beach. It was perfect and beautiful and carefree, except for when it was time to eat: Max taste-tested everything for me, trying to detect any trace of peanuts, because I have a nut allergy that I'm careless about even when I'm awake. I sighed dramatically every time, but on the inside, he made me feel loved and safe. But now I feel awful. Seeing him each day while he treats me like I don't exist. Watching him with someone new as though I never existed in the first place.

I scramble to turn off the alarm and throw myself back down on the bed in resignation, causing all the pillows to fluff around my head. I beat them down angrily with my fist, then hop out of bed, pull on a gray sweatshirt, and stare at myself in the mirror of my mother's vanity table. My caramel-colored hair is sticking out in so many directions you'd think I went through a car wash in a convertible, and my eyes are bright and intense, sitting somewhere between green and honey colored in the morning light.

"You really have to get over this," I say.

"Are you up, Bug?" I hear my father's deep, pre-coffee voice call on his way to the kitchen. "I know you're up. I can hear you talking to yourself again."

I run a brush through my wild strands and trot down the three flights of stairs to the kitchen. I find my dad seated at the large chef's prep table, just opening the *New York Times*.

"Good morning," I say, leaning down to give him a peck on the cheek, then crouching under the table to do the same to Jerry's fat face. Jerry barely blinks as my lips graze his furry wrinkled skin.

The coffeemaker pops and gurgles in the corner, and I walk toward it, breathing in the delicious smell.

"Sleep okay?" my father asks without looking up from the Opinions page.

I turn around slowly from the counter to face him. "Why do you ask?"

"Bags under your eyes, an unhealthy attention to the French roast," he says simply. "When our REM cycle is disrupted—"

"Thanks, Dr. Rowe," I say. "I know how it works."

My father glances up at me from behind his glasses. "Irritability is another sign of sleep deprivation, for the record," he mutters.

As soon as the coffeemaker beeps, I fill his favorite grad school mug and slide it across the table to him in apology, waiting until he takes a sip as a signal that he forgives me. Then, after filling my own, I slump down at the table, facing him. He's wearing his old flannel robe over navy pajamas and the same worn penny loafers he's had for as long as I can remember. He's obviously worn this costume outside to get the paper. Meaning he's been seen. By *people*. I wince, and I watch as he flips through the paper, mumbling to himself as he skims, reaching up to stroke his beard when he comes across an article of interest. I know all of his habits, his idiosyncrasies. I understand things about my father he doesn't even realize, and probably wishes I don't. Like how he still misses my mother.

"Do you think I'm going to like it here?" I ask finally. "I mean, eventually?"

"Where? Boston?" my father answers, clearly fixated on something in the Science section.

I tilt my head to the side. "No, Cuba. *Wait*." I throw my hands up to my face in mock horror. "Where *are* we?"

"Very funny," he says, folding the paper and looking at me directly for the first time. Then he switches to a topic he finds more interesting. "Odd you're having trouble sleeping again."

"What do you mean?" I ask. "I've always had the best dreams."

"Now you do," my dad says. "But after your mom left . . ." He stops for a second.

"Dad . . ." I say. I'm starting to feel a little noodly again.

"You had nightmares that you were lost. You'd wake up hysterical and I'd have to hold you until you fell asleep again. Until I found CDD."

"CDD?" I ask. Why does that sound so familiar? My coffee hasn't kicked in, but it's on the tip of my tongue.

"Center for Dream Discovery," my dad says. "You don't remember? Dr. Petermann?"

I stare at him a long moment, and then it clicks. "Wait, these?" I run to and from the front hall and dump the post-cards on the kitchen table.

My dad picks one up and makes a face. "I can't believe your grandmother saved these."

"Dad, can you please tell me what you are talking about?" I ask. "I have no recollection of this place. I'm going to feel like I've had a lobotomy if you don't explain."

My dad pours another cup for both of us. "As I said, after your mother left, you started having nightmares. You were only six. I think you felt vulnerable. It got so bad that you were barely sleeping. I was barely sleeping. So a colleague of mine at Harvard recommended a sleep study on brain mapping." He pauses. "Is this ringing any bells, Alice?"

"Um, only of a bad science fiction movie," I say, transfixed. "Go on."

"Not science fiction, just science." Dad gets very touchy about the difference. "As you know, much of the brain is still a mystery. But one advance we've made is in the monitoring of brain activity—what sections of the brain light up when we see or feel different things. Some scientists figured out that if they monitored brain activity during dreaming, then had subjects relay the stories afterward, they could actually—at a very rudimentary level—put those stories together."

"So basically you turned me into one of the monkeys in Madeleine's lab."

"I wish you would call her *Mom*," my dad corrects me, and I don't have the heart to tell him that at a certain point, *Mom* just didn't feel right anymore. "But you're not wrong."

Monkeys are why my parents met. Apes, actually. People are always mixing up monkeys and apes, when they are in fact two different species. Madeleine was at Harvard, studying the evolution of language. All beings have ways of communicating, of expressing themselves, but not all beings use language, which has grammatical rules. Madeleine wanted to figure out how it all came to be, why some do and others don't. She worshipped Jane Goodall and Dian Fossey, the young women who ran around the African jungle in the seventies documenting gorillas.

So she spent most of her days with a cumbersome boom box playing repeated sound patterns to apes in a lab. *Beep-beep-honk, toot-toot-whistle. A-A-B, A-A-B.* Madeleine believed that if she changed the pattern all of a sudden from *A-A-B* to *A-B-B* (*beep-honk-honk, toot-whistle-whistle*) and the ape noticed, it would mean they had noticed a pattern in the first place. She was a real geek about it; she couldn't get enough. She went to this lecture on how language is mapped in the brain, and that's where she met my dad, who was actually giving the lecture at the ripe age of twenty-eight. They stayed behind talking for hours, and were basically never apart again.

Until they had me. And six years after that, Madeleine's research grant in Uganda came through and she went alone, and never came back. Now she lives in Madagascar with Javier. Javier is a research student half her age from Barcelona. She says they are just friends, but I have seen pictures of Javier, who I Googled on the internet, and I say otherwise. Not that I ever tell her this, since we only communicate about six times a year.

"Anyway," my dad is saying, "a couple of Saturdays a month at CDD and suddenly you were sleeping like a baby. You were happier. An odd group of people over there, but they were passionate about what they did for you guys."

"You guys?" I ask. "There were others?" I am staring down at the balloons on the birthday card. I feel like my mind is full of puzzle pieces and I'm trying to put them all together without being able to use my hands.

"Sure," my dad says. "You know how studies work, Alice."

"Does CDD still exist?" I ask.

"Well, someone is still sending you those postcards, aren't they?" he says, going back to his paper.

I stand up quickly, feeling awake for the first time all morning and more hopeful than I've felt in days. I go to hustle back upstairs and change, but jerk my foot back when it touches the first step. I could've sworn it just sank right in, like a couch cushion. I stare at the step for a moment. It looks normal, like, you know, a step. I take a deep breath, then gently press my toe against it, followed by a few gentle prods. Nothing. The same wooden step as ever, covered in blue carpet.

Apparently the French roast is taking a long time to kick in this morning.

5

law & order: special cookie unit

THE THING IS, I can't possibly be expected to go through the school year like this. Longing for a guy I feel, deep down, that I truly know, who in reality acts like I don't exist. I might as well be the main character in some stalker movie on Lifetime. I imagine the trailer in my head. *In a world where nothing makes sense, how far will she go for the boy of her dreams—LITERALLY?*

So obviously I have to do something about it, which brings me here, to the Bennett cafeteria. Actually, Bennett doesn't have a cafeteria. It has a dining hall. Floor-to-ceiling windows, long oak tables, and massive chandeliers. There are vegetarian options, vegan options, and gluten-free options. There is a waffle maker at breakfast, a panini press at lunch, and more kinds of cereal than you'd find in a General Mills factory.

What's even more uncanny is the fact they serve *dinner*. So you can head to class and sports afterward and then grab a bite before hitting the library all night. If that's your kind of thing. A SOUND BODY IS A SOUND MIND! a sign above the bagel station proclaims. But right now I'm not even hungry. Right now I'm only here on business.

The phone call I received from Sophie during free period is what really set me in motion.

"I Googled him!" she proudly announced when I answered the phone.

"Who?" I asked.

"Who do you think?" she said. "Dreamboy, obviously. We couldn't do it before, because we only had spare defining characteristics: name, age, height, and . . . hot. But now we know so much more! Last name, hometown, even high school!"

"And what did you find?" I asked, my heartbeat picking up a little bit. Sophie was a total genius.

"Not much, I'm afraid," she said, her tone going flat. "At least nothing that links him to you. He's gone to Bennett since kindergarten, he's a scholar-athlete, captain of the soccer team—a pretty big deal for a junior, by the way—and he spent the spring of his sophomore year in Costa Rica—some kind of student travel program. Impressive."

"Glad you're so fond of him," I muttered.

"Could you lose the attitude, please?" Sophie said. "I just went full-on Nancy Drew for your butt."

"Sorry, Soph, you know I appreciate it. I'm just disappointed. I'm dying to figure out how I know him. Especially since despite all my best efforts, he's made it pretty clear I'm nothing more than some new girl who showed up in his psychology class."

"You're getting closer," Sophie said. "Don't lose hope. Now if you'll excuse me, Miss Tassioni is giving me the evil eye."

"Where are you?" I asked, chuckling.

"As a matter of fact, I am in the first row of English class," she said. Then in response to a voice in the background, her tone turned slightly hostile. "Okay! God! The world didn't begin and end with Jane Austen, you know." Followed by a click. I put my phone back in my bag with a sad smile and tried to ignore the ache in the pit of my stomach. Sophie was bold and unapologetic. But she was also as loyal as they came. I missed her too much to even think about.

And as much as I appreciated her help, it had gotten me nowhere. So I've been looking for Max all day, and I've finally tracked him down at dinner. And currently Dreamboy is picking up a plate and moving toward the food line, and my mission today is to see what he eats. Because if I can figure out if he shares the same likes and dislikes as Dream Max—a hatred of cilantro, a love of hamburgers, ambivalence about sweets in general—I'll know I'm actually dreaming of a real person . . . and then maybe I can figure out *why*. Maybe I can figure out what all this has to do with this mystery place CDD and what to do about it.

"Mmmm!" I say with way too much enthusiasm, coming up next to Max in line and reading the menu. *"Brazilian* Night." My old school had two kinds of food. Edible and inedible. This place is silly.

Max just nods as he places some steak on his plate and doesn't look up.

I tap my fingers on my tray nervously and scoot it along the line, feeling relieved when I come to the fried plantains. *Here it is. My "in."* Once when I was little, my dad had to go away to a conference and left me in the care of a Brazilian lady who lived in the apartment downstairs. I'd felt pretty great about it at the time and planned to watch all the television my eyeballs could stand before they melted into their sockets. But Beatriz was surprisingly strict, and to make matters worse, every night she cooked plantains and spiced ground beef. I'd smile as I chewed, then spit it into my napkin and feed it to Jerry under the table when she wasn't looking.

I went to sleep at night feeling an intense hunger and impossible loneliness for my dad.

But in my dreams, Max would always be there. "Fried plantains are actually really good by themselves," he said as we sat in a tree in the Amazon rainforest, watching a lime-green sunset. "Have you ever tried them with cinnamon and brown sugar? Here." He popped one into his mouth and passed me the brown paper bag, smiling as I gorged myself on the greasy chunks of fruit. Then we hopped down to explore and ended up discovering a new species of fish that had fur instead of scales.

"Have you ever tried these with cinnamon and brown sugar?" I ask now, pointing at the plantains with a serving spoon and looking at Max out of the corner of my eye. *Please say yes.*

"Nope," Max says casually. "Are they good?" But he doesn't even wait for my reply and just moves to the next station.

"Yeah, they are, actually," I say to nobody while my body deflates. "Thanks for asking."

I follow him to the soda station, where he doesn't get soda but instead fills six small cafeteria glasses with ice water that he organizes in a neat row on his tray. I can't help but make a face. So boring. So not Max.

"What about the Amazon?" I push further. "Ever been there?" Max finally looks at me, but the expression on his face isn't exactly what I was hoping for. It's quizzical, not kind. I glance away, placing a glass under the milk spout and pulling the lever a little too roughly. Chocolate milk spurts all over my tray. I sigh. "I guess I'm about to find out how plantains and chocolate taste." I smile feebly.

Max is still looking at me with his brows furrowed together, but this time I swear there is the slightest hint of a smile playing across his lips. Like he's biting the inside of his cheek to keep from laughing.

"What?" I ask.

"Nothing. You ask a lot of questions," Max says.

"The Amazon is in Brazil, and it's Brazilian Night," I explain.

He starts picking up utensils. "Never been."

"What about Thailand? Or Egypt?"

"Nope." He starts to lift his tray again, nodding to a table of soccer players who are motioning him over.

I take a deep breath, giving it one last shot. "Me either," I say. "But the Metropolitan Museum of Art has a pretty great Egyptian tomb . . . I went there once." I swish a plantain around in chocolate milk for a second before peering back up at him. "Have you?"

Max puts his tray down a little too roughly. His silverware clangs against the plate, and now people are looking over and conversations have become hushed. I'm sure everyone wants to know why one of the most notable guys in school is looking at the random new girl like he wants to swat her with a piece of rolled-up newspaper.

"I was just . . . making conversation . . ." I mutter. "Sorry."

Max shakes his head, inhaling deeply. "No, I'm sorry. I'm just really hungry, low blood sugar, and a rough practice today . . ." He takes the napkin on his tray and hands it to me. "You might need this. I'll see you in class."

My face burns as I take the napkin, wiping my hand on it and then using it to dab my tray. I feel dozens of eyes slowly turn away from me, and the chatter of the dining hall resumes. What was I doing? Because all I've actually accomplished is alienating the one person I am trying to get close to, who very clearly isn't the person I so badly want him to be. How many times did he need to brush me off before I got it in my head? Of course Max isn't the same guy I dream about. It's not possible.

"Alice Rowe?" A tired woman's voice comes over the school intercom. "Could Alice Rowe please report to the dessert section of the dining hall? I repeat, Alice Rowe to the dessert section of the dining hall. Thank you."

Confused, I run a hand through my hair and do as instructed. Oliver is standing by the confections, arms crossed and chin resting atop a fist, studying them as though this decision will affect the rest of his life.

"Do I want a brownie or fro-yo?" he asks aloud, then turns to look at me, eyebrows raised, like it's a perfectly natural question.

"Did you just page me?" I ask. I'm still totally confused, but I'm also relieved.

"You're right, fro-yo is pretty girly," he says.

"How did you just page me if you are standing right here?" I say.

"Fro-yo is for babes, but I feel like a man can get away with a sundae. No?"

"Oliver."

"Pick a pastry, Alice," he says. "Then we'll talk."

A few minutes later we are peering at each other over the

biggest sundae I have ever seen, piled high with everything we could get our hands on—gummy bears, sprinkles, cookie crumbles, fudge sauce, and a mother lode of whipped cream.

"Roberta," Oliver says with his mouth full. "The dean's receptionist. She hides it well, but she loves me. I texted her and asked for the loudspeaker announcement. You looked like you needed it."

I can't help but notice that this is the second time Oliver has saved me when I "needed it." I really hope I won't be in a position to need rescuing again. "Why do you have Roberta's number?" I ask, taking a giant bite of mostly whipped cream.

"Why wouldn't I?" Oliver asks.

I snort. "I just can't believe you paged me to the desserts. I thought we were in an episode of *Law & Order: Special Cookie Unit*."

Oliver smiles. "Well, until I paged you, I thought you were in an episode of *The Young and the Restless*. What's with Captain Douche?" He gives a quick nod in the direction of the door-way, where Max is putting his tray away.

I just shrug and take another bite of ice cream that takes for-ever to swallow. How can I tell him that I thought I knew Max from a lifetime of dreams, but I somehow managed to imagine everything? That even though I really feel like I know Max, he's not actually the Max I know. That the Max I know . . . well, that Max doesn't even exist.

"You don't wanna talk about it?" he asks.

I just shake my head.

"In that case, may I Segway you home?"

*

It turns out Oliver lives four blocks from Nan's house, which I know I should start calling my house. But my house is a floor-through walk-up on 119th Street, a strange hybrid of teenage lair and perpetual man cave. Not an endless maze of Oriental carpeting and paintings with heavy gold frames. My house has restaurants representing six different countries within a one-block radius. Nan's has a place called Beacon Hill Fine Linens.

"Is there anything more ridiculous than a store specializing in five-hundred-dollar sheets?" I ask Oliver when we pass it on our way home. "It makes sleep, one of our most basic needs, elitist." I am walking Frank beside him, and he is walking his Segway, because it ran out of juice.

"You want ridiculous?" he asks. "I went to the corner store to grab some milk for my cornflakes last week, because my parents forget I need to eat sometimes, and the lady said they only carry organic sheep's milk. She told me that with a completely straight face. I just turned and walked out."

"Your parents sound busy," I say.

"They run their own packaging company, so they're always running off to China at the last minute. They aren't around a lot."

"Do you get lonely?" I ask.

48

"Sure, but a guy finds ways to entertain himself." He gives one of his charming Oliver smiles. "Like doing poorly in school and getting into trouble all the time."

"I get it," I say. "My mom took off when I was little, and my dad isn't much of a talker, so I developed a pretty active imagination."

I expect him to feel awkward after my admission, or ask where my mom went. But instead he just says, "Like what?"

"I dunno, I was a curious kid," I say.

"Give me an example," he presses.

"I can't tell you!" I cry. "It's embarrassing."

"Alice Rowe, so secretive," Oliver teases. "You could be a Russian spy, for all I know. Have you already stolen my identity?"

"Okay fine!" I say when we stop at a crosswalk. A man walking a pair of poodles stares at Oliver's Segway. Oliver just nods hello. "For example, I used to follow our dog Jerry around like we were in one of those National Geographic documentaries, recording his every move on my dad's old tape recorder. He's a bulldog, and they aren't exactly energetic, so you can imagine how interesting it was."

"Please tell me you still have the tapes," Oliver says.

"If I do, you will never hear them," I reply.

*

"I think I know what's bugging you," my dad says over paella that night. He learned to make it when we were in Portugal two summers ago for one of his conferences. Besides scrambled eggs, it is basically all he can make.

"Oh yeah?" I say absentmindedly, staring into a prawn's eyeballs. He can't just make it with the store-bought shrimp. It has to be *authentic*.

"The boy," he says then, and I almost drop my fork. "The one from New York. Come on, you can't fool your dad."

"You're right." I nod, though of course he has it all wrong. Because there is no boy from New York. "It's the boy from New York."

My dad sits there quiet a moment. "Did you know the brain processes emotional rejection the same way it processes physical pain?"

I raise my eyebrows. "I did not."

"Well, it's true." He always lights up when he discusses the brain. "When you're in love, your brain has an influx of dopamine. The same effect people get from doing drugs. You're basically an addict. But when love, the person of your affection, is taken away from you, we process it in the same part of the brain that tells us if we've burnt ourselves, or broken a bone, or scratched our skin. So what I'm telling you, Bug, is not to worry. Heartache is not just a word we use. It has a scientific basis. So you don't have to feel bad for missing him. It's totally normal. But all broken bones or burns or hearts . . . well, they all heal up eventually."

I reach over and give my dad a pat on the forearm, just short enough so neither of us gets uncomfortable. Sometimes I wish he was the kind of dad that would just ask where the guy lived, drive to his house, and grab him by the collar. But I know this kind of dad is better.

6

mRs. peRRy Requested peacocks

THERE IS NO number 1.

I'm circling the interior of Dunham Court at MIT, peering at all the names and numbers like an old lady, while students shuffle by me. Dunham is made up of a central lawn bordered on four sides with university buildings, not unlike Bennett's main quad, except it's a fully closed square. CDD is listed at 1 Dunham Court, yet there is no number 1. The building at the most northwestern corner of the quad is number 2, and they increase in number as they circle around, with the highest, number 15, meeting right up with number 2 again.

I sit down on a bench and am just about to give up when I notice something peculiar. In the center of the quad is a small cupola-like building that looks as if it was removed from a rooftop and placed on the ground. It's solid white and has a dome on top, surrounded by pillars. A woman in a copper-colored sweater has just ducked out from behind one of the pillars and is skittering in the direction of Massachusetts Avenue, books clutched to her chest.

I approach the rotunda, and begin to walk the exterior. Sure enough, next to a set of heavy wooden double doors is a sleek metal sign, almost undetectable. It reads, CENTER FOR DREAM DISCOVERY. GUSTAVE L. PETERMANN, PHD.

I press a small button just below the placard and am jolted backward when a loud intercom voice comes out of nowhere.

"Yes?"

I hesitate, not sure how to begin.

"Do you have an appointment?" The voice is female and impatient.

I think for a second. "Um . . . Sure?"

"Name, please."

I roll my eyes, knowing this isn't going anywhere good. "Alice Rowe."

There is a long pause.

"You don't have an appointment."

"Is this an automated machine?" I ask. And what I think is another pause turns out to just be no response at all.

"I used to be a patient," I finally say, smacking my hand on the button again. "I need to speak to Dr. Petermann."

"Then you will need to call the number listed in your CDD handbook," the voice says matter-of-factly.

I think for a second. "Is there a security camera out here?" I ask.

"To your left," she eventually responds.

I look, and just above the door is a sleek white camera pointed directly at me. I pull the stack of postcards from my bag, fan them out like a poker hand, and hold them up to the lens.

"I don't have a handbook," I say, "because I haven't been here in ten years. All I have are these and some whacked-out dreams of a guy that I thought was a figment of my imagination, but turns out is a real person. So like I said, I want to speak to Petermann, and I am willing to wait. There can only be one way out of this funky little rotunda, and I'm standing in front of it."

After a moment of silence, the door clicks open. I enter the circular main floor of CDD. Across from me is a reception desk, with two sets of stairs ascending on either side behind it, meeting at a doorway at the top.

"Cool place," I say to the girl behind the desk, her hair in a smooth bun, her face serious. *Charm her*, I think. So I also say, "And that is a nice . . . dress." It is not a nice dress. It's a hideous brown pattern with a rounded collar. It looks like something someone's grandmother would wear. This girl is not much older than me. She's pretty, but this dress is not doing her any favors.

"It's the old observatory," she explains. "And my grandmother made this for me. May I see the cards?" She holds out a hand.

I wait patiently as she examines them, then types a few things into her computer. "You can sit over there," she says without looking up, and points aggressively to a bench on the side wall, its back curved to fit the shape of the room.

As soon as I sit down, I understand why she exiled me here. Due to something about the acoustics, I am unable to hear what she is whispering into the phone, no matter how far I lean in her direction.

"He's coming out," she says finally.

When Dr. Petermann descends one of the staircases, he is everything and nothing I expected. Expected are his fluffy white hair and thick spectacles. Unexpected are his spandex cycling shorts, racing top, bike shoes, and charm.

"Alice," he says, extending a leather-gloved hand. "What a pleasure. I knew both your parents way back when." He smiles heartily. "Please forgive the outfit. One must take advantage of these last warm days before the winter tundra sets in, correct? I'm just about to take my bike out for a spin around the river."

"I'm sorry to bother you, Dr. Petermann," I say. "But I recently found these cards, and understandably I had some questions…"

I realize I'm not holding the cards, that the blond vintage-loving cyborg still has them, so I take a few steps over to the desk and hold my hand out expectantly. She finally rolls her eyes and gives them back.

"Of course you must!" Petermann says jubilantly. "And I would be more than happy to fill you in on what we do here, if you'd just make an appointment." He purses his lips in such an exaggerated smile that I stop finding him sincere. "I am quite booked up at the moment, but I'm sure we can figure something out in the next couple of months. Right, Lillian?"

"Months?" I say. "No. This is slightly more time-sensitive than that. If I could just have a moment of your time, or perhaps take a look at my files?"

"I'm afraid not." Petermann laughs nervously. "You see, we've just recently upgraded to a new computer system, and not even half of our records have been logged. It's an arduous process, I'm sure you understand." He waves his hand in the air and begins to head for the door.

"Please, Dr. Petermann," I say, stepping in front of him. "I've been having the craziest dreams, and I'm starting to question what is real and what isn't. My dad says you guys helped me when I was little. I want to know exactly what you did."

Just then there is another buzz at the door, and Petermann stiffens slightly. Lillian looks up at him from behind the desk, her nostrils flaring.

"Should I—" she asks.

"No," he says quickly. Then turns back to me. "I'm sorry, Alice. Like I said, I'm very busy."

Another buzz. Petermann closes his eyes. Then a banging at the door.

"Expecting someone?" I ask.

Petermann grits his teeth. "Do not let them in," he orders Lillian.

"But, doctor," she hisses. "They may do more harm out *there* than in *here*."

Petermann looks at her hard. "You're right," he finally agrees. "Go ahead."

I hear a faint click before the heavy doors shove open and a male voice hollers, "I've got seven peacocks out here. Could you have taken any longer to open the door?"

To my utter astonishment, he's not kidding. A guy with shaggy brown hair and thick glasses strides in, a peacock squirming under one arm. Behind him, a girl with a copper sweater pushes a dolly with six more, stacked in cages. They flutter and shake and cry out again and again, their green tails sticking out every which way.

"I know Mrs. Perry requested peacocks," Dr. Petermann scoffs. "But next time we have to think of a better substitute." Suddenly he stops, remembering me. "Alice, this is Miles, one of our research assistants, along with Lillian and Nanao."

"Hey," Miles says.

"Nice to meet you." I look from him to Nanao, who merely

stares back at me while a peacock pecks at her fingers.

"So about the files," I try again.

"I'm afraid it's just not going to be possible right now, Alice," Dr. Petermann replies. "As you can see, we sort of have our hands full."

I want to tell him that having your hands full with peacocks is not a legitimate excuse coming from a medical professional, but I bite my tongue and try another angle instead. I didn't want to have to go here so soon, but I'm not sure I have a choice. "It's just that there's this boy. I keep seeing him in my dreams . . ." I stop short when I hear an incredulous snort from behind me, but when I look, Lillian is staring at her computer with deep focus. *"Anyway,"* I say. "I know this is going to sound insane, but I think he might actually be . . . real."

I brace myself for Petermann's response. Will he look at me with wonder or shoo me from his lab? But before I get to see the look on his face, the peacock beneath Miles's arm breaks free, heaving itself onto the marble floor before running wildly around the room, making absurd yodeling sounds as Miles and Nanao chase frantically after it.

When Petermann turns to me now, he seems actually agitated. "Like I said, Alice." He clears his throat. "Now is not a great time. But if you'll make an appointment with Lillian, we will get to the bottom of all this."

He is lying. It's all over his face—the tightness in his features, the clenching in his jaw. His voice, once upbeat and welcoming, is becoming short. He just wants to get me out of here, that much is clear. Which can only mean one thing: He's scared.

"I'm sorry." I give my sweetest smile, tilting my head to the side. "I didn't mean to waste your time. I'd be happy to make an appointment with Lillian. She's been so kind already." I slowly turn and give the same smile to Lillian, who I notice is eyeing me warily. The other thing I notice is her employee ID card on her desk. And in the shuffle that occurs in the next three minutes as Miles and Nanao maneuver the peacocks up the stairway, I have just enough time to grab it.

SEPTEMBER 16th

Everywhere I look there are bubbles, fat and wobbly, as though someone gave a class of preschoolers too much candy and then handed them bubble wands. The shiny spheres glide toward me like happy Martians. *We come in peace.* I try to pet one, but it pops.

"We have to turn off the washing machine!" my mom cries. She is standing by the overworked appliance, which gyrates and gurgles, dripping foam like it's right out of Fantasia. She's wearing a green safari jacket and camo boots. But the binoculars that hang around her neck are bright blue and bedazzled, sparkling endlessly.

"I'll get it," I offer, and climb inside the washer. But it catches me, whirling me to and fro like a riptide, until I tumble out into a clear blue ocean. All around me, floating in the water, are rubber duckies and plastic tugboats and also some bras and socks.

"Alice," I hear Max call out to me. His voice is muffled through the water, but he sounds happy. "Alice, come here! I think I found it." The surface of the water seems like a million miles away, but I am never out of breath.

When I reach the top, I'm at the edge of a swimming pool. I hop out, soaking in a gold one-piece, and Lillian from CDD is there, holding a fuzzy golden retriever puppy and smiling.

"Here," she says. "This is for you."

I take the puppy, but it squirms out of my arms and runs to a set of lawn chairs, where a guy is holding an iPad in front of his face.

"Max?" I say, pushing the iPad out of the way. But it's not Max, it's Oliver.

"What are you watching?" I ask.

He holds up the iPad and doesn't say anything. He just smiles. On the screen is Max, and he's talking to me.

"Alice, I found it!" he says to the camera. "Come here!"

"How?" I say desperately. "I don't know how to get inside!"

"Don't be silly," he says. "You know how."

"Max, I can't!" I cry. But he just shakes his head and walks off screen. Frustrated, I hurl the iPad into the pool.

"That was rude," Oliver says. But when I turn to apologize, I see Oliver is now a peacock, and it's wearing glasses.

7

and, they're vegan!

"TODAY WE'LL BEGIN our discussion of one of social psych's most popular topics," Mr. Levy is saying. I am barely listening, because I'm totally distracted by Max's eyelashes. They're so long that even though he is sitting one row in front of me, just to the left, I can still see their tips peeking out past his profile. I *know* these lashes. Beyond today, beyond last week. I've known these lashes forever.

But that doesn't mean these eyelashes know *me*. Ever since I left CDD, the stolen ID tucked into the back pocket of my jeans, I've been thinking about those peacocks. Clearly, the Center for Dream Discovery is an eccentric place, and I had been a part of it. What's more, I'd apparently had such vivid nightmares as a kid that I'd actually required professional help to fix them. What does that say about how far my imagination can go? Who knows what my mind is capable of? I can't explain it yet, but I must have seen a picture of Max somewhere and my brain handled the rest. Which is not just embarrassing and pathetic, it also breaks my heart. To know that, really, I've been alone in this all along.

"The topic we'll be discussing today is love," Levy says now, and I finally look up at the board.

"But first we have to start with the basics," he continues. "Attachment. Can anyone tell me who is responsible for the study of attachment? Kevin?"

"Um, Freud?" Kevin MacIntire mumbles almost inaudibly. He's a big kid who has yet to grow into himself. I catch him staring at me sometimes in class with a dazed expression, but he's never even said hello.

"MacIntire, you've answered Freud to almost every question I've asked this year. I commend the perseverance, but do your reading. Max, what do you have for me?" Levy jerks his chin upward slightly, giving Max the go-ahead.

"John Bowlby," Max says without so much as a pause. As usual, he sits up straight in his chair, never looking anywhere but the board, Levy, or his notebook to take neat, concise notes. I would know, because I'm usually watching him. He has these perfect wrists. Strong but delicate at the same time, with smooth skin, the joint sitting well past the cuff of his oatmeal-colored sweater, which he has pushed up below his elbows. I'm transfixed by them, how beautiful they are, and how funny it is that such a vulnerable, intimate part of a person can be in front of us every day, yet we rarely take note of it.

"Bowlby!" Levy says loudly, raising his arms like *hallelujah* and jerking my mind back to attention. "That is correct. For those of you who did the reading, like Max, you might recall that Bowlby believed early experiences in childhood have an important influence on our development and behavior later in life. Yes? And our attachment styles are established through the infant/caregiver relationship, or, to put it more simply, your relationship with your parents. Make sense?"

I nod and wonder briefly what happens if you barely had a child/caregiver relationship. If your mom moved halfway across the world, so you spent most afternoons putting your overweight bulldog in a tutu and pretending to interview him on *Oprah*.

"Can anyone tell me why we form these early bonds in the first place? What purpose they serve us?" Levy asks. He is met with silence.

"Survival," I say without raising my hand.

Max shifts in his seat but doesn't turn. Levy looks pleasantly surprised. "That's right, Alice," he says. "Care to elaborate?"

"Okay," I say, suddenly a little self-conscious. "I mean, it's pretty obvious, right? We're born these tiny things, unable to do anything on our own. So we need someone to do it all for us. Attachment to another person guarantees we will always be close to someone who can do that. Who will ensure we survive."

Levy nods. "But even though survival is the basis for these early bonds, it's not the only positive outcome. Attachment theory supposes that the child who has a supportive and responsive caregiver develops a better sense of security. The child knows that the caregiver is dependable, which creates a base for the child to then explore the world."

Levy turns back to the board and starts writing the stages of attachment, which is exactly the question I will get wrong on the exam, because it's exactly the moment I start tuning out. *A base from which to explore the world.* I keep turning the phrase over in my head. My mom was gone by the time I turned seven, and sure my dad was there . . . he just wasn't always well, *there.*

Suddenly I look up and notice Max staring at my bouncing fingers, which I didn't even realize I'd been tapping. I slap them down flat on instinct. He looks at me quizzically and directs his gaze forward again. My whole body tingles, a combination of embarrassment and the feeling of his eyes on me.

"What about other kinds of attachment?" Leilani Mimoun says. "Like in adults?"

"Miss Mimoun!" Levy teases. "So eager to discuss that beautiful and tragic thing we call love." He perches on the edge of his desk, his hands pressed to his heart.

Leilani blushes, removes her glasses, and starts cleaning

the lenses furiously. She is totally in love with Levy. She is the first one in class and the last one to leave, never misses a homework assignment, and cleans her glasses every time he asks her a direct question.

"We'll get to that next time," he says. "But there are many theories. Some think love is divided in two categories: passionate and compassionate. Passionate comes first, and lasts only a few years at most, followed by compassionate, which is stronger and more durable. Others have asserted that there are three components to love, intimacy, passion, and commitment, and different combinations of these three things produce different types of love." He draws a triangle on the board and starts writing words around it.

romantic love = passion + intimacy

liking = intimacy

empty love = just commitment

"That's sad," I say, before I can stop myself. "Empty love." I can't help but glance at Max. When I look at him, I can't even conceive that something like empty love is possible.

"That's BS," Max says. And when Levy turns to him with his brows raised, he clarifies. "Why bother trying to explain something as arbitrary as love? It's like the least definable thing in the world."

"Don't tell Celeste," someone calls from the back of the room, and everyone snickers. Everyone except me. I just feel nauseous. So Max and Celeste aren't just a couple. They're *that* couple. That perfect, everyone knows us, everyone wants to be us couple. Max and I don't even exist in the same sentence.

"It's human nature, of course," Levy says, ignoring the comment. "We want to define what we don't understand. But we'll cover that part, too. See, you guys, isn't social psych *so cool*?"

We all mutter and roll our eyes as the bell rings.

"Oh, and before I forget!" Levy says loudly as people start packing up their things. "I brought you hardworking young scholars a treat. I know what you are thinking: a genius *and* a chef? The answer is yes. Grab one on your way out." He produces a small Tupperware container from his desk and opens it to reveal surprisingly perfect-looking chocolate chip cookies. "And, they're vegan!" he says.

After hearing Celeste's name, I'm basically the opposite of hungry. But having never met a cookie I didn't like, I am one of the first to pick one up. It's plump and soft, and my mouth starts to water. I'm just about to sink my teeth in when someone suddenly grabs my hand, jerking it away from my mouth and pulling me out of my cookie euphoria.

"Don't eat that!" Max cries, his tone almost irritated as he throws the cookie into the trash can like it's on fire, more animated than I've seen him in days, more animated than I've seen him maybe . . . ever. Then his eyes shoot back to me, wide, as though he can't believe what he's just done. I swallow. We both look down at the trash can, and I can hear Max breathing heavily.

"Poor cookie," is all I can think to say. Because I mean it, it does look so sad there all alone, and also because I have to fill the silence.

"It's made with almond flour," Max finally replies, lowering his voice back to normal and not taking his eyes off the trash. "He brought them in last year, too." There's another pause before Max asks, a little quietly, "Are you okay?"

"Yeah," I manage to say, still not daring to meet his eyes. "Thanks."

"Don't mention it," he says, running a hand through his hair. Then he clears his throat and strides out of the room, as though leaving the scene of the crime will erase it from ever having happened.

"That was rude!" Leilani Mimoun says as she walks up next to me. "Are you guys even friends?"

But I can't manage a response, because my mind is far, far away, standing at a street cart in Bangkok.

He remembered my nut allergy.

Because he remembers everything.

Because he was there.

Because he is the Max from my dreams after all.

8

CREW is a sport, Rowing is a movement

WHILE I'VE BEEN trying to puzzle everything out the past two weeks, he's been there all along. My Max. It's really him. Through all my second-guessing and anxiety, he's just been there the whole time, literally within my reach. One desk up and to the left. I'm walking down the hall in a haze, trying to grasp exactly what that means, when I catch sight of Oliver's curls through a doorway in the science building and pause to catch his eye.

"Jeremiah," Oliver is saying heatedly to a chubby kid with a *World of Warcraft* T-shirt on. "I don't know any other way to explain this. The existence of dinosaurs does not in any way prove that dragons once walked among us."

"I'm merely asking you to admit that just because we have

yet to uncover any bones does not mean they are a purely mythical creation!" Jeremiah wrings his undoubtedly sweaty hands. "How else do you explain the burned ruins in Romania I showed you last week?"

"Show me a wing bone and we'll talk," Oliver says dismissively. That's when he notices me. "Speaking of medieval maidens." He grins.

I smile. "Don't stop on my behalf, this sounds interesting."

"We're just finishing up anyway," Oliver says. "This is our weekly *Game of Thrones* Fan Club." He points to Jeremiah, who I now see is the only other person in the room. "Jeremiah, meet Alice. It's a little too soon to tell, but I'm pretty sure she is going to be my first wife."

Jeremiah crosses his arms. "No girls allowed."

"We do allow girls to join, Jeremiah," Oliver says. "It's just that none of them want to join *us*."

*

"I'm having a party Friday," Oliver tells me as we walk to our two-wheeled vehicles. "My parents are out of town . . . again."

"And you didn't want to invite Jeremiah?" I say with mock incredulity. "But he seems so friendly!"

"Oh, I invited Jeremiah," Oliver says. "Everyone is welcome at my parties. I don't buy into that high school exclusivity crap. Unlike some people . . ."

He looks to where Max is standing by Frank, acting equal parts awkward and annoyed. My heartbeat picks up as I look at him for the first time with the understanding that every-thing has been real. All of this is real. Then he meets my eyes and I look immediately down at the path again.

"Wolfe," Oliver says, taking out his keychain and unlock-ing his Segway with a *beep-beep* like it's a Porsche. He's either oblivious to the tension or he's just being polite, and since it's Oliver, it's most likely the latter. "I was just telling Alice that I'm having a party, and because I'm not exclusive, even people like you can come."

"Thanks for your generosity," Max says.

"So will you, Alice?" Oliver ignores Max. "It's Friday. Come early if you want, so we have some time together alone." He looks at Max and rides off.

"Why is he always with you?" Max frowns.

"Maybe I'm always with *him*," I say, and Max's frown deep-ens. Then he looks down at his feet for a minute. When he looks back up at me this time, his eyes are wary but his expres-sion is kind.

"So," he says. "Can we talk?"

*

I barely knew what the sport of rowing was until I got to Boston, but it's everywhere. At least everywhere on the Charles River, and since the Charles River snakes right down one side, divid-ing Boston and Cambridge, you basically can't avoid it or the crew boats that dot its shoreline. The sport looks boring and beautiful all at the same time. Boring, I imagine, for the people

71

swinging the oars back and forth, all in a line like a bunch of muscular ducklings. Beautiful for the rest of us, who get to watch them glide along, working together in perfect unison.

"That's a lovely crew," I say, referring to a man moving past Max and me along the river in a shiny caramel-colored boat. I want to dangle my legs in, but the water looks a little too murky for that, so I settle for poking at leaves with a stick.

"That's actually a scull," Max says.

"A what?"

"Crew is the sport; rowing is the movement. A boat is a shell. But if it's a single-person boat, it's a scull because he's using two oars. Rowing with two oars is called sculling." At the look on my face he says, "I know, it's ridiculous."

"How do you even know all that?" I ask.

"I dunno." He shrugs. "I just do."

I use my stick to pick up a piece of trash and set it on the side of the dock. "Do you think there are any dead bodies in here?" I ask. I have this habit, whenever I'm in a remote location, of wondering if this would be a good place to drop a body. With all the unsolved murders out there, where are people putting them?

Max bursts into laughter. It's the first time I've heard him laugh in reality. In my dreams, he laughs all the time. "You are *so weird*," he says, and leans back onto his elbows on the dock.

"Yeah, yeah," I say. "Heard it before." But I want to say, *Why are we dodging the subject?* I turn halfway around, leaning on a hand to look back at him. "So?" I'm doing my best to remain cool and casual, but despite my efforts, I am positively grinning from ear to ear. I couldn't help it even if I wanted to. I bet if we had an unexpected solar eclipse right at this moment, my whole body would glow in the dark. I can't believe that Max is real and he is here and we are merely inches apart.

"So, what," he replies, giving me a sidelong glance. He seems totally at ease in this moment. Is he teasing me?

"Don't make me beg," I say. "I've waited long enough." My coyness surprises me, and that's when I realize I'm not nervous anymore. This isn't Max Wolfe, captain of the soccer team, resident babe. This is just Max, as he's always been. And deep down, I knew it all along. But I need to hear him say it.

Max smirks and shields his eyes with his hand as he looks at me. "So, okay, I remember."

"Remember what, exactly?" I ask, playing dumb.

"I remember the dreams, Alice!" he says, exasperated. But he's smiling, like he can't help it. "Happy?"

I am happy. Deliriously so. But I can't let him see that yet. "Can you elaborate please, Mr. Wolfe?" I ask, doing my best Levy impression.

"Fine." Max pulls his sweater off and leans back, stuffing it behind his head so he can stretch out on the dock. I catch just the glimpse of his stomach and forget what we are talking about for a moment, before he continues. "I remembered you the second I saw you. You started popping up in my dreams when I was little. You looked different back then. You had that funny bowl cut and Jerry was always following you around." The corner of his mouth twitches, which causes mine to break into a full-on smile.

"Blame the hair on a single dad," I reply fondly. "He couldn't figure out how to braid it, so he just chopped it all off."

"I didn't care about the hair," Max says. His eyes are closed. "I just thought you were the coolest. I still do."

I let his words sink in, my face feeling warm. Then I lie down next to him, propping my head on my bag. "I thought you were okay," I say. "Truthfully, I was just using you to get close to Horatio."

"May he rest in peace," Max replies. "He was the best box turtle this side of the Mason-Dixon line."

We lie there in silence for a little while, feeling the sun on our faces. If this were a dream, I'd flip over on my stomach and twirl pieces of his thick brown hair around my fingers. Or flick his earlobes playfully. When we dream, we are always connected. But this is not a dream. I wonder if he misses it the way I do. A time when there wasn't this distance between us.

Out of the corner of my eye, I watch a few pieces of trash float down the river: a newspaper and then, more peculiarly, an athletic sock, followed by a lime-green bra. But what comes next is really odd—a rubber ducky. I am about to point it out to Max, but when I glance back, it's so far away, it looks more like a juice box or can of soda.

Instead, I tell him about the birthday cards from CDD, the peacocks, and Dr. Petermann's cycling outfit. I'm rambling, I know, but I can't stop. Being with him, knowing he's just lying here listening to me and only me—it's invigorating. I could talk forever. But there are more important things to discuss . . . like why any of this is happening at all. "Ever heard of it?" I ask hopefully. "The Center for Dream Discovery?"

Max doesn't say anything, so I glance over to find him just staring at me, his mouth slightly agape.

"Are you being serious?" he asks.

"About which part?" I ask, genuinely confused. "The peacocks?"

"You went to CDD, too." He says it like he's getting used to the notion. Like he can't even believe it.

"That's what I just said . . ." I start to say. "Wait, *too*?"

Max looks back up at the sky and shakes his head. "This just keeps getting weirder and weirder."

"You went to CDD, too!" I nearly shriek. This is even better than I was hoping for. If Max and I dream about each other, and we both went to the same place to have our dreams monitored as kids, CDD must hold the answers to our questions.

"I did," Max affirms. "I had pretty bad nightmares when I was a kid, and my mom heard about the CDD from my pediatrician. But I didn't save the birthday cards. Unlike some people I know . . ." He opens one eye and smirks.

"My grandma saved them!" I reach out to give him a shove,

but Max catches my hand before it is actually able to make contact with his shoulder and holds it for a moment. I swallow, and my heart starts to flutter at the feeling of my hand in his, somehow warm and cool at the same time, before he gently places it back along the dock.

"How'd you know I was going to do that?" I ask.

"Come on, give me some credit," Max says. "You always hit me when I tease you. Over the years a guy learns to protect himself." I wish there was a casual way to dunk my entire head in the river to make me stop blushing.

We hear some noise behind us and see that a few members of the crew team have already begun to arrive for afternoon practice.

"That means I'm already late for soccer." Max winces, hopping up. "I better go."

"Wait," I say. "Can we meet back here afterward? I was thinking you could come with me to CDD."

"But I thought you already went?" Max looks confused as he loops his backpack over his shoulder.

"I did, and I'm going back," I say, standing up and swatting some dried leaves off my butt. "Tonight."

"I thought you said Petermann wouldn't see you?" Max asks, his tone a warning.

"I did say that . . ." I hesitate, studying a leaf as I break it into tiny pieces. "He doesn't exactly know I'm going to be there."

Max tilts his head to one side. "What did you do, Alice?"

"Why do you assume I did something?" I ask.

He shakes his head. "You are terrible at taking no for an answer. How exactly do you plan to get in?"

"I may have stolen a key card?" I raise my hands on either side of my shoulders like, *whoops*.

Max just sighs.

"Come on," I plead. "Don't make me go alone. All of this affects you, too."

Max turns and starts walking away toward practice. "I'll think about it," he calls back.

"Fine," I call after him. "But just remember, if you don't come with me, who else is going to keep me out of trouble?"

Max turns and walks backward on his heels. "Maybe you should consider not getting into trouble in the first place." He smiles. He looks like a heartthrob in an eighties high school movie.

"Why would I consider that?" I yell after him. But he's already gone, around the side of the boathouse, and I am left grinning, awake and happy for the first time in weeks.

9

we're looking for us

"MY LIFE IS basically lying in a pile in the corner with a pair of dirty socks on top," Sophie says when she answers the phone.

"Do you ever just say hello?" I ask.

"Rarely," she replies. "Anyway, I failed my Spanish test and Zeke Davis is apparently dating Marla Martinelli. I see no other option but to move to Iceland. Or Greenland. Wait— which one is actually green? And why are you whispering?"

"Because," I hiss, holding my phone between my chin and shoulder as I clip my bike lock on. "I am sneaking into CDD tonight, potentially by myself, so if I get arrested or murdered, you will need to tell my dad what happened."

"You are really hard-up for friends, huh?"

"There's nobody I've quite reached the breaking-and-entering level with," I say. Well, I bet Oliver would be up for it, but we're really starting to become friends now. No need to ruin it by convincing him I'm insane.

"Alice, I have been your best friend for a very long time, so I know the chances of you listening to me right now are basically a negative percentage, but are you sure you want to do this?"

"I have to, Soph. Petermann is hiding something, and I've got to figure out what. Especially now that I know Max remembers, too." I can just make out the CDD building squatting in the distance, all dark except for blinking red alarm lights along its circular perimeter. It looks like an alien spacecraft, if the aliens had been turn-of-the-century architects. Or a giant statue of R2D2, the robot from *Star Wars*. I zip up my hoodie a little tighter.

"I still can't believe he's not coming with you," Sophie says. "Also that he's . . . you know. *Real*. Still pretty weirded out by that fact, if that's okay."

"He didn't say he *wasn't* coming," I reply defensively. "He just didn't say he *was*. Anyway, he's not totally like the guy in my dreams. Although lately the guy in my dreams isn't totally like the guy in my dreams either . . ." I think about Max's color-changing eyes. His face separated from mine by the glass of an iPad.

"You're giving me a headache," Sophie says. "Sometimes

when I get off the phone with you, I realize I've lost all sense of reality."

"Try being me," I tell her. I arrive at the front double doors of CDD and pull out Lillian's ID, swiping it through a box to the right of the door handle. This is too easy. I feel like a Bond girl.

Except nothing happens.

"You've got to be kidding me," I say.

"What's happening?" Sophie asks.

"I stole an ID from the girl at the front desk when I was here on Monday, but it isn't scanning. She must have deactivated it already." I continue running the ID over and over again. *Nothing nothing nothing.*

"Try flipping it over," another voice suggests, and I turn to see Max standing behind me. "You're scanning the wrong side."

"Call you later, Soph," I say, and hang up.

*

"Tell me what we're looking for exactly?" Max asks. We've ascended the double staircase behind the front desk and are searching the research office, having risked turning one desk lamp on. I'm rifling through some drawers in the hopes of discovering a Post-it with a computer login, and Max is sorting through a giant wall of green metal filing cabinets.

"Us," I say. "We are looking for us."

"But we're right here," Max says with a quizzical frown, and

I chuckle. He's so literal. We are right here. And he showed up tonight. And it all feels sort of surreal.

"You know what I mean," I say. "Our files. Names, dates we attended CDD, that sort of thing."

Max opens a cabinet and a bunch of papers go flying to the ground. "Not the most organized institution," he observes critically, picking up the papers and giving them a quick once-over before filing them again.

"Which makes me all the more certain Petermann was lying before about the computer updates. Why invest in something like that when you can't be bothered to file anything in the first place?" I look to Max for his response and notice he is doing more shuffling of papers than he is reading.

"What are you doing?" I ask.

"Refiling," Max says, frowning as he pulls files out and rearranges them on top of the cabinet. "These folders are all messed up. I can't put the F back in its proper place if the E and G aren't even where they are supposed to be."

"Yes you can," I warn. "And you have to, or Petermann will know we were here."

Max looks over at me and sighs. "Fine," he says, shoving the files back in the drawer sheepishly and opening another. Papers come flying out again, but strangely this time they don't fall right away. They actually seem to fly up toward the ceiling, like doves that have just been let loose from a cage, before eventually floating to the ground.

Max nearly jumps. "Did you just see that?" he asks.

"Um, yes . . ." I manage, my throat a little dry. Max glances warily at the cabinets, then opens another drawer and it happens again. Like an invisible person is tossing the paper out from inside the cabinet. I watch Max peer inside and know he must be thinking the same thing. He tries a third door, but this time, nothing happens. No whirlwind of falling sheets. Just another poorly organized drawer.

"I don't get it," Max says.

I shiver a little. "Me either."

"No, Alice," Max says again, as though I haven't understood him. "I don't *get* it. Papers just flew upward toward the ceiling, and I want to know why."

I shrug. "This place is nuts."

But Max just stands there, his look of disbelief forming into an incredulous grin.

"What?" I ask.

He shakes his head. "I don't think it's this place, I think it's you," he says.

"*Me*? No way." I laugh, walking over to the scattered papers.

Max thinks for a second. "Then maybe it's us." Our eyes meet, and we hold each other's gaze for a moment. His hair has been blown a little out of place from the file cabinet gust, all fluffy like a baby chick, and I can't help but think that even imperfect looks perfect on him. I reach out and run my hands through the front piece, smoothing it down against his head, suddenly very aware of the way Max is breathing, his chest heaving in and out. But then I think about Celeste's hair, falling over his face as she kissed him on the bench at school, and I stop myself.

"This could take a while," I say, clearing my throat and kneeling down on the paper-covered floor. "Why don't you keep looking in some of the other rooms while I try and get this organized?"

"Are you sure?" Max asks, kneeling next to me to begin gathering documents of his own. We accidentally grab the same stack, and when I look up at him, he's so close I can smell him. I want to make a pillow out of his sweater.

"I'm sure," I say.

Max replies with a nod, before getting up and strolling into the next room. I'm creating piles by last name when I hear him whisper-shout my name from the next room. I find him standing in the circular space below the old observatory dome. The opening for the telescope has been permanently removed and replaced with glass, so you can see the stars above.

"Wow," I say as the sky sparkles down on us. "This is just like—"

"The Met," Max finishes my sentence. We look at each other. I can almost hear the symphony music in the background, and suddenly I'm craving Oreos. "You looked good that night," Max says slowly, subtle emphasis on the *good*, and even though his words send me into a state of sheer bliss, I still roll my eyes.

"You've always sucked at taking a compliment," he observes, trying not to smile.

"I know," is all I can think to say, because he's right.

Max puts his hands in his pockets. "I went there once. To the Met. We took a train down from Boston as a family. I dared my sister to touch a Rothko and she actually did it." He laughs. "Needless to say, it was a short trip to the museum."

Sister? I open my mouth to ask—she's never been in any of our dreams—but Dr. Petermann's voice rings out instead of mine, and the overhead lights flick on.

"What is this?" Petermann asks. He's standing in the doorway in shockingly small white athletic shorts with a canvas duffel bag slung over one shoulder and a sweatband in his hair.

"Dr. Petermann." I falter. "What are you doing here?"

"I have squash doubles on Wednesday nights, and saw the light on as I was heading home," he says. "And now I'm calling security." Miraculously, he manages to pull a cell phone out of his tiny shorts.

"Go ahead," I say. "But it will be a complete waste of your time. I'll just keep coming back." I can feel my nerves start to stand on end and a flush rise to my cheeks. He can't take this away from me. Not when we are so close.

"I don't appreciate your tone, Alice," Petermann says.

"And I don't *care*." I'm trying to control the level of my voice, but it's not going well. This always happens when I feel cornered. All my manners go right out the window. "I'm not giving up. If I have to set up camp outside the building or burn this whole operation to the ground." I don't mean it, of course. I just get carried away sometimes, the words come out before I have a chance to think about what they mean.

"Hang on," Max jumps in. "Nobody is burning anything."

"Speak for yourself," I tell him.

Max ignores me. "Dr. Petermann, please excuse Alice. She gets fired up sometimes. My name is Max Wolfe." He walks over to Petermann and extends a hand, which Petermann shakes reluctantly. "I'm not sure if you'd remember, but I was a patient at CDD about ten years ago, at the same time as Alice. I promise we aren't looking to complicate things. We're just looking for answers, about what happened to us, and why we dream the way we do—of each other." I don't know how he does it. So self-assured and charming. It's impossible to say no to him.

Nevertheless, Petermann looks stunned. "You really dream about each other?" The smoothest person on Earth couldn't soften the news that two of his former patients know each other from their subconscious. He slowly returns the phone to his pocket, glances from one of us to the other, and his mind seems to go elsewhere. "It was a very long time ago," he says, lost in thought. "But I might have an idea. Come . . . have a seat."

As we follow Petermann to his office, I mutter in Max's ear. "Of course he listens to *you*."

10

for normal people

"GROUP ATHLETICS ARE a great way to meet people," Petermann explains when I ask about the trophies.

There's a floor-to-ceiling bookshelf spanning an entire wall of his office, filled with equal parts books and awards, like tiny gold figurines of people about to hit a tennis ball or dive into a nonexistent swimming pool. "As you can imagine, it takes quite a bit of funding to keep an operation like this afloat. Connections are good for business." He gives his signature smile, and I almost expect one of his teeth to sparkle like a toothpaste ad. *Ding!*

Behind Petermann's desk hangs a giant photograph of an enlarged brain scan. He sits directly in front of it and kicks up his white sneakers. He opens his mouth to speak, but the words come out in Italian.

"Idiota!"

"Did you just call me an idiot?" I ask.

Petermann shakes his head. "Sergio." He points to a large birdcage in the back corner of the room by the doorway, where two giant blue parrots sit side by side, staring at us intently.

"And the one on the left is Brunilda. Aren't they gorgeous?" Petermann asks. "They only speak Italian, from the last person they lived with, an orthodontist in the North End. I'm trying to learn, but you know how it goes, busy-busy." He sighs dramatically. We don't really know how it goes, though. I've never seen any other patients in the building.

"Quest'uomo non è uno scienziato. Lui è un pagliaccio!" one of the birds cries, and what little Italian I learned during a summer my dad and I spent in Rome at a neuroscience conference tells me that it just called Petermann a clown.

"Exceptional," Petermann says, looking at them fondly. Then he redirects his attention to us. "So tell me about the dreams. How often? Any distinctive patterns? Are they recurring, as in same place, same subject matter? Or are they individually unique?"

"The only thing recurring about my dreams is Alice," Max explains, and I blush. I should be used to hearing him say my name out loud by now, but I'm not. "Ever since I was young, she's always been there. When I was little, she was little, and as I grew, so did she. But we'd never actually met. I never told anyone about it. . . . I figured other kids had imaginary friends, so Alice must be mine. By my sixteenth birthday we'd climbed a volcano, won the World Cup, built a life-size gingerbread house—remember that one?" Max turns to me, chuckling. "Jerry kept eating all the doorknobs."

"Who is Jerry?" Petermann frowns. "I don't recall ever having a patient by that name."

I open my mouth to answer, but Max answers first. "Jerry is Alice's bulldog," he says excitedly, as though talking about an old friend. "He's the best. Okay, he has a little bit of an attitude problem, but he calms down if you scratch just below his chin. He loves fetch."

"Maybe in your dreams," I mutter, thinking that I can't remember the last time Jerry had actually retrieved a tennis ball and dropped it at my feet.

"He's in about half our dreams. Wouldn't you say?" Max looks at me again.

It takes me a minute to respond because I'm too busy gazing at him, delighting in how much he seems to be enjoying this. To hear him describing the time we've spent together with the same pleasure that I feel. How despite our rocky real-life start, this has all clearly meant as much to him as it has to me.

"It's true." I nod. "I think I dream almost every night, and about three nights a week are about Max. And yes, often they are very exotic—riding pink elephants through the jungle, exploring underwater cities—but they can also be completely normal, like visiting a museum or eating really delicious ice cream. One of my favorites takes place on a rainy cobbled street. Just walking under a big umbrella."

"A red umbrella that's also a heat lamp," Max adds. "I love that one."

"This is astounding." Petermann is now leaning forward on his desk, his large fluffy head balanced between his thumb and forefinger. "What we did here was simple dream mapping, followed by some cognitive behavioral therapy. Yes, you were both here around the same time, but sessions are private. There's no reason for you to have known of each other."

"So you have no idea why this is happening?" I ask.

"I don't." Petermann begins tapping a finger against his skull, then stops. "But that doesn't mean I'm not willing to try and figure it out. The brain is a real mystery, but I'm sure we can get to the bottom of whatever it is, figure out what wires are crossed, so to speak."

Petermann's theory bugs me. Max isn't just a brain malfunction. Some thing that got put in my head and can be explained away.

"Is it possible this is something that science doesn't have the answers to?" I ask.

Petermann shakes his head. "Science is the explanation for everything. We just have to ask the right questions."

"This is the car you drive?" I ask, surprised.

Max has just pulled up next to me in an old turquoise-colored Volvo wagon. I'm struggling to put the blinking safety light on the back of my bike.

"Sentimental value. C'mon, let me drive you home. It's not safe at this hour."

I let him get out and lift Frank with one hand, as though the bike weighs as much as a marshmallow, and place it in his trunk, while I hop in the passenger seat. As he pulls onto Memorial Drive, we are silent, the river speeding by to our right. The car is warm, the seats are plush, and I feel safe in this space with Max.

"In my favorite dream of you and me, all we do is drive. Just open road. Sometimes we're in the desert, other times swerving around woody mountain ledges, this feeling of total wonder and excitement coursing through me. In the dream I always know we are going somewhere great. But even if we never get there, it doesn't matter, because I'm with you." He glances over at me, and I wish we were in that dream now. I wish we would never wake up from it. "Have you had this dream?"

"Of course," I say. "It's one of my favorites, too."

Then, I honestly wonder if we are dreaming. Because Max does something so unexpected that every hair on my body stands on end.

Slowly, so slowly I didn't notice it at first, he reaches for my hand. And suddenly there are two hands on top of my left knee. Mine and Max's, intertwined.

I stare at them, like if I look away, they'll cease to exist. How is it possible that even though only our hands are touching, the feeling of warmth has spread up through my elbow and into my chest? I don't take my eyes off them until we pull up outside my house, when Max is forced to release his grip so he can put the car in park. We sit in silence for a moment staring straight ahead, the interior of the car crackling with something beyond either of our understanding, my left hand feeling empty and cold.

I hesitate before turning to face him, and notice he has done the same thing. Max is giving me an odd look, his head angled down, his eyes peering up at me warily.

Is he going to kiss me? I consider how dry my lips are for a second, then realize I'm biting them and wonder if he knows what I'm thinking about, and am instantly mortified.

"Alice," Max says, tilting his head to the side and leaning it against the headrest as he watches me.

"Hmm?" is all I say, because I don't trust myself to form sentences or, for that matter, even whole words right now. *But when does the kiss part happen?* I want to ask.

"I don't think I can do this," Max says instead. And then all the air gets pushed out of my body.

"I don't understand . . ." I start to say.

Max shifts his jaw back and forth, as he tries to find the words. "Alice, there is so much about me you don't know," he says. "What we had, what we *have*, is awesome, but it existed in our dreams. What about everything we missed when we were awake?"

"So tell me," I say, putting a hand on his knee. "I want to hear it all, Max. Whatever I missed. Whatever I need to know."

"That's not what I mean." Max shakes his head, shifting so he's facing forward again, and letting his right arm rest on the back of my seat. "I mean for so long, you were the only good thing in my life. You were what I looked forward to every single day."

I lean toward him. "It was the same for me."

"No, you don't get it," Max says, his tone taking on an edge. "I mean the dreams were *all* I had. I wanted so badly for you to be real, and it just got so hard. Especially on those nights I didn't dream about you . . . It was like I'd become addicted. To the dreams, the world, and you. One day I woke up and I just knew I had to give it up. Maybe I couldn't stop the dreams—and I didn't want them to stop—but I could work to make my reality better. And I did. I worked harder in school, I got more involved in sports, I met . . . new people." He looks away and a feeling of panic begins to creep slowly into my chest.

"You mean Celeste," I say, so low it's practically a whisper.

"I mean Celeste," Max admits. He pauses like he's waiting

for me to say something, but I don't know what to say. We've switched places now. Max has turned to me, pleading, trying to make me understand, while I stare straight ahead, unable to look anywhere but the changing traffic light up ahead.

"Alice, you were the girl of my dreams," Max says. "But Celeste was with me in reality. She saw all the hard stuff. She saw a quiet kid who kept to himself, and she opened me up, opened up a whole new world to me. She introduced me to her friends and had me over to her house for family movie night and got me out on the weekends. And somehow I became a fully functioning teenager. I owe her so much for that."

"You owe me for some of that, too," I say, stung. "And just because I only saw the good, that doesn't mean I wouldn't have seen you through the bad."

"I know," Max says. "But you weren't there for the bad, and she was."

At this point I would rather be dangling on a rope from the Empire State Building completely naked than listen to Max talk about Celeste anymore, so I shove open the door of his car and head for my house. Jerry is scratching madly from behind my front door, so I open it, but he bypasses me and scoots right to Max, who has just unloaded my bike, sniffing his ankles.

"Hey, Jer," Max says, leaning down and giving Jerry a pat. Jerry plops directly at his feet. "I missed you."

Max looks up at me then, and I hate it, because now when he looks at me like that, all I can see is Celeste's face beside him.

"I'm sorry." He steps forward like he wants to touch me, but stops himself. "I can't go back to living in my dreams, Alice. I've worked too hard for my reality."

"Even if your dreams are standing right here?" I ask, my voice coming out all broken and squeaky, moments from collapsing into tears.

Max just shakes his head.

I don't say anything. I lean down and scratch the top of Jerry's head, so Max can't see the tears welling up in my eyes. This must be what breakups feel like. For normal people in normal relationships.

Max seems to get it, because he doesn't wait for a reply. "I'll see you," he says, before getting back in his car.

It hurts all over again when I realize he doesn't say "soon."

SEPTEMBER 17th

I am wiggling my toes in the grass of a lush green lawn, gazing up at a wooden tower, several stories high. As I look closer, I notice it's made entirely of Jenga blocks.

"Your turn, my dear!" Petermann cries. He's reclining behind me on a chaise with ease, sipping a cocktail with a giant pink flower floating in it. Far in the background appears to be the palace of Versailles, but its façade is inset with giant gemstones, like a family of My Little Ponies bought it and just finished renovating.

"But how do I get high enough?" I ask, eyeing the perfect move—a loose block about twenty feet up.

"Sergio will help you, of course!" Petermann replies.

Just then Sergio comes whizzing around the side of the tower, his blue feathers looking nearly electric in the afternoon glow. But it's not the Sergio I remember. This Sergio is the size of a teenage dragon, and he's wearing a beautiful Italian wool scarf around his neck.

"Ciao, Alicia!" he says enthusiastically. "All aboard! Veniamo!"

I climb up on his back, and he gives me a twirl around the tower as I lean down and point him to where I want to go. Then I slide the block out and carry it in my arms as he flies me to the top, where I carefully set it down.

"Brava!" Sergio cries, and from below Petermann raises his glass in approval. Sergio returns me to the ground and I have a seat as I watch Brunilda take her turn, wearing a big emerald necklace that perfectly complements her plume. She uses her beak to pull a block out with dexterity and gracefully places it atop the tower, giving me a wink when I congratulate her.

"Pretty fun, huh?" someone says next to me, and I turn to find Max sitting closely by my side, his elbows resting on the tops of his bent knees.

"When did you get here?" I ask, sliding closer to rest my chin on his shoulder.

"I'm always here, Alice," he says quietly. Then he leans his cheek against the top of my head.

It surprises me, how a gesture so small can feel so very big. How sometimes you don't realize the nervousness or sadness you were holding deep inside until the touch of someone you love lets it all out of you, like your entire body is exhaling. That's what this feels like. I close my eyes to savor it completely.

"Watch out!" someone cries from above, and we look up to see Petermann speeding down atop Sergio's back, as pieces of the Jenga tower begin to fall. "Take cover!"

But when the first block lands, bouncing and tumbling along the lawn, we realize there's no danger. They're actually just giant sponges cut in long thick strips, and suddenly we are swimming in a foam pit, like the one at my old gymnastics class in the Bronx.

"Max?" I say. "Max? Where are you?"

But before I truly panic, his head pops out of the pile with a huge grin.

"I'm here!" he cries. "I already told you. I'm always here." Then he tackles me into a sea of sponge.

11

fetal

I AWAKE TO the feeling of dead weight pressed against my back on the other side of the duvet, and know it must be Jerry, who apparently believes we are members of the most peculiar puppy litter in town. My knees are tucked up into my chest and I'm holding them against me almost desperately. Sun streams through my bedroom window, setting the whole room in a kind of angelic glow.

One unusually balmy day last fall, my dad asked if I wanted to come and watch a soccer match at Columbia. He's not big into sports, but he likes soccer more than the rest, and one of his students was playing. Unfortunately, that student ended up taking a pretty rough fall, flipping over and landing on his shoulder. The whole crowd quieted down as the coach and referees dashed to his side, the player curled up in a little ball, legs tucked into his chest as he held his shoulder with his opposite hand.

As they escorted him off the field, my father explained to me in a hushed tone that in times of extreme stress or trauma, humans of all ages will resort back to the fetal position, because it is an instinctual way to protect all our vital organs and because it reminds us of the safest place we all began, the womb. As I gave my usual nod to signal that I had heard and understood his latest factoid, he added, "And, in case this information should ever prove crucial to your welfare, it is also the best position to survive a bear attack in the wild."

As I lie under the covers now, in a position that can only be described as completely fetal, I see his point. It does seem to hurt a little less this way. The pain that started thudding through me when I opened my eyes. That even if Dream Max would always be here, Real Max had broken my heart.

But if that's the case, then what is he doing in our dreams? How can he wrestle with me in piles of foam and remind me of the parts of him I love, if he's only going to take it away?

"Make up your mind, Max," I say out loud.

"Bug?" My dad's voice comes through quietly and crackly out of nowhere.

"Dad?" I ask. "Where are you?"

"Bug, if you can hear me," he continues, still sounding a million miles away, "find the large rectangular phone that looks like it was purchased for a corporate law office in the early to mid nineteen-nineties."

Am I still dreaming? I think to myself as I stand on my bed in my PJs, scanning the room, until my eyes fall on a beige phone with a million lines and lights on a small table in the corner, a real eyesore among the painted Chinese lamps and silk pillows.

Cautiously, I pick up the receiver. "Hello?"

"You found it!" my dad says, sounding loud and clear now, and far too jovial for this early hour. "Exciting stuff! Aren't these neat? I think Nan bought them after we left."

"What is it, exactly?" I ask, rubbing my eyes and peering down at the phone. "And seriously, where are you?"

My dad lets out a laugh. "I'm in the kitchen. And it's called an intercom. It helps you call directly within the house, from floor to floor. Beats shouting up the stairs. Cool, right?"

"Yeah, really cool," I say tiredly. "Was there anything else?" I wince a little at my tone. It's not his fault I feel this way.

"Yes, as a matter of fact, there is," he says dryly. "Two things. One, I am your father and you will not sass me so early in the day. Two, as a result of point one, it is my legal obligation to tell you that you're going to be late for school if you don't get your butt downstairs in the next ten minutes."

*

If you Google "how to mend a broken heart," which I did on my phone while brushing my teeth this morning, you get more search results than you could probably read in a year. Some of the advice is okay (Make a list of everything you hated about them! Don't be afraid to laugh! Go to the gym and Work. It. Out!). And some of it is terrible (Find someone new immediately! Post pictures of you and that person on social media to make your ex jealous! Make a voodoo doll of them and Light. It. Up!). But I know of a much better cure-all: music. I scoured my library until I found the perfect genre for my mood, and currently I've got a bunch of folk rolling around in my ears. Somber thoughtful fellows like Nick Drake, Jeff Buckley, Elliot Smith, and James Vincent McMorrow. They sing about love and loneliness and you know they just get it. What it feels like to lose something. Of course, half of them are also dead. I listen to them all as I bike to school and keep listening as I trudge up through the main stairway of the administrative building and make my way down the hall.

Which is where I am unfortunately forced to stop short, once I see Max waiting for me up ahead. Truthfully he looks a little ridiculous, just standing there watching me, his eyes large and maybe even a little glassy. Today he's wearing some dark brown khakis and a gray-blue sweater, which makes his eyes pop against his skin. Max opens his mouth as though he's about to say something, and I realize that his presence, set against my overindulgent heartache mix, makes me feel like we might actually be the main characters in a romantic drama. And now is the moment where he starts crying and I start crying and we run to each other and then—

And then suddenly a door flies open between us and Dean Hammer pops his head out, straightening his glasses and peering in my direction.

"Alice. Excellent. I was hoping I'd catch you. I saw you walking up the stairs from my window. Any chance you have a moment?"

"Sure," I say, hesitating slightly. Was Max going to say something? Do I even want to hear it?

"Great," the dean says, stepping aside and motioning to the open doorway. Reluctantly, I lead the way inside.

"So, how is it all going?" Dean Hammer says with both brows raised, the most enthusiastic I've seen him yet, as he sits down across from me in a leather armchair in his office. I realize this is actually the perfect place for me to be right now, in my heartbroken and jaded state. With someone whose own natural demeanor mimics my current internal apathy. Sometimes people with too much enthusiasm make me wonder: Are they actually that excited, or are they acting excited in the hopes that it will make them feel that way? That whole "Smile and you'll feel happy" thing.

Like crap, I want to say.

"Pretty well," I reply instead. If you say "pretty good" in my house you practically go without dinner. *You are not good, you are well!* I can hear my father correcting me as though he were standing at his lectern.

"I've checked in with a few of your teachers, and they say the same." The dean nods. "Mr. Levy in particular is a fan."

This actually does elicit a small smile from my lips. Levy may be fulfilling some kind of *Dead Poets Society* fantasy, but he's smart, I'd give him that. I want him to feel the same way about me.

"So now comes the next step," Dean Hammer says. "I didn't want to throw this on you right away, but we need to set you up to talk with our college counselor. All the other juniors got assigned one at the end of their sophomore year."

"One?" I say. "You have more than one college counselor?"

Dean Hammer nods solemnly again. "Another *Bennett benefit*," he says like he's advertising car insurance he doesn't believe in. "We actually have four. Most of them are at capacity, but not to worry, I found just the one for you. She had a little space."

*

As I approach Delilah Weatherbee's office, I can tell immediately that, like me, she does not belong. For one thing, her office isn't even in the administrative wing. It's in the attic of the creative arts center, and I have to push past fashion mannequins and forgotten sculptures and broken easels to even knock. Also, it smells like incense, and the sound of New Age flute music is whistling from beneath the door.

Delilah opens it almost instantly. "Alice," is all she says, her face glowing and rosy and tilted to one side, her arms stretched wide. I understand almost too late that I am supposed to embrace her. Which I do, and she smells like patchouli. She pushes me away but, still gripping my shoulders, whispers, "Welcome."

Delilah ushers me in, all effortless beach waves and bare feet, her long linen skirt trailing on the floor. "Have a seat," she says, nodding to the corner as she pours some tea. I look over, but there are no chairs. Then I notice the floor pillows.

"So," Delilah says when we are seated cross-legged, facing each other, each clutching a small mug of fragrant green tea. "Who is Alice Rowe?"

"I don't think I understand the question," I say.

"Exactly," Delilah says, which only confuses me more. "I know you met with Dean Hammer and discussed your academics. Good work, by the way." She gives my knee a squeeze. "But now I want to ask you: What else?"

"What else what?" I ask.

"What else is there to Alice? What are your interests? What clubs have you joined? Who have you been hanging out with? You see, Bennett is a great school, but in order to make you a good candidate for college, we really need to cultivate a sense of self. I like to encourage my students to practice a certain kind of *mindfulness*. Taking time, paying attention to your likes and dislikes, your behavioral tendencies, to help you figure out who you are."

I don't think she really wants to hear my answer to who I am hanging out with, because currently it's Oliver, the school's biggest troublemaker; my father, a middle-aged neuroscientist; Jerry, a geriatric bulldog; and golden boy Max Wolfe, but only in an subconscious state. It also strikes me as amusing that she and Dean Hammer could be so very different and yet very much the same. This is not far from asking me what I want on my tombstone.

"Um, I think I must have missed the signup deadline for clubs?" I try. "I hadn't really thought about it . . ."

Delilah studies me, her head nodding over and over. Her stare makes me uncomfortable, so I glance out the window, and that's when I see Sergio and Brunilda, watching me from a tree outside. Sergio lifts a wing, salutes me, and they both fly off.

What in the—? Am I asleep? I blink a few times.

"Well, what did you do at your old school?" Delilah is asking.

Explored. Visited the museums. Played chess with some old guys in Central Park. Tried to keep Jerry from eating the ducks in the pond, at which I had only a ninety-eight percent success rate.

"I spent a lot of time outside," I say. And then instantly realize it sounds like I do a lot of drugs.

"That's helpful!" Delilah says. "What about the orienteering society? They organize weekly camping trips, hikes up local mountains . . ."

My eyes go wide with horror. "Not that kind of outside. I grew up in New York City."

Delilah raises her eyebrows. "How very cosmopolitan!" she says. Then she reaches into the bookshelf next to us and pulls down a giant stack of fliers. "Here, why don't you review some of these. They might give you some ideas."

"Can I just take them with me and decide later?" I ask.

Can I just take them with me and throw them out? I think.

Delilah smiles knowingly. "I'd prefer if you picked three before leaving my office today. I promise you will find something you'll like. We have over forty clubs and societies here at Bennett."

I glance down at the fliers, and the first one I see says, "Amateur Juggling Coalition."

"I'm sure I will," I say, flipping the page immediately. "Eventually."

12

please choose an orb

IN ANOTHER ONE of her infrequent letters from Africa, my mother described a German explorer who, in 1878, wrote about being led by a tribe called the Mkodo through the Madagascar jungle. The explorer claimed he watched a giant pineapple-shaped tree strangle and then ingest a woman, its tendrils wrapping themselves around her body while its huge leaves slowly folded over her like some sick cocoon or, in my imagination, some horror movie from the fifties with poor set design. The entire story, the tribe that led him, and the explorer himself were later deemed a fraud, but that didn't stop others from still suspecting the killer plant's existence.

At the moment, while I sit on a bench within the Bennett Academy greenhouse, a beautiful run-down building composed entirely of glass walls and a green metal skeletal structure, I am willing to admit that I am one of those people. Because in the corner of the greenhouse farthest from the main entrance is a plant that doesn't just appear to be looking at me; it also looks like it might try to bite me if I get too close. As I watch, I actually think I see it lean closer to sniff the hand of a girl standing next to it in a purple skirt, like Jerry sniffs a treat he's about to devour. But when I look again, it hasn't moved, and the girl is unharmed.

I really tried everything to avoid coming here. I don't think I have so much as watered a flower in my entire life. But Delilah told me that joining the bocce team wasn't enough, and my attempt to join SASM yesterday—Students Against Social Media—didn't go very well.

At the first meeting we went around the circle introducing ourselves, and when I told them my name, a girl named Gigi typed something aggressively on a laptop.

"Alice Rowe, formerly of Manhattan?" Gigi asked.

"That's correct," I answered.

"I see here you have a Facebook account." She looked up at me over the top of her sleek silver glasses. "Is it active?"

"I never go on it," I said.

"And what about Instagram?" she asked. "JerrysWorld?"

"Does that really count?" I answered, suddenly feeling a little hot. I'd taken chemistry exams easier than this. "It's just photos . . . I really like photography."

"So do I," Gigi said. "But I don't need the whole *world* to 'like' my photography to feel a sense of satisfaction and belonging." When she said the word *like*, she took her pointer finger and jabbed it into the air in front of her, as though poking an invisible heart icon on an invisible Instagram feed.

"I don't use it that much . . ." I try.

"So you did not post a photo just this morning of a bulldog lying in a pile of leaves?" she asked.

"He was really excited about the first day of fall," I say, a little more defensively this time.

"And the Spotify? I see you have over one hundred followers."

Needless to say, it was suggested to me that I not return to Students Against Social Media.

"Okay guys," a guy named Parker says now, standing up and facing the handful of students that are seated around the shelves of plants and potting soil. He's wearing a short-sleeved plaid shirt, those strange sneakers that have individual spaces for your toes, and is screwing on the cap to a Nalgene bottle with a sticker on it that says, MAY THE FOREST BE WITH YOU. "Really psyched to see such an excellent turnout for the Terrarium Club. I'm going to assume you all know what a terrarium is, but in case not, it's basically a small-scale ecosystem within a container. Just plants, no animals or reptiles of any kind. We'll begin with closed terrariums, where sunlight and the closed environment are used to circulate water to be self-sustaining, and move on to open terrariums toward the end of the semester, which focus primarily on plants like succulents, which require drier air."

"I have a question," someone says, and I recognize the nasal tone and poor voice modulation immediately. "Could we actually start with open? I want to make a desert vacation home for my lizard, Socrates, and I'd like to give it to him for his birthday in November." Jeremiah pushes his glasses up further on his face and blinks a few times.

"Jeremiah, what did I just say?" Parker replies, his patience already waning. "Terrariums are meant to be independent ecosystems. They aren't meant to house creatures."

"You're not the boss of me," Jeremiah says matter-of-factly. I wonder if Jeremiah gets beaten up every day.

"Sorry I'm late," Celeste says as she hustles through the doorway, and Parker's face changes from annoyance to deer-in-headlights in a matter of seconds. "I was coming back from third period when I found this injured baby squirrel on the side of the path. I brought it to Mrs. Hakes, and she's going to nurse it back to health. You should see its tiny cast!" She throws her leather bag down by a turquoise planter and plops her butt casually on the dirty floor, crossing her legs. "What did I miss?"

I study Celeste, wearing perfectly distressed jeans, embellished boots, and the kind of T-shirt that looks like a hand-me-down but was actually purchased for at least fifty bucks, and wonder if, like Sleeping Beauty, she is dressed by a band of merry bluebirds every morning. Except these would be merry hipster bluebirds with tiny fedoras and vests. And Max would be her prince.

Ugh.

I'm not the only one staring. So are Parker, Jeremiah, and the handful of other students in the room, because just my luck, Celeste seems capable of actually producing a near-celebrity reaction. She glances around, smiling at everyone. Then she looks at me. I freeze, wondering what's coming next. A watchful stare? A look that says, *Stay away from my boyfriend, dream-freak?*

"Oh, hey!" Celeste calls out with a wave.

I smile feebly and am startled to see her turn next to Jeremiah, of all people. Aren't people like them supposed to mutually loathe each other? "Hey, Jer," Celeste says. "How's Socrates?"

Jeremiah glares at Parker. "Homeless."

Parker rolls his eyes. "Forget it. And it's no problem, Celeste. I was just explaining what we'll be up to for the rest of the semester. We'll start by building a basic, small-scale terrarium today, just something easy, and then I'm going to ask you guys to actually cultivate your own plants, because I have a sur-prise . . ." He bites his bottom lip as he rocks on his heels a bit, trying hard to contain his excitement. "I spoke with Dean Hammer this morning, and, with work on the new science center being finished soon, he has commissioned us for a project—a large-scale succulent wall!" Parker holds his hands out like *ta-da!* and everyone *oohs* and *aahs,* and I try to Google *succulent wall* on my phone without anyone noticing.

"Now, if you'll all please choose a glass orb and grab a bag of rocks and soil from the back table, I can begin the terrarium demonstration," Parker says.

Once we've retrieved our materials, Celeste comes to take a seat with me at one of the workstations. "How's it going?" she asks. "Dean Hammer got you down?"

I look up at her. "How did you know?"

Celeste giggles. "Because I was new last year. Let me guess. Potential and opportunity?" I nod slowly, and she puts a hand on my forearm and says, "Don't worry, soon there will be someone else for him to mold into the perfect Bennett candidate. Just hang in there."

I'm beginning to get it, why people react to her the way they do. I mean, she's dating the guy I've been in love with my whole life. I should hate her . . . but for some reason I don't.

"Thanks," I say, then lean in closer. "By the way, what's a succulent wall?"

Celeste pulls out a blue sketchbook covered in ink drawings and opens to a page with pasted photos. They're of beautiful murals on the sides of buildings, but made entirely out of cactus-like plants, in shades of purple and green and gray-blue. Bordering the images are sketches of flowers and vines, long tendrils reaching from one page to another.

"Cool," I say, and I mean it.

"They are pretty cool." Celeste nods, putting her sketchbook away. "So, why did you pick this club if you didn't even know what a succulent was?" she asks. It's not accusatory; it's interested.

"Honestly? Mrs. Weatherbee told me I had to choose three clubs, and this was one of the first I saw." I shrug. "How about you?"

"My parents have a farm about forty-five minutes outside town," Celeste says. "That's where we live. I've had my own garden since I was practically old enough to carry a watering can. And I'm pretty into design . . . it just seemed like kind of a cool comingling of the two."

I study Celeste's gorgeous olive skin and her earnest, deep brown eyes, and I realize with only mild dismay that she is, like, the coolest of cool. And more importantly, she's *nice*. The idea of her and Max forming some superhuman dynamic duo is easier to picture than I'd like to admit.

"So, I feel like we should talk about something," Celeste says as she removes some soil from a bag and puts a thin layer in the base of her orb. I follow her lead, my hand jerking involuntarily and spilling some on the table. Celeste doesn't even comment on it. Here it comes. Has Max told her something?

"It's about Max," she says, giving a shy smile.

Oh God. I put down my bag of potting soil. "You don't need to worry—" I start to say.

"No, no, let me finish," Celeste says. "I just feel like he gave you a really dumb impression on the quad the first day of school. Oliver just brings out a . . . pretty unattractive side of him."

"Oh?" I say, relieved that this isn't about me. "Why?"

"They used to be friends a few years back, but then they started to grow apart. It's kind of a long story, but Max was different then. More reserved."

I run my tongue along the inside of my bottom teeth, something to distract my mouth from saying *I know*. That he told me all about it last week, right before he broke my heart. But explaining to Celeste that Max and I were hanging out would require me to also explain where, and I am definitely not getting into CDD with her. It's the only thing I share with him that's just ours . . . besides the dreams, of course. And if she ever shows up in one of those, I will resolve to never fall asleep again.

Celeste is still explaining the history. "Anyway, one day he started to change. He started to focus more on school, joined the soccer team—which, turns out, he's really good at!" She laughs like it's the craziest thing ever, like, *Oh, that Max, isn't he a hoot?* and I force myself to laugh, too. It comes out more like a chest cough. "And then he got a whole different group of friends . . . I don't think Oliver was very happy about that. And Max was disappointed that Oliver didn't want him to be happy."

"Wow." I feel like I'm reading a story where Oliver and Max are fictional characters. I've never even heard of the book, but Celeste knows it all. And she's really nice. And I am a horrible person for even entertaining the idea that her boyfriend should be mine.

Except he was mine first, whispers a tiny voice in the back of my mind.

"Anyway," Celeste says. "I know I'm talking your ear off. I just didn't want you to get the wrong impression of Max. He's actually great, once you get to know him."

Is this really happening? Celeste is giving me advice about a guy I've known longer than she's been able to spell her own name? But the irony is that she's kind of right. I'm beginning to realize that maybe I never knew him. Not entirely anyway. And that dreams and reality are far from the same.

13

welcome to the
bat cave

"HEY, ALICE!" I hear Celeste call out after Terrarium Club, just as I'm unlocking Frank to head home. It's moments like these when I really wish I had my earbuds in and could peel out of the parking lot and never look back like I hadn't heard her at all. I'm exhausted. Between the dean and Delilah and Celeste, there's a lot I need to process. But my earbuds are, as always, tangled in an impossible knot at the bottom of my bag.

"Hey!" I say, turning and putting on my biggest smile.

"I have kind of a big favor," Celeste asks, biting her lip as she walks over to me. "Is there any chance I can come to your house before the party tonight? You must live nearby if you biked here, right? It's just that I live pretty far outside the city, and I don't really want to go out and back. It could be kind of fun! We could get ready together and I could give you the lowdown on who will be there . . ."

There are a lot of thoughts running through my head. For example, as one of the most adored girls in school, doesn't Celeste have about a million people she could be hanging out with? I wonder if she's doing the whole "keep your friends close and your enemies closer" thing but wipe the idea from my mind almost instantly. She's just not that girl. Does she actually just want to be my friend? I push all those questions out of my mind, because there's only one that's actually on the tip of my tongue.

"What party?" I ask. Then, "Are you sure I was invited?"

Celeste laughs. "Oliver's thing," she says. Then she looks nervous. "Wait, aren't you guys friends?"

I close my eyes, letting my head fall back in exhaustion. "Is it Friday already?" I ask.

"I know how you feel," Celeste says. "But you should go! I'm making Max go, too. And then you could get to know him better, so he can prove he's not as much of a *doof* as you saw this last week." She raises her eyebrows and laughs.

I force a laugh, too, but something about this statement sends a tiny flame through my limbs. Yes, I am well aware that Max and Celeste are dating. We've been talking about him all afternoon. But the idea of him making a date with her, an actual prearranged time to see her, when I can practically still feel his head resting on top of mine below the Jenga tower, when the image of his stare in the hallway is still so fresh in my memory, makes me want to throw up, or break something expensive, or both.

Don't freak out, Alice, I say to myself. *You can do this. Celeste is genuinely cool, and she's asking you to hang out, and you could use some friends. And besides, you deserve some answers.*

"I'd love to," I say, even if it is the last thing I want to do.

* * *

"This is better than Newbury Street!" Celeste exclaims for possibly the tenth time, looking around with awe. We're camped out in the middle of Nan's giant walk-in closet, a box of pepperoni pizza on the floor between us. "Your grandmother had impeccable taste."

My dad wasn't kidding when he said that Nan saved everything. We're surrounded by clothing on three sides. And he wasn't kidding about the color-coding either. It's a ROYGBIV of textiles. The beautiful wool suits she wore in her older age, creams and fine tweeds and moss greens. And pieces she couldn't have possibly worn in years, like silk strapless gowns and mod minidresses and heels she could never have managed after the age of eighty.

Celeste and I were getting ready in my room when she asked if she could borrow something "funky," and I, too afraid to tell her I don't own anything even remotely interesting, directed our attention here.

"What's so great about Newbury Street?" I ask. I'd been

there a few times since we moved, once to pick up some decent coffee at a French bistro when our grinder broke, and another time to buy a new pair of leather booties.

"It's arguably the best vintage in the city," Celeste says, getting up and rummaging through a vanity that's built into the wall, with giant lightbulbs rimming the mirror like you'd see backstage at a Broadway theater. "By the way, this light makes your skin look flawless. Okay, what about these?" She whirls around from the mirror, waving her arm with a flourish, a series of chunky art deco bracelets extending up her arm.

"I love it!" I say, and take another bite of pizza. Whoever invented pizza, I'd like to kiss them on the mouth. "Take them."

"Alice." Celeste looks scandalized. "I will *borrow* them. I can't take them! Don't be ridiculous."

I shrug. "It's not like anyone's going to claim them," I say. "My mom's not around."

Celeste takes a seat across from me on the floor, tucking her legs underneath her body. "Is it okay to ask why?"

"She's a primatologist," I explain, just enough to hopefully skirt the issue. "She's studying lemurs in Madagascar."

But then Celeste asks the dreaded question, the question I hope most people will just let slide. "Well, when will she be back?"

"Um . . . she left ten years ago and hasn't come home yet . . ." I shrug, then glance over at Celeste from the corner of my eye. But she doesn't look uncomfortable at all.

"So your parents are divorced?" Celeste asks.

"Not really . . ." I say. I can't believe I'm telling her all this. These are the kinds of things I only tell Sophie about. "They just sort of never dealt with it. Their marriage. But they definitely aren't together."

"So you have not seen your mother in ten years."

I want to be annoyed at this statement, and at Celeste for pushing the issue, but oddly I'm not. There is judgment in her tone, but I can tell it's not at me.

"I mean, I've *seen* her . . ." I stretch my legs out, knocking my feet together like a little kid who's just been asked a tough question. "We Skype once in a while . . . but it's usually too awkward. We do better in writing. I get a letter or postcard from her every couple of months, telling me about her latest adventure and any new exciting findings in her research."

"And what do you tell *her*?" Celeste asks.

I pick up another slice of pizza. "She never really asks," I explain. Then I take a huge bite so I don't have to say any more. But Celeste doesn't say anything, either, and I feel a need to fill the silence. "So the point is, the jewelry is up for grabs," I say, waving my slice toward the vanity, my mouth still a bit full. "I mean, look at me—it's not like *I'm* gonna wear it." Currently I'm wearing a worn-in chambray shirt, black jeans, white Keds, and zero "funk."

Celeste gazes at me, resting back on her hands with her head tilted to the side. "Actually," she says, "you are going to wear it. And while we're at it, you're going to wear some eyeliner, too."

I smile and wish I wasn't growing fonder of Celeste by the second.

*

When Oliver told me he lived a few blocks from my house, I assumed he meant a house just like mine. Old and dusty, with so many stairs a real estate agent could advertise guaranteed glute definition in the listing. I did not assume what he actually meant was the penthouse apartment at the Taj Hotel, with suited doormen, a gracious concierge, and an elevator that moved so smoothly and soundlessly that at first I was afraid we'd gotten stuck.

When Celeste and I arrive, pushing our way through a lushly carpeted, crowded room of our schoolmates, we find Oliver alone on the balcony overlooking the Public Garden, a glass of something dark balanced perfectly in his left hand.

"Yes, that's correct," he says politely into his phone, as though making a dentist appointment. "I want thirty-six pizzas delivered to the Taj. Half cheese, half pepperoni and onion. Oliver Healey. You have my card on file. And what's your name? Denise? Thank you ever so much, Denise. You're an angel."

Oliver hangs up the phone and turns around, his eyes lighting up at the sight of us. "Laaaadies!" he says, wrapping an arm around each of our shoulders. "Welcome to the Bat Cave. May I offer you a beverage?"

"It's just that he's so dreamy," Leilani Mimoun gushes, and I can barely hear her. We—she, Celeste, and I—are wedged into a tiny corner of the kitchen counter as the party continues to grow around us, because apparently the whole world knows about it. "He knows *everything*. And oh my *God*. When he wore that Black Watch shirt and Levis on Tuesday? I thought I would faint." Leilani fans herself with a stray oven mitt. "I love a man in good denim. I know he's our teacher, but it's not like he's *that* much older, you know?"

"What's Black Watch?" I ask.

"It's a type of plaid," Celeste explains. "Anyway, I dated a college guy when I was fifteen. Summer camp. It was no big deal." She takes a swig of beer. Celeste is totally the girl who dated a college guy when she was fifteen and knows so much more about life than any of us ever will.

I open my mouth to say something when Max walks through the doorway to the kitchen, stopping dead when he sees me and his girlfriend shoulder to shoulder in conversation.

"You think I'm super creepy, don't you?" Leilani pesters when I don't respond.

"No!" I assure her. "That's not it at all. I totally get it. Levy is adorable."

"Hi, babe!" Celeste coos, slinking over to kiss Max on the cheek. "You remember Alice, right? We met on the quad. I guess you know her from psychology, too. Duh."

And the time we broke into the Louvre and had a picnic with the *Mona Lisa*. And the time we raced a 1960s Porsche through back roads in Italy. And the time we rode pink elephants along the Great Wall of China.

"Hey," I say, smiling with just my mouth.

"Hey," Max says back, smiling with even less of his, and I blink. I know things are awkward between us, but why is he being so cold? After all, he's the one who broke *my* heart, and after all that, I'm the one standing here being nice to *his* girlfriend.

And that's when I realize: He's *scared*. When he first saw me in psych class and walked the other way. When he was cold to me on the quad. When he slammed his tray down in the cafeteria. And now, here, when he thinks I'm becoming friends with his girlfriend. Max hates uncertainty, and I make his world less certain.

And he has no idea how to handle it.

"Alice was cool enough to have me over before the party tonight to play a little dress-up," Celeste says, brandishing her arm candy once more. "Cool, right? Oh my God, Max, you should see this house. And her grandmother's closet. It's like that store I love, Second Time Around, but better!"

"Nice," Max says, raising his brows as his eyes bounce from Celeste to me, trying to look happy but still looking panicked.

"What'll it be, Wolfe?" Oliver asks.

Max blinks. "Excuse me?" he asks Oliver.

"What do you want to drink?" Oliver replies slowly. "It's not rocket science."

"Oh," Max says, swiping a hand through his hair. "I'll just take a Coke. I have a game tomorrow."

"Bo-ring," Oliver says. Then he turns to a tall kid with dark brown hair who is leaning against the fridge. "Jonathan, one Coke." He holds up a single finger, and Jonathan obediently opens it and begins rummaging inside.

"As long as it's not diet," Max and I say at the same time, before glancing at each other uncomfortably. Max would rather drink acid than drink Diet Coke.

Celeste laughs. "That's so weird! How did you know Max only drinks regular?" she asks.

"I didn't," I say quickly. "I just want one, too." I clear my throat. "Um, Jonathan, one more, please?" I call out, and Jonathan tosses two cans from the fridge.

Celeste pulls Max to her and wraps her arms around his waist, leaning her chin on his chest and looking up into his eyes like a baby deer. My stomach starts to churn, and I feel like I'm watching it all in slow motion, like a violent scene in a movie I just want to fast-forward through. I thought I could handle this. I thought I was angry enough at him to show up, maybe stay long enough just to make him feel awful. But Max is smiling down at Celeste, and now he *is* smiling with his eyes.

You've never been good at hiding how you feel, I hear Sophie say in the back of my mind. *It shows on your face like turquoise eyeshadow.*

The can of Coke is shaking in my hand, and I know I have to get out of here.

*

In the grand scheme of things, I would say I'd rather be almost anywhere in the world than in an elevator. The definition of claustrophobia has never made much sense to me, because that's like saying it's the space itself that bugs you. Small spaces don't necessarily bug me as long as I have a way to get out of them. I would rather be in a small room with an open roof than in a stadium with the doors locked. I just don't like to be in a spot that I have no control over getting out of. It goes against my natural composition or something. I need to run free.

So I am already preparing myself for a heart-fluttering ride back to the ground floor as the doors to Oliver's elevator slide shut, when a hand reaches in between them. Max gets on, his eyes boring into me, as I resolve to glare straight ahead. The only problem with this plan is that the interior of the elevator is completely mirrored, so when the doors shut, a thousand versions of me just end up looking back at him anyway.

"I offered to make an ice run," Max says, and then pauses. "Are you okay? I know how you feel about enclosed spaces."

I ignore him.

"Alice . . ." he starts.

But I interrupt him. "Don't."

"You don't even know what I was going to say." Max sighs. "I was going to say, this is hard for me, too."

"I don't want to hear it," I reply. "I'm sorry it's hard for you. But have you thought about how it actually feels for me? To watch you with her?"

"I know," Max says.

"And what about her, by the way?" I'm starting to lose my cool, which is exactly what I promised myself I wouldn't do. "Because she's great. I genuinely like her. But what would she do if she knew that when you go to sleep at night, you're basically just switching girlfriends?"

"I know," Max says again. The fact that he sounds remorseful only makes me angrier.

"Do you mean to?" I ask softly. "In our dreams. Do you mean to act the way you do in our dreams, like nothing has changed, when during the day I'm barely allowed to look at you?"

"I can't help it," Max says quietly. He meets my eyes, this time not through the mirror but in person, tilting his head slightly to the side to gaze down at me. "I know what's right, and what I should want, but when I'm in the dreams, I can't control it. The way I act, it just happens. You know that as well as I do. What happens in the dreams isn't our choice."

I break away from his gaze and stare at a corner of the floor, where I won't have to meet his eyes again. I know he's basically right, but it's also not good enough. We ride in silence for a while, before Max finally speaks.

"You look different tonight," Max says, even though he's not looking at me. He's looking at the elevator buttons. "You did something to your eyes. It's pretty."

By now the doors have opened, and we've reached the ground floor, and my face is burning with rage. "Just because we can't help the way we act in the dreams doesn't mean what happens in the dreams doesn't matter," I say coldly as I walk out. "Especially to me."

"I know," Max says one final time as the doors close again.

SEPTEMBER 23rd

It's a gorgeous day at the flea market, and I am gazing into a cracked antique mirror, trying on a neon alpaca poncho.

"It looks great on you," the vendor says, and when I turn, I realize it's Kate Moss.

"Would you wear it?" I ask.

"Darling, of course," she coos in her sexy British accent.

I pull at the yellow fringe, unsure. "I want to know what Max thinks. Do you know where he went?"

"I think I saw him heading toward the books section," she replies, straightening some vintage lace dresses.

I wander off, still wearing the poncho. Up ahead I spot Max striding away from me among the brightly colored tents. I yell his name, but he doesn't turn. It's busy today, and I am dodging shoppers left and right. Eventually I lose him.

I make it to the book vendors and Max isn't there. But Dean Hammer is.

"Have you seen Max?" I ask.

"He said he wanted to grab some ice cream," the dean replies. "What do you think of these?" He turns to face me, wearing red, heart-shaped sunglasses.

"Love them!" I cry. And this time I don't walk, I run. I can feel panic rising up within me. I look by the food trucks, the smell of fresh Nutella crepes following me. I sift through a wall of colorful scarves, scrambling to get to the other side. Everywhere I go, he seems to have just left.

"You just missed him," my grandmother says in the jewelry section. She is standing at the stall next to me in a pink Chanel suit, trying on a diamond brooch with gigantic peacock feathers. Jerry is on a leash by her side in a velvet bow tie.

"Where did he go?" I plead.

"He seemed unhappy," Nan says. "Did you get in a fight?"

"Nanny, listen to me." I put a hand on her small, fragile shoulder. "Where did Max go?"

"I think he said he wanted to take a swim." Nan smiles, her mind somewhere else already.

I run out of the market and down Vanderbilt Avenue until I reach the Navy Yard, somehow knowing exactly where to go. He's waiting for you, like he always is, *I tell myself as I sprint out onto the docks. But when I reach the end, breathless, there is still no Max. Just endless water. When I turn back the way I came, I find water there too, gray and unwelcoming. There is no way back, no way forward, and, worst of all, no one here to tell me everything will be all right.*

I am utterly alone.

14

We are all surrealists

IT'S NOT LIKE I don't know what a bad dream is. And I know, of course, that I've had them before, because bad dreams are why I went to CDD in the first place. It's just that I've never been able to *remember* any. It's as though all that CDD did, the magical worlds they created, didn't just give me something new and something better, they wiped away all the bad, too. Until now.

The entire day after the flea market dream I feel off, like I'm coming down with something. Like someone slipped something weird into my coffee or, worse, like someone has been slipping something in there all along, something to make me happy, and today they decided to stop. And nothing is making it better. Not the three coffees I've had since breakfast, not the bike ride to school in the brisk fall morning under a piercing blue sky. Not the A I got on my English paper or the fact that in Terrarium Club I actually managed to build an arrangement with nobody's instructions. It's not like I'm depressed or anything, I'm just not right. Which makes me all the more eager to get to CDD today and start to fix it.

"Upstairs." Lillian just points to the ceiling when I dash through the door of CDD. I realized when I arrived at Frank after Terrarium Club clutching my newest orb that I had nothing to store it in safely, and I had to rest it carefully in Frank's basket as I walked him the two miles from Bennett to MIT.

"Thanks," I say. "By the way, this is for you." I set the tiny ecosystem down on her desk and don't look back as I dash up the stairs, where Petermann is waiting patiently in his office and Max's leg is jiggling.

"Sorry I'm late! I had a precarious terrarium situation, don't ask," I announce, looking at Dr. Petermann. I'm afraid to look at Max after our elevator run-in. I'm not fuming anymore, but I'm still angry. And even though last night was just a dream, I still can't help but feel hurt by the way he ran from me.

"It's no trouble, Alice," Dr. Petermann says, and I'm surprised to see he's wearing the same heart-shaped glasses Dean Hammer was wearing in my dream.

"Alice?" Petermann says.

I blink.

"Are you all right?"

I blink again, and his glasses look completely normal. "I think so . . ." Then I look over at Max and notice him smirking as he turns a silver skull paperweight over in his hands.

"What?" I ask.

"Nothing," he says, standing up straighter, like he's been caught, his face going serious again.

"No, tell us," I say, folding my arms across my chest. "I'm dying to know what's so funny."

Max sighs. "You're just exactly the same." He shrugs. "Generally forgetful, often late, blowing into the room with your hair all over the place." He flaps his hands around his head with a goofy smile but then clears his throat and goes serious when he notices the look on my face.

I am shooting daggers at him with my eyes, but I can't help but notice he seems to be staring at my hair like he wants to reach out and touch it. "Thank you for that observation," I say, trying to keep my voice steady.

Max gives me a look. "You're the one who asked for it," he says. "I didn't mean to upset you." We hold each other's gaze for a minute.

Petermann looks like he couldn't care less. "I was just telling Max more about the science of dreams, and why we study them. Do you have any idea?"

I think for a moment, about the parrots and the Jenga blocks, how happy I was in that dream with Max even though my rational mind should have known we weren't together anymore. "I guess because they're often so weird and dis-jointed, and they seem to come out of nowhere?" I reply.

Petermann claps his hands together. "Bravo, Alice. That's very close. Most people just say the first part. But it's the latter that's the real fascination. Recorded history tells us that from the very beginning, dreams have been just about the most universally fascinating subject on earth. Poets, philosophers, religious figures, and, of course, scientists have grappled with what dreams mean and why they exist." Petermann leans back in his chair, looking from me to Max.

"In the most basic terms, we define our dreams as a succession of images, ideas, emotions, and sensations that occur involuntarily in the mind during certain stages of sleep. In more specific analysis, Freud asserted that dreams were where we revealed our deepest fears and desires."

I look over at Max with an expression that says, *See? I am your deepest desire.*

"Ancient Greeks, for example, believed the dreams of a sick person would communicate what ailed them. But again, to me the real question is, why the obsession in the first place? Why the desire to prove what it all means?"

He pauses as though he is waiting for us to answer, but when I start to speak, he just talks over me. Petermann is in his element. "Turns out, it's not the content that gets under our skin, so much as the word *involuntary* in the definition. We don't like that dreams just happen to us. We don't accept or want to accept things beyond our control . . . especially when they come out of our own minds."

Max is staring at Petermann intently, and I realize that's the big difference between us. Max is that person. Max is here because he doesn't like the loss of control, the ambiguity, the disruption of his daily life. I don't mind what happens in my dreams. I don't even mind that my dreams are now part of my reality. But Max can't stand it.

Petermann gets up quickly. "So there you have it! That's why we're all here, and today we will begin to try and fix it. Follow me please." He walks out his office door without looking back.

Max and I reach the door at the same time. We gaze at each other coolly before he steps aside, making an *after you* kind of motion. I respond by shaking my head and mimicking his motion, extending my hand to gesture toward the door. But as I do, my iPhone goes flying, clattering to the floor with a sound that echoes through the halls.

"You should really get a case for that," Max says from above as I stoop down to pick it up.

I stand back up, clutching the phone in my fist. I know he's not teasing; he's serious. But I really don't need him butting into my life. "*Go*," I say.

"Fine," Max announces, following Petermann down the black-and-white-tiled corridor.

The walls are lined with paintings. I peer at a picture of a clock that looks like it's melting into a desert landscape, and then a larger painting of an eyeball with a cloudy blue sky where the iris should be, followed by a portrait of man wearing a large black bowling hat, but his face is obscured by a big green apple. The objects in the paintings are clear and distinctive, but put together, nothing about them seems to add up.

"Why paint someone's portrait if you are just going to cover their face with a piece of fruit?" I say out loud.

"They're surrealist," Max says from up ahead.

"I knew that," I shoot back. *Sort of.*

"Why the fascination with surrealism, Dr. Petermann?" Max calls out.

At this, Petermann turns on his heels to face us, arms outstretched. "Because in our dreams, we are all surrealist painters, creating narratives and pictures that are often as beautiful as they are nonsensical."

Petermann motions us inside a room, where we find Nanao looking bored, holding a clipboard. To her left is a machine that looks like a giant glossy white donut, with a center the size of a manhole.

All I can think is, *Nope.*

"Will I be expected to get in there?" I ask, my body suddenly frozen where it's standing.

"I know it's hardly a hammock on a tropical shoreline, but I need to get a standard read of your brain activity before we begin putting you to sleep and seeing how it changes when you dream," Petermann explains.

In response I just start nodding quickly, over and over again, unable to form any words.

"Alice is a little claustrophobic," I hear Max clarify, and when I glance his way, I find him smiling at me. It's infuriating.

"Is my anxiety humorous to you?" I ask, and feel my face growing hot.

"No," Max says, in a tone that sounds like he's giving up. "But you have a small piece of cactus in your hair."

Horrified, my hand shoots up to my waves, where I find a stowaway from Terrarium Club. I am always getting things stuck in this rat's nest. "Then maybe you should stop *looking* at me," I mumble, and attempt to stealthily pull the leaf out. Max is still sort of smiling, though it looks like he's fighting it.

"Did you get it?" he asks.

"Shut up," I say.

"I'll go first," Max announces to everyone.

*

As we watch Max's long frame retreat into the depths of the evil donut monster from behind a glass partition, Petermann explains to us—over a speaker, so Max can hear, too—exactly what the machine does. A functional MRI maps the blood flow to the brain to show what parts are the most active. In dream mapping they use an fMRI in combination with an EEG. The EEG monitors the electrical activity in the brain, which determines when the subject is in early REM cycle and likely to have the most image-filled dreams. The fMRI then maps what parts light up in the brain, to help us understand how the brain dreams. Then the person is awakened to describe what they saw.

When Max is finished, I pull my phone out of my pocket in a dramatic fashion. "Oh, would you look at that," I say loudly. "Six p.m.? We should probably wrap it up soon, right, Dr. Petermann? It's okay, I can come back another time."

"You are going to be fine, Alice." Petermann puts a hand on my shoulder. We'll be here the whole time, just behind the glass. And you just tell us when you need to come out."

"Okay," I say quietly, looking at the machine from five feet away. "I'm ready to come out."

Petermann gives me a look. "First you have to go *in*."

*

I told myself it would be better once I was lying in the machine, that it would be over and done with before I know it, but it doesn't feel any better at all. I understand I'm not enclosed, that there's a hole where my feet are, that I could, theoretically, scootch my butt out of this death trap if the power went off or everyone in the room was suddenly rendered unconscious by a freak accident or alien invasion. But staring up at the roof of the fMRI just makes it feel like it's closing in on me . . . which it sort of is.

"Just lie perfectly still, Alice." Petermann's voice comes on over the intercom.

"I am," I say.

"Your left foot is jiggling like there's a mouse up your pant leg," I hear Max observe.

"Can you make him leave, please, Dr. Petermann?" I ask.

"This isn't going to work," I hear Petermann whisper. "She's too frightened."

Despite my suspicion that all the blood had drained from my face long ago, my cheeks still manage to burn. I feel so embarrassed. This test is part of the research I insisted we do, and I can't even go through with it. But that doesn't stop me from wanting to get the hell out of this thing anyway. My breath is starting to come too quickly and my lungs feel like they are the size of sandwich bags. Am I feeling light-headed, or is that just my imagination?

"Alice?" Max's voice is like the eye of the storm. The one calm place right in the center of the hurricane, breaking through all the noise of my mind. "Are you still with us?"

"Yeah," I manage. My voice comes out so quiet it scares me even more.

"What's the one place in the world you would like to go but have never been, in a dream or otherwise?" Max asks.

I take a shallow breath and focus. Easy question. I can do this. "Pig Beach," I say.

I hear a chuckle from Petermann. "Did I hear that correctly?"

Max explains, "Pig Beach is an island in the Bahamas, filled with clear blue ocean and palm trees, but inhabited entirely by giant, fuzzy, friendly . . . pigs. It's Alice's favorite place in the world, but she's never been. She talks about it all the time."

He's right. Most people fantasize about a vacation in a tropical destination, and so do I. It's just that my tropical island also has a bunch of fat jolly pigs on it. And it really exists! But my dad refuses to take me, dismissing it as an obvious tourist trap, not to mention unquestionably filthy.

"Legend has it the pigs were dropped off on the island by a group of sailors who intended to come back and cook them, but never made it," Max says soothingly. "Or that they survived a shipwreck and somehow swam to shore. Either way, they survived something and now have a happy ending, fed by tourists and locals."

My body relaxes as I listen to the lull of Max's voice describe my happy place.

"How remarkable," Petermann says. "How did you know all this?"

"She told me once in a dream . . . we were in Thailand . . . and Alice turned to me and just said, 'I wish there were pigs here.'" Max lets out a low laugh, like he can't help himself. I smile.

"Looks like we've got all we need," Petermann says over the speaker. "You can come out now, Alice. Next session we will start putting you guys to sleep."

I want to thank Max for stepping in to calm me down, but he leaves while Nanao is still unhooking me from all the wires. When I come back down the stairs to the main hall of CDD, I expect to find my terrarium in the trash, or right where I left it. Instead, Lillian has made a special place for it on the bookshelf behind her desk, nestled in among some tiny cacti pots and a photo of a handsome guy with a man-bun.

Lillian doesn't say thank you for the terrarium, but she does say, "Your boyfriend left his phone here."

"He's not my boyfriend." I turn around.

"I couldn't honestly care less what dysfunctional scenario the two of you are carrying out." Lillian looks back down at her paperwork. "But I imagine he'll need it." She hands the phone out, still not looking at me.

"I don't even know where he lives," I whine.

"You go to the same high school," Lillian says. "I'm sure you can figure it out."

15

attack of the pekingese

"ALICE IS ONE of the most forgetful people I have ever met," I say out loud to nobody. My Max impression sounds more Neanderthal than teenage boy (if there's a difference). "Who's forgetful now, Max?" But when I look down at his phone in my hand, I see that unlike mine, his has a case. And it looks like the same material that the Batmobile is made out of. Indestructible. "How responsible," I observe.

It's eight p.m. and I'm standing on the stoop of Max's house. It's a lot like mine, four stories high with a black doorway and shutters (Doesn't anyone have any creativity around here? What I would give to see just one door painted blue . . .), but Max's house has a curved façade, as though the building ate too much for dinner. I half expect the front door to come popping off like a button from the strain.

Without warning, Max's front door opens, and it startles me. I haven't even pressed the doorbell yet.

"Alice, what are you doing here?" Max asks, furrowing his brows together while he stands a few steps above me. He has on a charcoal-gray collared shirt, untucked, and green khakis. It must be nice to wake up in the morning and just look great in whatever you put on.

"How did you know I was here?" I ask, ignoring his less-than-welcoming welcome. Dream Max loves surprises, but Real Max probably hates them.

"I heard voices," he replies, and looks around while I cringe. "Or . . . voice."

"How come nobody ever paints their door blue?" I ask, nodding behind me to the other houses on the street. But Max has already started walking inside, back down the hallway.

"Historic preservation," he calls out. "It's basically illegal to change the exterior of your house at all." Then he turns back and gives me a look like I'm a puppy who needs training. "Come on," he says with a small motion, and I follow.

Soon I'm seated on a stool in Max's gorgeously renovated kitchen, while he rummages in a drawer for something. The exterior of the house may look like any other on the hill, but the interior is all modern fixtures and clean design. Nothing is out of place. Not the white throw on the cream-colored couch, not the architecture books on the coffee table, not even the spice drawer I just pulled open. *Who has a clean spice drawer?* I think, before shutting it. In our house, you're lucky if your cinnamon pancakes don't accidentally taste like cumin.

Max reveals a wine opener and pulls a bottle of something white and crisp out of the fridge. The cork gives a swift pop, followed by silence, and I suddenly feel very awkward, standing in Max's house with nobody else around.

"Oh, no wine for me, thanks," I say, putting out a hand as if to stop him.

"Good, because it isn't for you," Max says, and raises an eyebrow at me. "I'll be right back." Without explanation, he exits the room and I hear the sounds of voices and forks scraping plates increase and then decrease in volume as he opens and shuts a door.

Finding myself unsupervised, I use the opportunity to take in my surroundings, which, apart from the tasteful décor, mostly consists of photographs. They are everywhere: lining the mantel in polished silver frames, hanging from the walls in perfectly curated rows. The images are mostly of a woman I assume to be Max's mother, because of her brown hair and large almond-shaped eyes, with some people I know (government figures, a few celebrities), and a lot of people I don't know. There are also a lot of Max—one in his soccer jersey, sweaty after a game, a man I assume is his dad with a hand on his shoulder. One looking dirty but happy on the side of a mountain with some Nepalese guides, and one proudly brandishing a silver plaque that must be some kind of honor or award.

"Bet he didn't get that for hula-hooping," I say.

Then I'm glancing at the lushly carpeted staircase out in the front hall, and before I can help it, I'm wondering what Max's bedroom looks like. I bet it's classic and adult, with dark wood furniture and a well-organized closet. An immaculate desk with his textbooks on one side and a smudgeless computer on the other. Max is not the kind of guy who still has his old racecar bed. The idea of being inside it makes me even more nervous than I feel right now. A space that's wholly his, where everything is all Max. I shiver.

"Are you cold?" Max asks, walking back into the room, looking confused. "You still have your coat on."

"Nope," I say, quickly changing the subject. I turn to the first thing I see, a silver and black device set into the wall with a glass pane at the center, displaying a keypad. "Is this your intercom?" I ask. "We have one in our house, too! I just learned how to use it."

"That's the alarm system," Max replies from across the room, hands in his pockets. His face twitches as though he wants to smile, but is being polite about it.

"Oh," I say, pursing my lips together seriously. "Did you know that in ancient China, an emperor's last line of defense against an intruder was a tiny Pekingese dog hidden up the sleeve of his kimono? Maybe you should get one of those." I read about that the other day on one of my animal-lover blogs, designed solely for weirdos like me. "You know, if you're worried about security . . ." I trail off.

Max shakes his head, but now he finally does smile, and I breathe a sigh of relief. "I didn't know that," he replies. "But I'm not surprised that you do."

"What's going on in there?" I nod to the doorway he just came out of, with the symphony of clanking plates.

"Just the millionth dinner party of the season. My parents have a lot of friends," Max answers, sitting down next to me at the island. He sounds exhausted. "So what is this, Alice. Twenty questions? What are you doing here?" He folds his arms across his chest, then places them on the countertop, before ultimately letting them rest in his lap.

I give him a look. "I have your phone," I say. "Relax. Why are you being so weird?"

"I'm not being weird," Max says, in a voice that's uncharacteristically high and squeaky. "You have my phone?"

"That's why I'm here," I reply coolly.

"So, can I have it?" he asks impatiently.

"You know what?" I reply, sliding the phone across the marble countertop so fast I think it might fly off the other side, and I sort of hope it does. "I came here tonight to do you a favor. And I'm getting kind of tired of your manic behavior."

146

"What do you mean?" Max asks, looking genuinely confused. He snatches the phone with ease before it can shatter on the floor. *Of course.*

"I mean one minute you're a jerk at Oliver's party. The next you're apologizing to me in an elevator, then you're coming to my rescue when I think I might suffocate in the MRI machine, and now you're acting like I'm some stalker who just showed up at your home. I mean really? Pick a side, Max. I feel like I'm living through some vampire romance where you can't be near me because my blood smells delicious."

I'm obviously kidding, but Max suddenly looks more uncomfortable than ever. He stares awkwardly down at his hands.

"What?" I ask, watching him. Then my mouth falls open slightly. "Is that it? You're afraid to be alone with me?"

Max still doesn't say anything, and his jaw clenches. "Kind of," he admits.

It takes me a moment to find my voice, and when I do, it comes out small and unsure. "Why . . . what is it you're afraid will happen?"

Max finally meets my eyes with a look that says, *What do you think?* And I think I might actually pass out.

Instead we're interrupted by a voice from the hall. "Max? Could you bring a bottle of red as well?" Max's mother appears in the hallway between the dining room and living area. She's immaculate with a friendly, open face. "Oh," she says when she sees me.

"Mom, this is my friend Alice. She was just leaving," Max says quickly, standing up from the table.

I can take a hint. "It's very nice to meet you, Mrs. Wolfe."

"Not so fast," Max's mother says. "Alice, first of all, it's lovely to meet you. And please call me Katherine! Secondly, I'm sorry Max is in such a foul mood. He hates our dinner parties. Why don't you come in and join us for dessert? Someone canceled at the last minute and we have an empty seat."

I look to Max, but he's intentionally not meeting my gaze.

"I—I'm not sure . . ." I stammer.

"Well, I am," Katherine says, putting a sparkling diamond-clad hand on my back. "Besides, we have a flourless chocolate torte for dessert, and if more people aren't here to eat it, I'll do it all myself." She winks.

*

The chocolate torte is what dreams are made of. Like a brownie that's been cooked just right, warm and gooey at the center, with a deliciously crisp crust. I would swim in it if I could. Or just dig a hole and sit inside it with a spoon and eat my way out. Maybe tonight when I fall asleep, I'll dream about this cake.

"So, Alice," Jacob Wolfe says. Over the course of dessert I learned Max's dad is the head of pediatric surgery at Mass General Hospital, a few blocks away. His mother, meanwhile, works for the largest philanthropic foundation in the city.

No pressure or anything. "How come we've never seen you before? Where have you been hiding?"

I put my spoon down, embarrassed to realize it hasn't left my hand since I sat down. "I just moved here, actually."

"Alice is in one of my classes at school," Max says. He's acting different, like he's playing a version of himself. His speaking is more formal and enunciated, his posture more rigid. Like the way you speak to someone who is hard of hearing. Not the way you talk to your father.

"Yes, psychology," I add. I was only trying to participate, but immediately I see Max wince.

"Psychology?" Jacob asks. But he's not speaking to me anymore, he's speaking to Max. "I thought you decided not to take that this semester?"

Max takes a deep inhale, nodding, and I realize I've made an error. "We did discuss that, yes, but this is the only semester Mr. Levy teaches Psych 201, and I didn't want to miss the opportunity. Especially if I want to get into his three-hundred level next year."

Jacob clears his throat, his posture still like stone. "I just thought we agreed you'd wait until your senior spring to take the fluffier courses," he says.

"He just said it wasn't offered in the spring, dear," Katherine says in that same soothing tone. A tone that says, *I'm putting out this fire, and don't bother trying to light it again.* She brushes a strand of Max's hair out of his eye. "And besides, you have such a great relationship with Levy. It will look even better on your transcript to show a continued interest in a specific subject."

This conversation stuns me. In my house we talk about the things we saw or learned that day. The new bicycle share in Harvard Square, or the coffee shop that just opened on Marlborough Street. Max's parents seem to know every detail of his life, and everything they don't know yet, they seem to have planned for.

"Max is by far the smartest in the class," I chime in. "I swear he knows the questions Levy will ask before Levy does."

In response to this Jacob beams. "That's great to hear. Good work," he says to Max.

"And he doesn't hesitate to make sure we all know it, either," I tease, and the whole table erupts in laughter, including Max, whose eyes shine at me gratefully from the other end.

*

After I thank Max's parents for dessert, Max walks me to the door. I am just turning to give him a wave when I see him putting on his own coat.

"What are you doing?" I ask.

"Walking you home." He shrugs. "It's late."

"I thought you didn't want to be alone with me?" I tease him.

"I think I can handle myself," he says with a laugh, playing along. But I notice he missed one of the buttons on his coat, and without thinking I reach over to fix it. Suddenly, a moment too late, I am aware of how close he is, and even though I refuse to look up and meet his eyes, something crackles between us.

"I'll be fine, really," I say, taking a step back. "I like to walk alone. It clears my head. Besides, my dad makes me use one of those apps where he can locate me whenever he wants." I sigh and wish I were kidding.

Max actually looks a little hurt. And a little silly, standing there in his brown waxed-cotton coat with a plaid scarf that's less wrapped around his neck than draped over it, where it won't do any good. "Oh," he says. "That's cool."

I wait for him to say something else, but he doesn't. "Okay, so . . . I'll see you at school." I turn to leave.

"Alice," Max calls out.

"Yeah?" I say.

"Thanks," Max says.

I smile at him, and as I make my way back down the hill, I can't help but feel like something between us is changing. It's not just about our memories anymore. We're getting to know each other again. We're building something in real life. And it's not always pretty, but I'd rather have that than have no Max at all.

september 26TH

The first thing I think is that I've obviously eaten the same mushrooms that Alice, the other Alice, eats in Wonderland. The ones that both shrink her and make her grow. I've eaten the first kind. I'm making my way through the living room at Nan's house, but I'm so small I'm able to walk directly under the piano without crouching an inch, and the carpet seems much softer than usual, squishier beneath my feet. I'm looking for something, but I don't know what.

I take the stairs slowly, flipping over onto my stomach and wiggling down each one. I cling to pieces of carpet with my fists to hold on for dear life. I can hear voices in the distance and want to go faster, but I don't know what I'm looking for.

In the kitchen, I hoist myself up onto a chair and lift a teacup the size of a kiddie pool from where it lies facedown on a saucer. I poke my head underneath it and see if anyone's inside, but find nothing. I'm disappointed, but then I'm momentarily distracted by a pile of cream puffs in the middle of the table. They are as big as loaves of bread. I pick one up and break it in my hands, then begin to nibble around the edges, and I take it with me as I continue on my way.

I hear a laugh, a woman's laugh, loud and full, and suddenly I'm excited. I smile and pick up my pace, hustling back through the dining room, checking beneath each piece of furniture as I go. But I can't find her. In the main foyer I catch a whiff of something lovely. Sweet and a little bit spicy. Familiar. Like shampoo. I close my eyes and breathe it in. But as soon as it comes, it goes again.

Where is she?

Anxious and alone, I wander over to the window curtains and wrap myself up in deep green silk. I wait; for what, I'm not exactly sure.

That's when I hear the breathing—large grunts and snorts. I think I should be afraid, but I'm not. I'm less afraid than ever. I'm relieved. They are getting closer, and I wait patiently. Suddenly the curtain is pulled away and I am face-to-face with Jerry, except he's as big as a buffalo. His wet nose wipes against my face as he sniffs, and then he nudges me, before picking me up by the collar of my sweater and carrying me back through the house.

He hops up the stairs and places me back in my bed, giving me a big slurp with his tongue and curling up next to me. I fall easily to sleep.

16

swans mate for life

JERRY HAS THIS unbearable habit of scraping at the front door for dear life every time he needs to go to the bathroom, and then taking an exhaustive amount of time deciding where to pee. Or worse, just standing on the sidewalk and staring at me indignantly, as though he is waiting for me to tell him what we are doing here in the first place, and why I got him up so early.

"Are you kidding?" I say, staring down at him with my hands on my hips. It's nine a.m. on Saturday morning and I am in bare feet, jeans, and an old lavender sweater I pulled from one of my mother's drawers. "You have exactly one minute to go to the bathroom. And then we are going inside, and I don't care if you have to hold it all morning." Jerry blinks once before hustling over to the edge of the sidewalk to handle his business.

"That's what I thought," I say.

This morning I woke up spooning him like he was a living breathing teddy bear, his little sausage-shaped frame nestled comfortably in the blankets, his giant head resting on the pillow like a person. I also woke up with an odd pit in my stomach. But not the kind of pit I felt the morning after the Brooklyn Flea dream. This one was different. Less heartbroken, more lost. Like I was missing something I couldn't find, but something I hadn't been able to find for a while. The feeling is fading little by little, but the memory is vivid. I stare up at the façade of our beautiful old house and then I just know. I was missing her. My mom. I'd been looking for her in my dream.

"Time to go back in, Jer-Bear," I say, turning around to discover that we are not alone. Oliver's fluffy head is blocking Jerry's face as he leans down to pat him on the back.

"Hi!" I say enthusiastically, but when Oliver raises his head to look at me, he just squints.

"I'm sorry, have we met?" he asks.

"Oh, come on," I say then, giving him a shove.

Oliver's blue eyes widen in shock, cradling his shoulders as if to protect himself. "Ma'am! Please. I'm just here to visit my friend Jerry. We were roommates in college." He turns back to the dog. "Jer, do you even know this woman?" I'm pretty sure dogs can't roll their eyes. But if they could, Jerry definitely just did.

"Very funny," I say. "What are you really doing here?"

Oliver grins. "Well, obviously I've come to take you both on an adventure."

I open my mouth, ready to protest—I am in bare feet, after all—before realizing that an adventure is exactly what I need.

"I'm only doing it for Jerry," I say. "He needs to have some fun." We turn to find Jerry lying on his side on the brick sidewalk, while a little girl with a butterfly balloon rubs his belly.

"Poor Jerry," Oliver says, shaking his head. "His life is so hard." Then he crouches down with his hands on his knees and says to my dog, "How do you feel about boats?"

*

Of all the wonderful books that exist about the city of Boston, *Make Way for Ducklings* is by far the best. The story is about a mother duck who gives birth to her babies on a small island in the middle of the Charles River, and must find a way to get them back to the pond at the Public Garden. So she marches them through town in a little row, and the whole city stops to "make way," until they safely plop their fuzzy bottoms into the water, and all is right with the world.

In the Public Garden, which is right across the street from our house, there are also swan boat rides. For three dollars you can climb aboard what basically looks like two green canoes welded together under six rows of wooden benches, followed closely by a giant swan sculpture, behind which sits your tour guide. Then you are pedaled around the pond, which has to be no more than half a mile in length, for fifteen uneventful minutes, and get off again.

"Isn't this kind of a tourist attraction?" I ask Oliver as we wait in line for a ride.

"Aren't you still kind of a tourist?" Oliver responds.

"I resent that," I say. "And so does Jerry."

Oliver doesn't answer, he just hands me an envelope. "Here, hold this," he says.

"Why?" I ask.

"Do-it A-lice," he singsongs nervously while eyeing the ticket taker, and for some ridiculous reason I obey.

"Oliver!" The ticket taker gives him a big hug when it's our turn. "We miss you around here. Are you coming back next summer? You were such a hit with the guests."

"How could I not, Sam?" Oliver says. "Best job I've ever had."

Sam raises an eyebrow. "Pretty sure it's the only job you've ever had, but I'll take the compliment. Unfortunately, what I cannot take is this guy." He points at Jerry, who is gently sniffing the back of a woman's calf in front of us in line, like she is an expensive piece of cheese. "You know the rules, no dogs unless they are a service dog."

Oliver gives an overexaggerated sigh. "Sam, what do you think, I just forgot everything I learned last summer? Jerry is an emotional support animal. He belongs to my friend Alice. She even has a letter from her therapist—don't you, Alice?"

Suddenly I understand the envelope. And I want to murder him.

Sam takes the letter from me and scrutinizes it, then glances sidelong at Oliver. "He doesn't seem like much support," he says.

We look over and see that a fat brown duck has swum up to the dock and Jerry is leaning toward it, right out over the water, emitting a low growl. The leash is the only thing keeping him upright.

"He's both an emotional support animal and a security dog," Oliver says quickly.

Sam sighs.

"This is ridiculous," I mutter, very aware of the fact that Oliver has put his arm around the back of my chair, as Jerry lies down below our seat with a grunt. "And wrong, on so many levels."

"But isn't it fun?" Oliver winks, and stretches out his legs in front of us. He belongs on a beach in Malibu, not a boat with a giant fake swan on it. I can't help but consider all the hearts he would break if he weren't always acting like the Energizer Bunny. "Did you know swans mate for life?" he asks, wiggling his brows.

I roll my eyes.

"So, where were you on Wednesday?" Oliver asks. "I looked for you after Terrarium Club, but Jeremiah said you ran off.

I thought we were going to that old record store in Harvard Square I told you about."

I lean forward and place my forehead in my hand. "I completely forgot," I say. "I'm sorry, Oliver."

"I'll be fine." Oliver waves a hand dismissively. "It's Sally who is heartbroken."

"Sally?" I ask, wracking my brain. I don't remember meeting anyone at school with that name.

"Sally the Segway. Don't tell her I told you, but she sort of had a crush on Frank . . . I think she just felt jilted is all. They lock up together one time at a bike rack and he never calls her again? Real classy, Frank."

I can't help but snort in response. We've just made our way under the small pedestrian bridge that crosses the pond, and a little girl in a green wool coat waves to us. We wave back.

"Seriously, where did you go?" he asks then, and I feel a pang when I see how earnestly he is looking at me.

I take a deep breath. "It's kind of weird," I say. "I'm not sure what you'll think." I can't believe I'm even considering doing this. Telling him everything. But Oliver always makes me feel safe. And I can tell right now he's a little hurt.

Oliver shakes his head. "Alice, since the day I met you, you've been nothing but weird. News flash, I like it. Tell me what's going on and maybe I can help."

"Okay, so . . ." I lean in closely, unsure. "It seems that Bennett isn't the first time I've ever met Max Wolfe."

Oliver's eyes go dark. "Well, when then?" His jaw twitches slightly. We've now reached the end of the pond and are curving around, heading back again. For the first time I notice the weeping willows dotting the shoreline, and they seem familiar, but I can't tell if it's from an actual childhood memory or a dream I had as a child.

I take a deep breath. *Can I trust him?*

"In my dreams," I say, ripping off the Band-Aid.

Oliver's face falls, and he removes his arm. "I know you like him, Alice, but don't you think it's a bit cruel to go on a swan boat ride with another suitor, only to tell him that someone else is the man of your dreams?"

Suitor. I choose to ignore the word. "No, you don't get it." I laugh and put a hand on his knee, then pull it away quickly when I see his eyes zero in on it. "Max and I actually dream about each other. We have been dreaming about each other since we were kids. But the thing is, we've never met before. In . . . reality." I go on to tell him everything, the full history, seeing Max for the first time at school, and how difficult it's been. "Okay, now is the part where you ask Sam to make an emergency stop so you can run for the hills."

Oliver's expression hasn't changed. He's still looking at me, but I can tell his mind is working eighty miles per hour.

"You and Max," he says.

"Me and Max."

"In your subconscious?" he asks.

" . . . Yes?" I respond.

"You're right, that is totally insane," he replies.

"I know!" I want to bury my face in my hands. I know exactly how it sounds. Too bad it's *true.*

"But I'm totally into it."

"You're what?" I ask. "I mean, you believe me?"

Oliver gives his shrug. "I'm into it. When I was a little kid, and would watch a scary movie, I'd wake up the next morning asleep in the hall outside my parents' door, with no recollection of how I got there. I mean, really, how do you explain that? And honestly, I like it better this way. You're so weird about Max, and I couldn't figure out why. Maybe you love him, but at least it's not love at first sight . . . That would be tough to compete with." He grins.

I blush and look down at my hands.

"Just one question," Oliver says.

"That's it? Just one?" I laugh.

"Have you ever had a dream about me?" Oliver looks me directly in the eye when he asks. Is he afraid of anything?

I think about the pool and the socks and the iPad. "Yeah, kind of," I say.

Oliver's whole body relaxes, and he sits back on the bench with a happy sigh, his arm finding his way to the back of my chair again. "Excellent."

And suddenly I realize, my whole body has relaxed, too. Talking to Oliver about Max and the dreams is such a relief.

I have Sophie, too, but she's so far away. Confiding in Oliver makes me feel like I'm not so alone.

Unfortunately the moment is ruined when we hear a splash in the water, and see that Jerry, having spotted his duck target once again, has launched himself off the swan boat and into the water, like a hairy little Ishmael after his own White Whale. It also appears that Jerry can't swim very well.

I turn to Oliver in a panic and realize he's not there. He's already in the water, grabbing Jerry around his thick middle and pulling him toward the boat.

"Don't even think about bringing that animal back aboard," Sam calls as he continues to pedal. "It's disruptive! This is highly unprofessional behavior, Oliver."

"But that's my dog!" I yell over the heads of horrified tourists.

"If you have a problem with the policy, miss, you are welcome to join them," he replies. He's obviously not serious. He doesn't think I will do it. But then I look at Oliver, treading water frantically, Jerry lying on his back with his bulldog tummy exposed, and Oliver's face just lights up. He raises his eyebrows as if to say, *Well?*

"You know, as a matter of fact, I think I will!" I say. And I dive in after them.

The three of us swim to shore, Oliver and me supporting Jerry as we go, and a small crowd has gathered to see if we're okay. But as soon as we've pulled ourselves onto dry land, we just burst out laughing.

"That was crazy," I breathe.

"That was fun," Oliver says. "Told you we'd have an adventure." I love how I feel right now. Like I just had a dream, but I didn't. It was all real. Oliver doesn't need the dreamworld to have fun. I think about Max and my mood darkens.

Then I glance to my left and see two gorgeous white swans, real ones, pruning themselves side by side.

"That's Romeo and Juliet," Oliver explains when he sees me staring. He gives his hair a quick shake, like a golden retriever that's just gotten out of the water. "They're famous. They've been together for ten years."

"They make a cute couple," I observe.

"They're also both ladies," Oliver says with a chuckle. "The parks department didn't realize when they put them together. They lay eggs every year, but none of them hatch. But they still seem to like each other a lot."

"There are many different ways to love someone," I say, observing the swans, and turn to find Oliver gazing at me. Then a shadow falls over his body and we look up to find Sam. He does not look happy.

Needless to say, Oliver is told he is not welcome back at the swan boats again, professionally or otherwise.

That afternoon, sopping wet, I let a soaked Jerry into the

foyer of the house and replace the spare key under the urn to the right of the door. My father and I are too forgetful to ever have our keys on us. Before I follow Jerry inside, I glance at the wet paw prints he just left on the stone steps.

They are the size of basketballs. Like they were made by a dog the size of a water buffalo. I remember the image of Jerry from my dream last night, parting the curtain with his giant head, ready to carry me away. Then I look back at the footprint, before walking inside and shutting the door, as though getting it out of my sight will make it disappear.

Something really weird is happening.

17

we missed everything

"DID YOU KNOW that every time we dream, we basically just become certifiable lunatics?" Max calls out.

It's another beautiful fall afternoon, but we can't see that, because we're in the Dozing Center, which is kept at a perfect level of dim for optimum comfort. I also can't see Max, so I crane my head over the top of my sleep pod. The pods are a genius solution that Petermann devised to help his subjects relax and eventually fall asleep. He was so excited when we came in today for our first day of real research that I thought he would short-circuit. "Now is where the real fun begins!" he said as he rubbed his hands together.

Sleep pods, by the way, are exactly what they sound like. Large couches shaped like seashells or the head of the flower in the Bennett greenhouse that looked like it was going to eat me. You wedge yourself right in the middle and it closes around you, submerging your body in total comfort, like lying on a cloud. It's so comfortable that even claustrophobes like me don't mind.

"I always say my sleep is where my true crazy comes out," I reply, then I chuckle.

"What?" Max asks. I like the way he asks, like he's already excited, like he trusts that whatever I'm going to say, it's gonna be good.

I pause to explain. "Just that we're talking about how sleep makes us crazy, while we lie here looking like a couple of hot-dogs in buns like it's totally normal."

Max lets out a genuine laugh, and I wonder why, after all this time, making him laugh still makes me feel like I just pulled the lever in a slot machine and millions of gold coins are spilling out on top of me.

"I did some reading about it," Max continues. "It turns out that the five main characteristics of dreaming can also all be attributed to mental illness. One, heavy emotion. Two and three, illogical thought and organization. Four, acceptance that what one sees, however bizarre, is true. And of course five, trouble remembering the experience. All of these things are also the experiences of patients with delirium, dementia, or psychosis. The only reason we accept ourselves as *not* being insane is because we are asleep at the time and none of it's voluntary in our minds."

I try to nod my head in understanding, but the pod doesn't allow for much movement and it's not like he can see me anyway. I think about Jerry's enormous footprints yesterday and wonder what this means for me.

"Sorry about the other night," Max says then. And it takes me a moment to figure out what he's talking about.

"With your parents?" I ask. "They were great." Then I wince. I forget that Real Max still may not know me very well, but Dream Max definitely does. And he knows when I'm lying.

"Well, they are certainly *something*," he says. Neither of us speaks for a little while, and all we can hear are the repetitive beeps of a machine that's attached to our pods, tracking our vitals and brain waves. Lillian asked if either of us wanted a noise machine. They have ninety-two varieties, everything from chirping birds to waves crashing on the beach, even just the sound of voices in another room. Max said he liked that one because it reminded him of being little and going to bed, listening to the sound of his mom's dinner party downstairs. But in the end we decided we'd rather just talk to each other.

"Your parents really love you," I try. "That's all. They just don't necessarily show it in the best way."

"Hey, kids," Miles pipes in over the intercom. "I'm really enjoying this heartwarming exchange, but I just want to let you know the clock is ticking, and you have seven minutes to fall asleep if this session is going to be useful at all."

"That's really helpful, Miles," I call out. "Nothing like a little anxiety to calm the body down."

"Whatever. I'm going to get a cappuccino," he says. "You better be asleep by the time I get back."

How was I supposed to fall asleep, lying inches away from Max? What if I talked in my sleep, or, worse, what if I talked about *him*? The good news is that for some reason he doesn't seem to be able to fall asleep, either. Max, the perfect student. So I don't feel so nervous. And the less nervous I feel, the closer I'm getting to falling asleep.

"Why did you come here?" Max asks out of the blue. "To CDD, I mean. When you were little."

"I don't really remember," I reply. "But according to my dad, it all started after my mom left to go do her ape thing." I haven't told Max the full story, but we've been to enough exotic places and seen too many rare species for Madeleine's research not to have come up.

"So she just left you? I don't think I ever realized that," Max whispers, and I'm surprised I never told him that part. I'm also surprised at how genuinely offended he sounds. But then his tone softens. "I guess we always had other stuff to talk about . . . like when we found ourselves scuba diving around that old pirate ship."

I smile. "Or how about when we floated down that milk

river on a raft made out of a giant piece of Cinnamon Toast Crunch?"

"Delicious," Max replies, and I giggle. But I'm reminded yet again that when it comes down to it, what do we really know about each other? How much have we already missed?

"Anyway, yes. I guess she left us," I say, before correcting myself. "I mean *yes*. She did leave us. My dad would say it's less definitive. But it's not. She definitely left." I think about the dream I had, lost in my house, how I felt when I woke up. I wonder if that's the kind of dream I had when I was little. I decide to switch topics. "So what about you? How did you end up here? I picture you as this perfect child with no problems. Like the kid who ate spaghetti without ever getting it on his white bib."

Max snorts. "I was never like that, not even close," he says. "But then there was the thing with my sister . . ."

"What sister?" I ask. "Is she at college? You mentioned her the other night, too, and I didn't even know you had one."

Max doesn't say anything for a long while, and I wonder if he's fallen asleep already. But deep down I know he hasn't. And something terrible is coming.

"That's because she died," Max says.

My heart clenches, and the sleep pod suddenly seems tight around my body. I want to go to him, but it has me in its clutches.

"Max," I say. "I am so sorry. I didn't know."

"Thanks," he replies, and I can just picture him stretched out next to me, gray eyes wide open and staring at the ceiling. "It was a long time ago. I was seven and she was fifteen." He pauses for a minute. "You would have liked her. She was a total free spirit. My parents couldn't control her, and they hated that. But she was always there for me whenever they weren't, which was most of the time. And then one of the many weekends she was grounded, she snuck out. And the other kid had been drinking, and Lila only had a learner's permit, so she couldn't . . ."

Tears are welling up in my eyes, not just over Lila, but imagining Max, just a kid, suddenly so alone. So much is starting to make sense. About who he was, about what Celeste said. About who he's so intent on being now. And how we didn't miss a little bit, we missed everything. Max experienced a whole life without me.

"That's why your parents are so intense." I understand it now. "If they can plan it all out, they can account for any unforeseen errors."

"I believe the saying is, 'all their eggs in one basket,'" Max says. "I am the basket. I guess that's when I became the kid who never spilled spaghetti on his bib. I just want them to be happy, you know? They've been through enough."

"But, Max," I say. "So have you."

Max clears his throat. "Thanks, Alice," he says again. Then he switches topics slightly, and I let him, because I can tell he needs to. "Isn't it kind of strange that we both went through this stuff when we were younger—your mom leaving, my sister . . ." He trails off at the end of the sentence, leaving it blank.

I step in. "Yeah, it is strange. But we came here for our nightmares. Right? And something's gotta give you nightmares in the first place."

"Right," Max says, his voice a little quieter, a little more crackly than before. He's falling asleep. Over the years you get used to the signs. Max usually trails off midsentence.

"Sweet dreams, Max," I say.

"I'll see you soon, Alice," he says. And then we're both out.

OCTOBER 10TH

FoR a moment I think I must be in a laundry detergent commercial.

All around me is a duvet. Soft and fluffy, smooth and cool against my skin. I inhale, stretching my arms overhead, and roll over on my side.

And come face-to-face with Max.

I'm not surprised to see him, and from the look on his face, he's not surprised to see me, either. We just grin, to the point where my smile isn't a part of my face, my face is a part of my smile. My mouth, my eyes, I bet even my dimples have dimples. Everything is just a little bit fuzzy. Like when I feel noodly, but in a really good way. That's how lying in this giant duvet and staring at Max makes me feel. Normally there's a point in a staring contest where people get uncomfortable, and someone will finally say something. It's vulnerable, staring someone in the face. But that moment doesn't come for us. I have no idea how long we've been here. Minutes, hours, days. I don't care.

Then just beyond Max's head I see a giant balloon float past. It's a million shades of purples and pinks, ranging from fuchsia to cranberry to grape. I sit up and realize that this is no duvet we're lying in. It's a cloud. And down below, covering the sky, are a million little hot air balloons in various stages of flight.

Max sits up, too. Neither of us speaks. I lean past him to get a closer look at the balloons, because I don't see any people in them, like the balloons themselves are acting of their own free will. Then I realize Max isn't looking at the balloons at all. I feel something in my hair and glance down to find his hand gently running through it, almost imperceptible. Except it's the opposite of imperceptible. I may not feel it in my hair, but I feel it in my stomach.

Ever so slowly, I turn to face Max. But I can't meet his eyes right away. We're too close. I feel drawn to him, like he's a refrigerator and I'm made entirely out of alphabet magnets. Finally I look up, and he's not looking at me, either.

He's looking at my lips.

I don't realize that we are slowly moving toward each other until his lips are almost touching mine.

18

wakey-wakey

I OPEN MY eyes, back to the *blip-blap-bleep* of the sleep pod.

"Wakey-wakey," Nanao says as she carefully helps me out of the pod, while my eyes adjust from the soft glow of the cloud to the dimly lit room. I realize it's the first time I've heard her speak.

"Where's Max?" I ask, glancing at the empty pod next to mine and trying to control the panic in my voice.

"Don't worry. Follow me." Not only is her voice kind and reassuring, but it's also British.

"Our data isn't clear enough," Petermann is saying when Nanao ushers me into the main laboratory. This time he's dressed in riding jodhpurs and a polo shirt. Out of the corner of my eye I see Max sitting on an iron windowsill, and I am nervous to look at him. But when I finally get the courage to do so, he's looking right back, a bit warily from beneath his eyelashes, leaning over his knees with his hands clasped together. My whole body jolts from the feeling of his eyes meeting mine, and I have no doubt that my cheeks have just changed from pink to fuchsia to purple.

Petermann leans over a desk, a pair of spectacles perched at the end of his nose as he looks between two large computer screens. Because they are made from renovated rooms of the old observatory, CDD's labs are far from the sterile environments you'd expect. They have black-and-white-checkered floors, huge windows, and classical moldings. If it weren't for all the technical equipment, you'd think you'd been transported back a hundred years. I like it here.

Petermann continues. "If our data isn't clear enough, I can't tell what you're thinking." He scratches his head. "See, Max, you just told me that this dream was about a hot air balloon." He points to a series of data on the screen to the left. "But all I'm getting on the monitor at the right, is a balloon from the Macy's Thanksgiving Day Parade." He's not lying. On the monitor on Petermann's right is an image of a giant helium-filled Snoopy dog.

The goal of today's session was to spend the first part sleeping in the pods while a monitor mapped our brain activity, then wake up and tell Petermann everything we dreamed about. He will line up the imagery we describe with what parts of the brain light up, and try to understand our dream logic and the pathways in our mind that got us there.

Except apparently there isn't much logic to be found, as the confusion over the Snoopy balloon can attest. It's as though our brains are trying to trick Petermann, because it doesn't want him to figure it out. And that makes me kind of happy.

Petermann rubs his face in his hands, looking worse for wear. "Alice, can you tell me more about the dream? Max doesn't seem to remember much at the moment."

"Sure," I say, taking the only seat I see, next to Max on the windowsill. "It was pretty simple, we were basically just sleeping on a cloud."

"Together?" Petermann asks.

I hesitate. Max stares at his shoelaces. "Yes . . ."

"And then what happened?" Petermann asks.

"Um," I say, glancing at Max.

Now Max breaks into a smile, still looking down at his feet. "Yeah, Alice," he says, furrowing his brows together mock-inquisitively. "Then what happened? Sounds like a pretty boring dream."

I want to whack him, but smile despite myself. "I don't know," I say. "I think I might have woken up just before it got good."

Max looks up suddenly, his eyes cutting into me, surprised and curious. I feel a shiver run through my body. Max smiles.

We should just tell Petermann about the almost-kiss. Why aren't we? This is why we're here. But to tell Petermann about the almost-kiss would mean giving up our moment, something only we share. And also admitting it had happened, something I'm not sure we're ready to discuss.

"How odd," Petermann says, oblivious to the tension. "Your dreams are usually so much more diverse. There's usually more material to work with. But our data is inconclusive regardless. The sleep pods are just not as conducive as I'd hoped. Never fear, I have another idea." He takes a seat on a stool facing us. "If anyone is interested in hearing it?"

Scratch that. Petermann now seems to have noticed that Max and I are looking at each other with googly eyes.

"Of course we are." Max shifts and sits up straighter, giving Petermann his full attention. I stay where I am, leaning back against the window where I can keep an eye on him, as though I expect him to lunge at me with his mouth at any moment. But I can't help it. We are inches from taking this a step too far. We woke up before it happened, sure. But what if he hadn't? What would have happened? Would he have let it?

When I was in the seventh grade, my cousin Jane came to stay with us in New York. Jane was starting at Barnard in the fall but had an internship the month prior, before the dorms opened. And for that month, she drove me mostly insane. She borrowed my books and gave them back with food stains all over the pages. She left her hair covering every inch of the bathroom sink. And she had about eight thousand dietary restrictions. For example, Jane was a pescetarian, but only if the fish was killed humanely. *Excuse me,* I imagined Jane asking a waiter at a fancy French restaurant, *but was this fish gently euthanized by syringe as soothing symphony music played? Or did it just die of natural causes immediately at the time the fishing boat came by, like a heart attack or brain aneurysm?*

In this moment, watching Max, I picture my heart as one of Jane's beloved fish. How many ways could it possibly be murdered before Max is through with me? I picture it now, swimming with a bunch of other little heart muscles down a stream, before they are all caught up in a net, jumping and wiggling around.

"So, what's the new plan?" Max asks, appearing calm and focused as ever, and I hate it. One moment I feel like I'm sitting next to my boyfriend, the guy I've known and kissed a thousand times before. And the next he's perfect Max, a Max I barely know, a Max I can't even kiss. I hate all of this back-and-forth. I'm so tired of thinking about it. Suddenly I just want this day to be over so I can go home and bury myself in my real, non-cloud duvet and try to make myself dream about something, anything other than Max tonight.

"I think we should try reenacting a dream you've already had about each other," Petermann says then. "A way to get you in the right mind frame. If you've been to a baseball game, go to a baseball game and try to get the same seats. Or if you went swimming, go and find a pool. Try to wear exactly what you were wearing and behave exactly as you did."

"Why?" I demand, and I realize I sound like a fitful child. But I can't help it. This isn't just the last thing I want to do in the world, it's the exact opposite of what I want to do. It's torture.

Petermann removes his glasses and begins cleaning them with a pale blue pocket square. "Because what we need is material. Stuff to sift through. I want the memories and images fresh in your mind before you dream again."

"Sure," Max agrees. "Though our dreams are kind of weird. I don't know if we can remember all the details . . ."

"I have it all written down," I say. "But even if I didn't, I'd still never forget them." The last part comes out a little more defensive than I mean it to, but Max doesn't seem to notice.

Petermann, however, turns in shock. "You keep a dream journal?"

I nod. "It's a notebook."

"Alice, this could have been incredibly fruitful information to have at the beginning of this process," Petermann says. "Why was I not informed?"

"Because it's personal," I say, crossing my arms.

"The way you write about and describe these experiences could be a goldmine for this experiment, and for dream research in general," Petermann says.

"The purpose of this experiment isn't just about science,"

I say. I'm not sure why, but suddenly I feel like I'm going to cry. He just doesn't get it. "You don't get to take my personal memories and distribute them to a group of research assistants. Max and I can use them as a script, but consider me the director."

Max is looking at me sympathetically. "It's okay, Alice," he says. "Nobody is going to do that. Are they, Dr. Petermann?"

Petermann purses his lips, but nods in agreement. "Understood, but here are my terms. You will go to the location and act out the dream, and then you will come back and spend a full night sleeping in the laboratory. No more of this afternoon nap business."

"The whole night?" Max and I ask at the same time. My voice comes out as small as a cartoon mouse, and his is the opposite: incredibly loud.

"The whole night," Petermann says firmly. "If this is as important to you as you claim it is, you shouldn't have a problem with that."

Max clears his throat, taking a sidelong glance at me. "I guess the real question is, which dream will we choose?" he asks. "We can't exactly hop a plane to Thailand right now."

"I'm not sure," I say. "We don't need something as exotic as Thailand, but it has to be more interesting than the red umbrella. Something that is exceptional, yet accessible."

Max stares out the window for a moment, thinking. Then he smiles. "I think I know just the place."

19

nocturne

THE SUMMER MY father and I lived in Rome, I was desperate for a trip to Venice. He was against this, even for a couple days, saying that like Pig Beach, it was a complete tourist trap at that time of year, and impossible to get around regardless. But I was fascinated by the place. It was a city unlike any other, where everything was old, and where the streets were made of water.

"Come on, we have to go before it sinks," I said, and there was no way for him to argue with this statement, although he did mutter something about how there'd always be scuba tourism.

Tourists aside, it was even more magical than I'd expected. My favorite part was how easy it was to picture exactly what life would've been like hundreds of years earlier. Being in Venice was like being one step closer to the life and energy that the paintings in my beloved museums only hinted about. The water flooding over the steps of a church at high tide, the pigeons in Piazza San Marco, the boats tied up alongside the canals. It was all too easy to imagine Venetians throwing grand parties in their waterfront palazzos, while their guests approached by gondola.

The late Isabella Stewart Gardner, who traveled there in the late nineteenth century, when that very world was still in full swing, apparently loved Venice just as much, because when she returned home to Boston, she designed an entire mansion around it, and then she filled it top to bottom with art. I don't think I have ever seen anything so beautiful in my life. Four stories of Venetian design surrounding a gigantic, plant-filled courtyard, topped with a glass roof.

"Over the course of her life, Isabella Stewart Gardner traveled the world and befriended artists, musicians, and writers, amassing a collection and creative network rivaling any other in the United States at that time," Emmet Lewis says wistfully as he tours me and Max around the grounds. Emmet was a guest of Max's parents the night I crashed their dinner, and I was immediately fond of him, his friendly smile, and immaculate tweed suit. He is also the director of the Gardner Museum. "But her favorite place by far was the Palazzo Barbaro in

Venice, where she would stay. And you see its influence here today." He waves a hand at the intricate architecture.

"Thank you for letting us visit after hours, Mr. Lewis," I say. "This is a dream come true."

"How could I resist?" Emmet exclaims. "I love young people taking interest in the arts. And when Max called and said you had a school project you needed to take care of right away, I was happy to help." He gives Max a pat on the shoulder. "Now, I've given all of security a heads-up. If you need anything from me, I'll be on the fourth floor handling some last-minute emails. I had them turn Isabella's private spa into my office." He bends over and whispers in my ear, "Sometimes I like to read in her clawfoot tub!" With that, Emmet winks and heads off up the staircase.

"I kind of love him," I say, watching his tweed-covered body disappear at the top of the stairs. Then I turn to Max. "And I can't believe you arranged all this."

Max shrugs bashfully. "I know how you feel about museums," he says. "It's the perfect place to reenact our dream at the Met."

We've just arrived in a room on the second floor, as gorgeous and ornate as the last, but with one major difference. On one of the lavishly papered walls, lining either side of a fireplace, are two large gold frames that appear to be framing nothing at all.

"This seems like an odd choice," I say, pointing at the empty frames. It's more something I'd expect to find in Sophie's parents' apartment, alongside a giant sculpture of a hamburger.

But Max looks thrilled. "These must be left over from the heist. In the nineties, a bunch of guys posing as police officers showed up to the gates of the museum after hours, saying they were responding to an emergency call from inside, and a guard broke protocol and let them in. The next morning the guard who was supposed to relieve the two from the night before found them duct-taped together in the basement . . . and a bunch of priceless works were missing."

"Did they ever catch them?" I ask.

"The *Boston Globe* occasionally posts a rumor or two . . . something spotted in a small gallery in Europe or in a private collection at a residence, but nothing official has ever turned up."

We make our way back downstairs and come to a small sitting room on the first floor. It's covered in sunny yellow wallpaper and paintings of portraits and landscapes, guarded by a very large Eastern European man wearing an earpiece and a blazer, who doesn't acknowledge us in the slightest.

"This is where the work I'm looking for should be," Max says, scanning the walls. "There."

I follow his gaze to a canvas in the far corner of the room by the window, a painting that is at first glance not at all what I expected. It's smaller than the others and painted in various shades of gray. Not the bright turquoise tutus and deep pink backdrops of Degas's ballerinas, or Monet's colorful lilies. But as I move closer, I see the gray is peppered with small flecks of fiery orange, as though appearing through a mist. NOCTURNE, JAMES McNEILL WHISTLER, the plaque reads. Somehow calming and slightly mysterious, it's one of the most beautiful paintings I've ever seen. Forget Petermann's surrealist works. As I stare into *Nocturne*'s depths, all I can think is that this is what a manifestation of a dream *really* looks like. I see why Max chose it, and I love him even more for doing so.

"Are you ready?" I turn to Max, and find him already gazing at me with a funny, almost wary expression, like we are thinking the same thing.

All I can manage in response is a nod. I can't believe we are doing this.

"Let me just change," Max says. "I'll be right back."

I remove my wool coat and place it under a carved wooden table in the corner that probably cost more than our car, revealing a long, plum-colored ball gown I found in my grandmother's closet. It's not exactly Beyoncé material, but it does bring out my complexion. Then I open to the entry about the Met dream and scan its pages as though running lines one last time before going onstage.

I hear a noise and turn back, finding Max standing by *in the doorway*, looking terrified. And also completely perfect in an elegant tux.

"You look . . . beautiful," he admits.

"Then what's wrong?" I ask.

"Nothing," Max says with a sigh. "Just read the journal, Alice."

I open my notebook and start from the beginning of the dream, describing the sparkling champagne, the fancy dress, and the elegant crowd, until I get to, "And that's where Max finds me, standing in front of the Degas ballerinas, in the Impressionist section."

I swallow at the next part, but press onward. "And this is where you say—"

"I know what I say," Max interrupts, his voice low, his eyes gentle. "You know, I can dance, too." He slips an arm around my waist. How I have missed this arm.

"Right, good." I flip a page. "And my whole body—let's just skip that part." I glance up at Max's face, which is way too close, and find him barely containing a smirk. It's like he's enjoying the fact that this is torturing me.

"And I say, 'Prove it.' And now you . . ."

Without hesitating, Max gives me a twirl. As I spin, I swear I see twinkle lights flying past, like little fireflies zooming around me. But when I steady myself again, it's just the glow of the candelabras.

"Good, good," I manage after the twirl, smoothing my skirt down in the back to make sure it hasn't flown up. So I'm already off balance when Max pulls me tightly to him, and I smell his neck and close my eyes for a second.

"And now you say . . ." Max's voice comes from far away, and I open my eyes again.

"You look good in a tux," I barely whisper, having sort of given up. I want to nuzzle my nose just below his ear.

"Thanks. It's the one Beyoncé wore to the Grammys." He says the line like he's tired, like he's given up, too, and I can feel his heart hammering in his rib cage. This time we don't laugh. We just stand there, because we both know what's next, and it obviously can't come next, we know that, because he has a girlfriend, and also because this is real life and not a dream, and because it would mean something more than maybe we are ready for. I swear from somewhere I can hear the hum of low chatter and symphony music, which makes negative sense since we are at a high-security museum after hours and the only people here are us and Emmet upstairs in a nineteenth-century tub and the security guard, who must think we are complete and utter mental patients.

"Okay, great!" I announce, way too loud, and use all my energy to pull away from Max. But just as I'm at a safe distance, I realize he hasn't let go. And firmly, almost forcefully, Max has pulled me back into his arms and tipped me backward.

And Max kisses me.

And his lips taste like Oreos. But the Oreos are an

afterthought. I know somewhere deep within my brain that when a woman finds herself on the receiving end of a gallant kiss, she should let herself just be kissed. Isn't that how it always works in the movies? But I'm unable to play the part. Nothing can stop my hands from reaching up and tangling themselves in Max's hair, my arms from pulling me to him and him to me, closer than we already were. As though I've never been kissed before. As though I'm devouring him. As though we're the last two people left on the planet and kissing is the one thing that can keep us alive.

Max pulls away far enough to lean his forehead against mine. "I missed you," he says. And I can't tell if we're on script anymore.

*

As the security guard, whose name I learn is Igor, lets Max and me out of the locked front door of the Gardner, I feel as though I didn't just talk about sipping the champagne in my dream. I feel as though I had it. Maybe more than one glass. Maybe more like twelve. When Max takes my hand, I think, *And there goes one more*, and I look back at the museum door to see Igor standing behind the glass.

He gives me a wink.

We drive back to the lab in mostly silence, because I can't think of anything to say. I stare out the window and wonder if he's regretting it all, except for one thing. Once again, there are two hands on my knee, and one of them is Max's.

"Where'd you tell your dad you were staying tonight?" Max asks.

"I told him the junior class had a lock-in." I laugh. "I could've told him I was going to Portugal and he would've barely heard me. What did you tell yours?"

"They're out of town," Max says. "What they don't know won't hurt them, as long as I keep my cell phone on."

I know we need to talk about it, but truthfully I'm afraid to ruin it. Right now, just the two of us driving, dressed up in ridiculously fancy clothes, we could actually be in a dream. We wouldn't even know. Who is here to tell us otherwise?

*

Turns out Lillian is, when she greets us in the circular foyer of CDD by the staircase, holding two sets of blue cotton PJ's—CDD standard issue—two toothbrushes, and two travel-sized bars of soap. It feels like summer camp. A really bad summer camp where you never get to go outside.

"Where's Petermann?" Max asks as Lillian hands us our toiletries.

"He'll be here soon," she says. "He had a fundraiser to attend. In the meantime, I'm on duty. Just yell if you need anything."

"Thanks, Lillian," Max says.

"You're very welcome," Lillian answers, shooting me a mischievous look when Max turns his back for a moment.

I shoot a look back. *What?* How could she possibly know?

But when I walk into the bathroom, I see why. I'm a mess.

My hair looks like I just woke up from a twelve-hour nap, and there is a redness around my nose and cheeks, no doubt due to Max's slight stubble.

But that's not even the most distracting part. Speaking of my cheeks, they are glowing. Not like I just ran six miles, more like I just swallowed six nightlights. I am positively lit from within, and my eyes are big and round.

Apparently love makes you beautiful.

I put on my pajamas, wash my face and brush my teeth, and finger comb my hair so it looks halfway decent again. Then Max and I climb into our side-by-side pods.

"I wish I could hold your hand," Max admits when we are all tucked in.

"Me too," I say.

"Do you want me to tell you a story?" he asks.

I smile. "Yes, please."

"Okay," Max says. "One day a little boy is sitting on the floor of his living room, playing with some toy trucks. *Vroom!*" Max makes the sound effect enthusiastically. "He shoots one across the carpet, but it goes too far, to the other side of the sofa. And then miraculously, it shoots right back. Surprised, the little boy peers around the sofa to find a girl around his age with a very attractive bowl cut, building a giant Lego castle. She asks him if he wants to play, before popping one of the Legos in her mouth, informing him that if he's hungry, they are made out of chocolate." Max pauses now, and his voice takes on a softer tone. "And the boy had never felt so happy in his whole life. They build the most incredible chocolate castle, with dragons and soldiers and a moat made of milk. And then they fell asleep side by side. The boy wakes up in his living room, and even though there is no castle or no little girl, he still feels just as happy. And he knows he will see her again."

"Was that me?" I say with a yawn.

"That was you," Max says, his voice a little hoarse. "The first time we met."

"I like that story," I sigh.

"I'll see you soon, Alice," Max mumbles.

"I'll see you soon," I say. And slide into a peaceful sleep.

October 11TH

"So what did you think of Nocturne?" Isabella Stewart Gardner says. We're seated facing each other in her empty bathtub, fully clothed, sipping chocolate milk shakes.

"I thought it was the most beautiful painting I've ever seen," I say breathlessly after swallowing a big mouthful of ice cream, careful not to spill on my plum ball gown. Isabella, in turn, is dressed in a gown made of deep-green velvet.

"I'm so glad you think so," she replies.

"Me too," Emmet Lewis adds. He's seated in the corner in an orange wing-backed chair, wearing a teal suit and perusing a book titled Tweed, Tweed, and More Tweed!

"Come on," Isabella says, hoisting herself out of the tub abruptly, before extending a hand to me. "I want to show you my latest acquisition."

Raising the hems of our skirts around our ankles so we don't fall, we tiptoe down the staircase to the third floor of the Gardner Museum, but when we reach the bottom of the steps, I see we're back at the Met, in the Impressionist wing.

"Isn't it lovely?" Isabella asks, pointing to a painting of a bright green field, where a purple hot air balloon is tethered to the ground. "It just arrived."

"It's striking," I say. There really is something extraordinary about it, but I can't put my finger on what it is. The colors and detail are so vivid they're nearly lifelike.

"Touch it," Isabella suggests.

"Are you sure?" I hesitate. "It's against the rules."

"Alice, I make the rules," Isabella says. "And I insist. You haven't seen the half of it."

Biting my lip, I reach a hand out to touch the painting and find that suddenly I'm inside it. And the hand I extended has landed on Max's cheek, where he stands in the basket of the hot air balloon.

"Wanna go on a ride?" he asks, a welcoming smile on his face.

"Okay," I say, taking his hand and climbing over the top of the basket.

"Lillian, will you do the honors?" Max asks. Lillian appears, holding a giant pair of golden scissors, and snips the rope with ease.

And just like that we are rising, up, up, and away, slowly at first and then a bit faster. I look down and see there's no longer a field below us but, instead, the city of Boston. Fenway Park, the Citgo sign, and a gleaming statehouse dome, the Charles River snaking through it all. Everything is bathed in a warm, dusky light.

"Where are we going?" I ask.

"Back to the cloud," Max says. "To finish what we started." He comes up behind me and wraps his arms around my shoulders, leaning down to rest his head on my shoulder blade.

I blush. "We don't have to go back to the cloud," I say.

"We don't?" he asks, spinning me around to face him.

"Nope." I take a nervous breath, gazing up at him.

"Great," Max says. "Because I've been dying to do this again all night." Then he places one hand at the back of my neck, and leans down to kiss me.

20

they're merging

WHEN WE ARE ushered into Petermann's office the next morning, I am shocked to see him dressed in something other than athletic attire, but relieved to see it's just as strange. Max and I aren't the only people in the room in pajamas. Petermann's are a silk cobalt blue.

"Good morning, sleepyheads," he says, removing his glasses and setting down the paper. "Please, take a seat and help yourself."

Spread out all over his desk is an array of breakfast items. Scones, cinnamon buns, bagels, and croissants. In other words, heaven. Lillian walks in looking tired, pushing a cart with a bunch of clinking cups.

"Would anyone care for coffee?" Petermann asks, gesturing to the cart, and both Max and I eagerly raise our hands.

"This is all for us?" I ask, genuinely excited.

"She has a thing for baked goods," Max interjects, and I nod enthusiastically.

"It's your reward for all your hard work yesterday," Petermann says, leaning over his desk and clasping his hands together. "I think it really paid off, because not only did you sleep soundly through the night, your brain activity was off the charts. Now I am dying to hear what happened!"

Max has already covered a bagel in cream cheese and taken a big bite, so I go first, smiling when I notice he put the other half of the bagel on my plate. There is something very primal about it, like we are prehistoric people and he went out and killed the bagel and brought it home for me. "Well, we dreamed about the hot air balloon again," I start to explain.

"No," Petermann says, waving a hand impatiently. "No, no. Earlier. Start at the very beginning, when you were conscious. Begin with the reenactment and go from there."

I hesitate, and look at Max. "Everything?" I ask. But Max just gives a *why not tell him* shrug, and Petermann insists. So this time, I don't leave anything out. I tell him about Emmet and the clawfoot tub, about the stolen artwork, about *Nocturne*, and about how we stood in front of her and went through the whole dream . . . even the kiss. I look down when I mention the last part, feeling weird talking about it in front of Petermann, of all people. But he doesn't seem fazed.

"Your idea must've worked," I say. "Because it all felt so real at the time. I could actually hear the symphony music from the Met dream."

"So did I," Max adds. "And your lips tasted like Oreos."

"So did yours!" I practically shriek in excitement, and Max, laughing, reaches over and lets his hand rest lightly at the back of my neck, giving it an affectionate squeeze.

But Petermann doesn't look excited. "I'm confused. You mean his lips tasted like Oreos in your dream."

"No," I say. "Well, yes, they did in the dream the first time, but then they also did in real life."

Petermann's brow furrows. "I suppose it would be silly for me to ask if you had in fact consumed any Oreos yesterday?"

Max and I shake our heads.

"What is it?" Max asks.

"I'm not sure," Petermann says, tapping his fingers on his desk. "Have either of you ever experienced anything like this before? A moment where something from your dreams seems to seep into your reality?"

The question makes the hair on my arms stand up. "I have," I say cautiously, telling him about Sergio and Brunilda outside my window, and Jerry's giant footprint. "Have you?" I ask Max.

Max nods. "The parrots have been stalking me, too. The

other day they were roosting on the goal during a game and cheered when I scored. And yesterday, when I went to switch my laundry from the washer to the dryer, I pulled a rubber ducky out with the load."

"Like the washing machine dream," I whisper. "I saw one in the Charles River a few weeks ago."

"Had either of you ever experienced this . . . dream bleeding, so to speak, before meeting each other?" Petermann asks.

Max and I both shake our heads again.

"They're merging," Petermann says under his breath.

"What?" Both Max and I speak at the same time.

"I don't want to alarm either of you yet," Petermann says. "But it's my concern that now that you've met in real life, your minds may not be able to tell the difference between reality and your dreams. It's possible that the longer this continues, if we can't stop you from dreaming of each other, it could become impossible to distinguish waking and dreaming, one from the other." He pauses and leans forward. "And you may slowly begin to lose your grip on reality altogether."

"You mean like, go insane?" I ask.

Max's hand, once tangled up in my hair, has dropped into his lap. "That doesn't make any sense," he says.

"Look around, Max," Petermann says. "What about any of this makes sense?"

*

"It's going to be okay," I say to Max as we walk to his car. It's still early in the morning, not even eight yet, and the whole quad is empty. Max is still holding my hand, but he hasn't looked at me directly since before Petermann told us his theory. "We'll figure it out. Petermann will figure it out." I stop, waiting for him to show he heard me.

Like the gentleman he is, Max doesn't go around to his door, but comes to mine first, opening it for me.

"I know we will," he says, placing his hands on the sides of my shoulders. "I just wish everything wasn't so complicated. I should be studying for a history exam right now, but instead I'm worried my dreams are taking over my mind. I know it's silly, but I just sort of wish that last night's dream balloon never came down to earth again."

"Why? What happened on the balloon?" I ask, pretending to be confused.

"Oh, you don't remember?" Max says, playing along. "Would it help if I reminded you?"

"It's not just helpful, it's important," I say, pointing a finger at him. "Crucial to research as a matter of fa–" But I don't even get to finish my sentence, because Max is already kissing me.

I pull away, feeling disoriented. "Sometimes when you kiss me, I become completely weightless," I say.

Then I see the look on Max's face. He's staring in horror at the ground. I look down too and realize we actually *are* weightless. We're floating. Just a bit, just a foot or so. I kick my feet and just like that, *whomp*, we're thrown back to the earth again, where we lean against the car to ground ourselves. My heart is pounding so fast I think it might burst through my rib cage, and I feel like I might throw up.

"Did you see that?" I ask.

"Yup," Max says, breathing hard.

"Did we . . ."

"We did." Max nods. "And I think it might've been my fault."

"How was it your fault?" I asked.

"Well, I said I didn't want to come down from the balloon again . . . so we started to go up."

Max is looking at me, terrified. I take his hand and squeeze it tight.

21

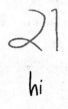

hi

OLIVER'S HEAD APPEARS upside down over mine with a quizzical expression, but I can't hear what he's saying through the musings of The Cure in my ears, so I pull out my headphones. If you are not familiar with postpunk or new wave music of the late 1970s, I highly suggest you amend this, particularly if you are hopelessly in love.

"What?" I ask, choosing not to sit up from my position on the quad, where I've been splayed out all free period just staring at the foliage above. I swear this one tree keeps turning from a normal fire-red color to various shades of hot purple and pink, which I could attribute to the fact that I'm dozing on and off. Or the fact that, you know, as Petermann said, I'm losing my grip on reality.

"I said, what's up with you?" Oliver repeats, still standing over me, his curls falling in his face like the first day we met.

"Can you be more specific?"

Oliver stretches out next to me. "You've got this funny smile on your face," he says. "Like you have a secret nobody else knows."

I have a secret only one other person knows.

"Oh," I say, trying to make my face more serious. "I didn't realize."

But I did realize. My dad said the same thing to me at breakfast, after I looked up from my Cheerios to find him giving me an odd look, and had to block his face with the cereal box when he wouldn't stop. I've been smiling like an idiot since I woke up, because I can't stop thinking about the kissing. Or our kiss last night, in our dream. Or our kiss yesterday, at the Gardner. So many kisses, and all of them incredible. I know I should feel guilty, and really a part of me does. But another part, a bigger part . . . feels great. Like something has fallen into place. I don't want to hurt Celeste. She's been nothing but nice to me. But I can't help how I feel, and Max can't help how he feels. And honestly, a part of me wonders if I feel this way because technically—and pardon me for sounding juvenile—I saw him first. He was mine first.

"Is this about Wolfe?" Oliver says now. "Please tell me it's not about Wolfe."

"It's not about Max," I say. "Why would you ask that?"

"Because he's right here," Oliver says, sitting up and leaning on his elbows.

"Hi," Max says, from where he's standing over us.

"Hi," I say with a little laugh that mortifies me, and I brush the hair away from my face.

"Hi," Oliver says in a tone he doesn't even try to mask as suspicious.

"*Hello,*" Celeste says loudly, and we all turn to where she is standing a few feet away, hands on hips, in the middle of the quad.

"Is it true?" she asks, sucking in her cheeks a bit as she looks at Max.

"Is what true?" Max says, his posture stiffening.

"You two," she says, looking at him but nodding to me. "I have to admit, I did sort of wonder about it. I could tell you acted strange around her, but I didn't think you'd actually . . ." She stops talking and just looks down, shaking her head.

"What's she talking about?" Oliver mutters to me under his breath, but I don't move a muscle.

"Where were you yesterday?" Celeste says to him, tears welling up in her eyes.

Max just keeps staring at her, his face like stone. As I watch him, I realize people might think he's being a jerk, or that he doesn't care. But I know better by now. He's shutting down. He's scared.

"Because the thing is," she continues, "you said you had to

go to some event with your mother. Some stupid event with those giant scissors and the big ribbon you hate. So did you?"

Max opens his mouth as if to speak, but nothing comes out.

"Did you?" she asks again, her voice breaking. I want to put my face in my hands.

Max exhales. "No," he finally admits.

Celeste's mouth is hanging open. "So it's true. When Francesca Dello Russo texted me this morning and said she'd just seen the two of you kissing on a quad at MIT when she went for a run this morning, I said, no way. She must be mistaken. But deep down I knew she was right." She looks to me now. "I was nice to you. I *liked* you, Alice."

"Celeste," I start to say, not knowing what's going to come out. "We didn't mean to hurt you. We just—"

But Max interrupts me. "It's my fault," he says. "Don't blame Alice. I kissed her. But it just sort of happened . . . we . . . I didn't mean it."

Now it's my turn to stare at Max in shock. I know what he means, it did just *happen*. There was the symphony music and the painting and my dress and the twirling . . . and yes, it was all a bit dreamlike and fuzzy. But it didn't end there. There was also the drive to CDD and the handholding. The bedtime stories and the kiss on the quad today. One thing was for certain—last night and today, I meant it when I kissed him back. I thought he did, too.

"You didn't?" I ask.

204

"As if that makes it better," Celeste scoffs as she starts to turn away. "And by the way, in the future, if both of you would be so kind as to never speak to me again, I'd really appreciate it." She marches off, and it's only at this moment that I realize the entire quad is staring at us.

Max doesn't chase after her, but he doesn't turn to me, either. He just stands there a moment, looking dazed, before walking off toward the boathouse. I turn to Oliver and see he's already long gone.

After all the mixed signals and emotions, the MRIs and EEGs and dream reenactments, I thought we were starting to figure it out. Not just the science . . . *us*. But we weren't. We're no closer than we'd been since the day I got here. As the quad starts to hum again, no doubt with the gossip of what a terrible person I am, I put my headphones back in my ears and slink away to hide out in a place where nobody will see me cry.

22

he's not your boyfriend

I UNLOAD SOME potting soil in Nan's garden, pausing to shoo Jerry away from a snail he is sniffing, when my phone buzzes. My heartbeat picks up speed as I look to see if it's a text from Max, but it isn't. It's about my mother. Apparently I forgot about the Google alert I set up for her a few years back. When we figured out what Google alerts were all about, most of my friends chose televisions stars or pop singers. *Who is he dating now? What did she buy at the supermarket?* But my mother was just as elusive to me as any celebrity, perhaps more so. It just never worked . . . until now.

PRIMATOLOGIST MADELEINE BAXTER
TO ATTEND ENVIRONMENTAL RALLY IN DC
AND SPEAK AT THE SMITHSONIAN ON THE ROLE

OF DEFORESTATION IN THE ACCELERATION OF

SPECIES EXTINCTION AND CLIMATE CHANGE

I stare at my phone, stunned, then put it back in my pocket and walk into the house, where my father is reading *National Geographic* in the living room.

He speaks before I can. "Did you know that in certain indigenous cultures of Papua New Guinea, yams are considered sacred?"

"I did not," I say. "But, Dad . . ."

"If a man grows a large yam among his crop, he must give it to his neighbor, thereby shaming him, until the neighbor is able to grow a larger one himself . . ."

"Dad," I say.

"I don't know if they ever even *eat* them!" he cries. "Really makes you rethink our favorite Thanksgiving dish, doesn't it?"

"Dad," I practically yell. I have no patience for his factoids today.

"Sorry, yes?" He looks up now, as though seeing me for the first time.

Now that I have his attention, I pause. He's not going to like this. Taking a breath, I decide to just rip the Band-Aid off. "Did you know that Madeleine is coming to DC?" I ask.

My father's face flashes from happy to grim to perfectly controlled. "I wish you would just call her *Mom*," he says. When I don't say anything in response, he asks, "How did you know that?"

"I have a Google alert for her," I answer matter-of-factly. The less I beat around the bush, the less he will be able to lead me off course in this conversation.

"I see . . ." he says, laying down the magazine and folding his hands in his lap, thinking.

"Do you think we'll see her?" I ask.

"It's possible," he says, glancing at his watch, out the window, anywhere but my face.

"Possible?" I ask. And I want to say, *That my mother might decide to swing by to see her own daughter for the first time in ten years?* But I don't say that part.

"Sure, of course," he says, looking back down at his reading again. "We should email and check."

"You mean you'll email her?" I ask. I know I'm pushing, but why is it up to me? He is my dad. He is supposed to take care of me. He is supposed to be able to ask my mother when she is coming home.

"Sure," he says, turning a page in the magazine. "I can do that."

He's being deliberately vague, noncommittal. And I want to scream. At him for letting me down, for being unable to talk about something so important. At my mom for being such a crappy mom in the first place, for never being here when I need her. At Max for saying he didn't mean it, for walking away on the quad and leaving me all by myself.

At all of them, for leaving me alone.

"You wanna cool it with that tiny shovel?" I hear Oliver say behind me. I'm crouched over the soil back in Nan's garden, planting succulents to grow in a cold frame for the wall at the science center. But now that I look, I seem to have been doing more harm than good. Less planting, more rampant soil stabbing with my trowel.

"Sorry." I peer around to look at him. "Rough morning. Actually, what are you doing today? I could really use an adventure right about now."

I stand up, wiping my hands on my knees, and only now do I see that something is off about Oliver. He hasn't moved from the front gate, and is standing a little rigid, his hands clutched to his sides.

"Actually, no," he says. "That's not why I'm here. I wanted to . . ." He stops, frustrated, then tries again. "Alice, how could you do what you did?"

I sigh. "I know. Oliver, I can explain. The dreams . . ."

"What, the dreams *made* you do it, Alice? The dreams control your mind now? I believe you when you say you and Wolfe dream about each other. But I can't believe that." Oliver is frowning at me, his shoulders clenched. He's never looked at me this way before.

"Oliver."

"He's not your boyfriend, Alice."

"I know that," I start to say.

"He's not yours, Alice. He belongs to Celeste. And Celeste is a good person; she doesn't deserve this. He's hers. He's not yours."

"But he was mine!" I finally yell. "He was *mine*. For years. For my entire life, he was mine. My best friend, my boyfriend. My partner. I can't just turn it off," I say, realizing suddenly that Oliver is not the person I want to be yelling this at. The person I want to be yelling at is Max. I also realize, when I say those words out loud, that while they are exactly how I feel about Max, they are exactly how Max feels about me, and what he was trying to tell me in the elevator that night. That sometimes you can't just turn it off, even when you know it's wrong. "People can't just turn off how they feel because someone tells them to," I say to Oliver now, more quietly than before. "You wouldn't understand."

"Yeah, I would, actually," Oliver says without meeting my eyes, and I now understand that there are two broken hearts in this tiny succulent garden. And that just because my feelings for Oliver were innocent, doesn't mean his were.

"I promise I will make things right with Celeste, first thing tomorrow. She deserves better," I tell Oliver. Then I hold my gaze on him until he finally meets my eyes, and add, "So do you."

Oliver waves a hand dismissively. "Whatever," he says with a smile. "I'll get over it."

"I'm sure you will," I say.

"But you have to be the one to tell Sally the Segway. Because I can't watch her pine for Frank anymore," he adds. "She's driving me crazy."

As Oliver leaves the garden that afternoon, I watch him nearly careen into an elderly woman on the sidewalk. Like a nineteenth-century nobleman, Oliver steps aside and bows gracefully, bidding the woman good afternoon, and she smiles back in delight. Oliver winks.

If I knew what was best for me, if I were someone else, I would fall in love with him. For his wit and charm and sense of adventure. The way he looks out for me, the way he's not afraid to say what he wants.

But unfortunately, I'm not someone else. I'm me. And unfortunately, I have to be aware of the fact that Max Wolfe exists in the world. And, unfortunately, nobody else stands a chance.

23

they were really smart birds

"LET ME SEE if I have this straight," Sophie says. "You and Max have been in love for years, and you finally kissed in real life. But in real life, Max is dating Celeste. And now Celeste is mad at you, and Oliver is, too, because he is in love with you, but you aren't in love with him, you're in love with Max, who you, incidentally, also haven't spoken to in two days."

"I would give anything in the world to tell you that even one sentence of that is wrong," I say into my phone.

"Jesus," Sophie exclaims. "My biggest challenge lately is how to get the new junior, Marco Medina, to notice I exist."

"Oh no," I groan. "What have you been doing?" I love Sophie, but she's not the most tactful, and she's extremely confident. It's not always a winning combination.

"My mom said to just keep saying hi to him, so I've been doing that," Sophie says.

"That doesn't sound too bad," I say.

"I may be saying it a bit too aggressively," she admits. "The other day he all but ran away when I greeted him. You know, all, *Hi!*" She shouts the last part into the phone. "Anyway, you haven't forgotten that I'm coming to visit, right?" she says.

"Of course not!" I say, reminding myself to go back into our last email chain and see which date we chose.

"Great," she says, sounding excited. "I can't wait to see all the drama in person."

*

Celeste isn't in Terrarium Club on Wednesday afternoon, and I feel sick about it. "Go ahead, eat me," I mutter aloud to the man-eating plant. "I deserve it." But then Parker dismisses us and I walk out of the greenhouse and find Celeste waiting by Frank, and then I feel sick all over again.

"It's highly likely that she's going to kill you," Jeremiah observes as he walks by me with his signature hurried gait, on his way to where his mom is waiting at the curb in a white BMW.

"How do you know?" I snap.

"Everyone knows," Jeremiah says. "Even me."

"Relax," Celeste says when I get closer, one hand on her hip. She's wearing another amazing outfit—black leather leggings and a draped gray wool sweater. "You look like a puppy that did something bad."

"That's because I did," I say.

"Of course you did," Celeste calmly replies. "But the only thing worse than kissing another girl's boyfriend is turning that girl into something to be scared of. Victimizing yourself is not cool."

I really wish she wasn't being so mature about this. It would make my life a lot easier.

"I know," I say. "You have no idea how sorry I am for what happened." And then I understand why Max said what he did. Because I *am* sorry. And he is sorry, too. And no matter how we feel about each other, you just don't do that to a girl like this.

"It's just weird, I thought I could spot girls like you," Celeste says. "The boyfriend stealers. They act like they're your friend but you can always sort of tell they aren't, you always know they aren't totally there. They have another agenda, another target, and you are just a prop to help them get to it." She reaches down and absently dings Frank's bell a few times as she chooses the right words. "But not you. You genuinely did not seem like that person to me. I was really beginning to think we could be friends. So I don't want to kick your butt, I just want to know . . . what happened? So I can readjust my sense of the world again, and go back to Terrarium Club in peace."

"I promise I'm not that kind of girl," I say. "I know it seems like I am, because I did what I did, but . . ." I bite my lip, frustrated. This is too hard to explain. "Can you come with me?"

"Where?" Celeste asks.

"I need to show you something. This will sound ridiculous without proof."

*

"This is what you wanted to show me?" Celeste asks as we approach the CDD rotunda. "Some creepy old building in the middle of MIT? What are you going to do, kidnap me and hide me here so you can have Max all to yourself?" She takes a deep breath. "Sorry, I have a pretty active imagination. It tends to alienate people once they get to know me."

"That actually explains a lot," I say, wondering if Max has a type. That's when I notice the neon-orange sign taped to the front of the CDD double doors.

THIS PROPERTY IS CLOSED PER ORDER OF
THE CITY OF CAMBRIDGE AND ALL ACTIVITIES HEREIN
HAVE BEEN SUSPENDED PENDING AN INVESTIGATION
—THE CITY OF CAMBRIDGE

"What the hell?" I say. I was just here three days ago.

"Seriously, why are we here?" Celeste says. "You've got two minutes to clear the air before I take off."

For a moment, I freeze. This is a disaster. I needed to show Celeste CDD for her to believe me. Oliver might have believed me without proof, because Oliver is Oliver. But not Celeste. I've done enough to make her doubt me already. I run the options through my head. I could sneak her in, but now that there's an official police warning outside, that seems unwise.

Just then I see Lillian rounding the rotunda, and I think all is not lost. But she turns around and starts walking the other way when she sees me.

"Lillian!" I cry out, rushing after her when she doesn't turn. "Lillian!" I say. "What is going on?"

I grab her by the oversized scarf she's wearing and spin her like a mummy until she faces me. "Ow!" she says, straightening her scarf again. "I wasn't going to break in or anything. I just needed to get something at my desk. I was going to be in and out. They kicked us out yesterday with no warning at all."

"Why?" I ask.

"Petermann," Lillian responds. She spits out his name like it's a bad grape, like she can hardly bear to have it on her lips.

"Who is Petermann?" Celeste has come up next to me by now.

"Who are you?" Lillian asks.

"Celeste," Celeste says.

"What do you want?" Lillian frowns. This girl seriously needs to take an etiquette course.

"I wish I knew!" Celeste says, exasperated, and looks at me.

I take a deep breath. I can make this work to my advantage. "Lillian, would you please explain to Celeste what our relationship is?"

"We don't have one," Lillian says matter-of-factly.

"No, we don't have a *friendship*," I say slowly, like I'm teaching a kindergartener how to spell. "What I mean is, how do you *know* me?"

"Oh," Lillian says. "You were a research subject at the Center for Dream Discovery, where I used to work."

"How often did I visit?"

"Twice a week."

"With who?"

"Your boyfriend, Max."

My jaw clenches at this, and I glance at Celeste out of the corner of my eye, only to find her looking at me with hatred. "No, as we discussed, Max is not my boyfriend."

"Whatever you say . . ." Lillian rolls her eyes. This isn't quite going as planned, but I can still fix it.

"And why were Max and I here exactly?" I press her.

Lillian has been looking around the quad absently, where people are reading on benches or hustling from building to building. But now she straightens up. "I thought that was confidential."

"I'm now giving you permission to explain," I tell her, crossing my arms.

Lillian sighs. "You and Max were here because you came here as children, for your nightmares, and somehow through the study ended up dreaming of each other. It's my understanding that you've dreamed of each other your whole lives, and you were coming to CDD so you could fix it."

"Great, thank you, Lillian," I start to say.

But Lillian isn't finished. "Because you had fallen in love and neither of you knew how to handle it. Anyway, who is this?"

I smile tightly. "Lillian, Celeste is Max's girlfriend."

Celeste's eyebrows shoot up and her mouth forms a tiny, perfect little pout.

"Oh," is all Lillian says in reply. "Anyway, I'd better go. I'd like to grab my stuff and get out of here before the police come back."

"Where is Petermann?" I ask again.

"Jail, I assume," Lillian says.

"What are you talking about?"

"Petermann was arrested," Lillian says. "It was the parrots. Petermann was involved in the illegal parrot trade. He was obsessed with birds, the rarer the better. They say he could go to jail."

"Jail for a couple Italian birds with attitude problems?" I ask.

"They were really smart birds, Alice."

＊

"So let me get this straight," Celeste says a while later as we each lean against a pillar by the steps of CDD. We've been here in silence while I bite my fingernails and Celeste has been chewing on her lip, as I wait for her to say something. It's all on the table now. She just has to believe it.

"You and Max came here to have your dreams analyzed so you could effectively be rid of each other forever?" She pushes herself off the building and pulls her leather bag over her arm. "Okay."

"Okay?" I ask.

"Yeah, okay, I get it. Frankly, because this crap is just too crazy to make up. But this doesn't mean we are friends. Plus, you have other stuff to worry about."

"Like what specifically?" I ask, and I really do want to know, because there are too many things she could be talking about.

"Like how you are going to fix this mess when the scientist performing the procedures is in lockup," Celeste answers, before walking off across the lawn.

I stare after her, because of course, as usual, she's right. If CDD is closed indefinitely, then we'll never get to the bottom of the dreams. And if we never figure out why we dream about each other, we'll never be able to stop it. All of this, the drama and confusion, will just keep happening again and again.

I look down at my brown boots and take a deep breath, and when I exhale, the ground ripples under my feet, like I just blew across a perfectly still lake. Except this isn't a lake, it's a lawn at MIT. *Not again*, I think, before breathing in deeply, pursing my lips, and pushing all the air out of me, this time harder. Sure enough, it's not just the grass that ripples, but the ground itself.

I pause for a moment, then raise one of my boots and stomp

it down on the grass, hard, and watch a wave of green earth rise and swell, undulating across the lawn. It would be beautiful if it weren't so weird. I stomp both legs down and the next wave is even bigger, maybe even knee high, which is when I look up suddenly and notice it's heading right for Celeste as she walks into the distance. It's just about to topple her over when I scream out her name like she's about to get hit by a truck.

"What?" She turns around, annoyed. And just like that, the grassy wave has disappeared.

"Um, I'm . . . never mind," I call out, feeling pathetic, and also mildly insane.

Celeste just shakes her head and keeps walking. "You really are a weird one, Alice Rowe," she says out loud.

This was about so much more than me and Max and all the drama we were causing. This was about our sanity.

OCTOBER 15th

I am not sure if I have ever felt something as wonderful as the sun on my face right now. I'm draped across an innertube on some windy river in Texas, my toes dangling in the water, my head and arms splayed backward across the other end. I adjust the big round sunglasses above my nose and sigh.

"You look happy," Max calls out, and I raise the sunglasses again and turn my head in the direction of his voice to give him a wink.

"You betcha," I say, and grin at him.

Max is floating along a few yards away in navy swim trunks and black Ray-Bans. He grins back. "Come here."

"You come here," I say, waving an arm out toward him. That's when I notice my fingernails are painted the most beautiful shade of sparkly sunset red. I wiggle my fingers in front of my face and marvel at the sight of it, the sun shining between my fingers.

I go to rest my hand down again and am confused by the texture of the innertube. It's rough and chalky to the touch, and it has big holes in the surface. That's when I sit up and realize I'm floating along in a giant Cheerio, and the river is now made entirely of milk.

"This must be great for our skin," I observe, and look at Max again. "Hey, how come you get a Froot Loop?" I demand to know.

"Because I'm more fun than you are," Max quips back. He reaches down and breaks off a piece of his lime-green vessel, dunks it a few times in the milk river like a donut, and pops it in his mouth. "Mmm," he says.

"Wanna trade?" I ask sweetly.

"No way," Max says, and now he's sitting up, too, because he knows better.

"Too bad," I reply, and start paddling madly toward him. He's going to give me that Froot Loop whether he wants to or not.

But no matter how hard I paddle, I can't seem to reach him. The river is picking up pace, and suddenly it's no longer white—it's rainbow-colored milk, like someone just finished a bowl of Lucky Charms and is pouring the remaining milk down the drain.

"Max, slow down!" I cry.

"I can't!" he yells back, moving farther and farther away, until he's just a dot on the horizon, and I've stopped moving altogether. Dejected, I pull my giant soggy Cheerio to shore and fall asleep with my head against it, my legs resting on a beach made of sugar.

24

they're just breasts

IT'S SAFE TO say that if you are a student at Bennett Academy who needs to get actual homework done, the last place you should go is the library. It's more social than the dining hall at lunch, the main quad on a Monday morning, or the bleachers at a Saturday afternoon football game, all put together. Most of the time students go there and pretend to work while they people-watch instead, and sometimes they don't even bother to take their books out of their bag. It drives the librarians absolutely nuts.

The library is the last place you should go to study unless, of course, you have the discipline of Max Wolfe. I almost don't want to disturb him when I find him sitting in a far corner on the second floor, surrounded by stacks of history books, the light of the desk lamp casting a glow over his handsome face. But then he looks up and spots me and I feel embarrassed for staring.

Hi, he mouths.

"Hi," I say back out loud.

Max shakes his head with a smile and motions me over.

"This is the silent floor," he whispers. "Do you want to sit down?"

I nod, and pull up a chair next to his desk.

Neither of us says anything for a moment.

"We have a problem," I finally whisper.

"I know." Max nods. "I know we have a lot to talk about, and I promise we will, but right now this exam is all I can think about–"

"No," I say, putting a hand out to stop him. "Not about . . . *that*." Because there's a lot to say about *that*, but right now there are more important things to deal with. "About Petermann. It seems he's . . . been arrested." I feel bad telling him this on the eve of his history test. After how nervous he was Sunday, it's going to throw him for a loop. But we have to figure out what we're going to do.

"I know," Max says.

I sit up straighter. "You do? How?"

Max pauses. "Celeste told me," he answers, and I slump again.

"Of course," I say, working hard to make my tone light. "Did she tell you I took her there? I was just trying to make things right, to make her understand."

"I know you were," Max says. "And it means a lot. Thank you."

"So things are okay between you two?" I ask casually, doodling with a pen on his worksheet and forgetting the real reason I came here for a moment. "You and Celeste?"

"We'll see." Max shrugs, and my doodles morph into furious whirling scribbles.

Max reaches a hand out, and I think he actually might brush my cheek, but instead he pulls something out of my hair, which turns out to be a dried Cheerio. *Not again*, I think, as I stare at it.

"Where did this come from?" Max asks.

"I have no idea."

Then Max does something that totally surprises me. He starts laughing. Hard.

"Well, I'm so glad I could entertain you!" I exclaim.

Max catches his breath. Then he speaks. "I broke up with Celeste," he says. "That's when she told me about CDD."

"You did?" I ask, looking at him and putting my pen down slowly. A girl with mousy brown hair at the desk a few feet away gets up in a huff, shoves her books in her bag, and walks off.

"Yeah," Max says. "I did."

I don't move. I'm not sure what this means. Did he do it for me? Are we going to be together now, finally? This isn't exactly how I'd pictured this moment in my head.

"So does that mean . . ." I start to say.

"It doesn't mean anything, except that I broke up with Celeste," Max says gently, but matter-of-factly, like he was expecting the question. "You know I care about you, Alice, but this has so far been the weirdest semester of my life. Right now, I think I just need some time to figure things out."

No, I think to myself, *this is definitely not how I pictured this going at all.* But I also know there are more important things to deal with. Like the matter of our sanity.

"So what are we going to do?" I ask. "About the dreams. Especially with everything Petermann told us on Sunday, we need answers now more than ever. And CDD is totally shut down. Things are only getting weirder around here."

Max just shakes his head. "I honestly don't know."

"But you always have the answer for everything," I say.

"I know," Max says. "But I'm not sure I have the answer for this."

*

When I walk into the kitchen that night, bossa nova is playing loudly from the record player, and it looks like there has been a mass murder of baking materials on the countertop. There is powdery substance covering virtually every surface. Sugar and flour, cocoa powder, chocolate chips, and large smudges of oily butter.

My father is standing at the counter in an apron, frosting a cake with the dexterity of a world-renowned painter. Except that when I look closer, I see the cake is basically concave, and he is using the frosting to piece it back together.

"Well, this looks like progress," I observe.

"Ha-ha," my dad says. "I try so hard, but I never get it right."

"Have you ever considered just accepting the fact that you are not very good at baking?" I ask.

My dad looks at me like I am nuts. "No," he says. "I have not. And I can't believe you would even ask me that." The seriousness of his statement is harder to accept when he turns to me and I see he is wearing the apron he purchased in Florence, which turns his entire body into a naked marble statue . . . of a woman.

"Ugh, Dad, gross," I say, putting a hand in front of my face. "But also, it's just a cake. You can buy them, you know." I sneak a little bit of frosting on my finger and lick it off. It's surprisingly tasty.

"They're just breasts, Alice," my dad says, removing the apron to reveal his usual cashmere-and-corduroy ensemble. "Also, I am a scientist. Do you think I just give up every time a result isn't satisfactory?"

"No," I grumble.

"What have I always taught you?" he asks, pointing a batter-covered spatula at me a little too closely.

"Never keep bananas in the fridge; they go bad faster that way," I tease.

"The other thing," my dad says, not taking the bait.

"Always answer every question, and always follow through," I say.

"Exactly. Good girl." He bops some frosting on my nose with the spatula, and I roll my eyes before scooping it off with a finger and sticking it in my mouth.

"The frosting isn't bad, you know," I say.

"It's just butter and sugar," he says. "If I somehow managed to make those two ingredients taste bad, I'd really be in trouble."

I trudge upstairs to try and make a dent in my homework, some reading and a short work sheet for Levy. But even though it's my favorite class, I can't seem to sit still, and I find myself being drawn to one of the tall, built-in bookshelves with beautiful half-moon moldings at the top. I've explored the items on these shelves dozens of times before. There are carved boxes, silver ring trays, and old postcards with nothing written on the back, showing they were purchased as souvenirs instead of as a means of communication. I pull a chair up and stand on it to see what's on the top shelf, where I discover a small canvas box. Inside are rows and rows of slides, and a small antique wooden slide viewer. I pull the box down and sit on my bed.

I suppose I was thinking that maybe just one baby shot of me couldn't hurt. Something to show she recognized my existence, something to hint that maybe she still does. Instead there are photos of exotic places, seascapes and windy plains, and animals, animals, and more animals. Giraffes and birds and turtles. No people whatsoever, in fact, not even a shot of my dad. Except one at the end, of her. Looking windswept in an old Harvard T-shirt and straw hat, sunburned and grinning as she sits in the bow of a small fishing boat that is taking her to wherever she was going.

"On to the next adventure, huh, Mom?" I tell the slide. "The next unanswered question."

Then I hear my father's voice in my head again. *Always answer every question, and always follow through.* I repeat it a couple times in my head, still gazing at my mother. She certainly always did, and this time, I was going to. I had a ways to go before I was done with this experiment.

25

it's called a gi

WHEN GUSTAVE PETERMANN answers the door of his quaint, mansard-roofed home just off of Porter Square, I should be more surprised to find him dressed head to toe in a karate outfit, but I am not. I also can't help but notice the large black cuff attached to his left ankle.

"Alice," he says, looking alarmed, adjusting the piece of cloth tied around his forehead. "How did you find me?"

"The internet," I say, before getting right to it. "Were you even planning on telling us? And why are you wearing a kimono?"

Petermann looks uncomfortable. "It's called a *gi*. Listen, this really isn't a good time," he says, not inviting me in. "My sensei is here, and Yoshi doesn't like interruptions."

"What happened?" I ask, ignoring him.

"I am not legally able to discuss it," Petermann says. "Per Yoshi's advisement."

"Yoshi your sensei?" I ask.

"He's also my lawyer," Petermann replies, as though I am too slow to keep up. "Two birds with one stone, pardon the expression under the circumstances."

I feel the sudden urge to take his headscarf and strangle him with it. Why isn't he taking this more seriously? "But what about me and Max?" I demand. "We need you. You told us yourself we are at risk of losing our sanity, and then you just abandoned us!"

"Alice, this is all just a silly misunderstanding," Petermann says, glancing behind him nervously. "It will be handled in no time and we can get back to the business as usual, I promise. I think we are very close to an amazing discovery."

"Dr. Petermann, the papers say you had over twenty species of rare birds lining the walls of your attic in cages!" I push.

"Yoshi Yamamura is one of the top criminal lawyers in Massachusetts," Petermann says. "If he can't get the charges dropped, I don't know who can. Now if you'll excuse me, I have to get back to my lesson. I'll see you in a few weeks, Alice. There's no way you'll have gone crazy by then. Trust me."

Petermann shuts the door in my face and I hear the sound of somber flute music resume in the house. I stand there a second, thinking. Petermann's reassurances are not comforting.

"No way," I say out loud. And then I start banging on the door again. I bang louder and louder, but the flute music only increases in volume. Eventually my hand starts to hurt and a few people on the sidewalk are staring, so I have no choice but to give up. I am almost all the way down the driveway when I hear the front door open again and a woman wrapped in a green cashmere cardigan and black leggings comes dashing out after me.

"Wait!" she cries. "Wait, please." When I stop, confused, she speaks first. "It's Alice, right? Alice Rowe?"

In response I am only able to nod my head. I feel a specific hopelessness building within me and am certain that the tears will come any minute.

"I'm Virginia Petermann," she says. "Gustave's wife." She extends a hand and I shake it slowly.

"I've heard all about you," she says. "This project, the work with you and Max, it reinvigorated Gustave over his research. The possibility of it all . . . you don't know how much it meant."

"He has a funny way of showing it," I say with a small sniffle.

"Well, here's the thing about Gus," Virginia goes on. "I already wanted to kill my husband half the time, even before I found out he was adding more parrots to the attic and giving me vague answers about where they came from, even before he got arrested and even before he hired that ridiculous lawyer who comes over every day with his flute music. But I can't murder him, because I love him. Even if the man spends eighty percent of his waking life in athletic attire. Even if he has entire chest of drawers filled with cashmere sweaters that I buy him for Christmas in the hopes that once, just once, he might wear that to the office rather than a poly-Lycra blend. So instead I'm going to help you."

I stare at this Virginia Petermann, with her wispy bob and her cuddly sweater, her sensible boots with just a hint of furry trim. "How can you help me?" I ask.

"Because I know who you need to talk to," she says, as though it's obvious.

At this moment behind Virginia I see a curtain whisk closed, and suddenly Petermann is running out the door in his karate outfit and a pair of LL Bean duck boots.

"Virginniaaaaaaa!" he calls as he takes each long leap.

"You're too late, Gus!" She turns around, practically shouting. "I've already told her about Margaret Yang." Virginia turns back to me. "Margaret Yang is the one who did it," she says quickly, excitedly. "And she can fix it all. She works at Wells College in Maine."

"Did what, exactly?" I ask, looking between them. Then to Petermann I ask, "What is she talking about?"

Petermann just shuffles his feet.

"Tell her, Gus," Virginia says.

Petermann doesn't say a word.

"Gustave Louis Petermann, you will tell this girl what she

needs to know, or I will walk out the door and I will never come back. And guess what—you've got an ankle monitor on that says you can't go past the front walk, so you won't be able to find me this time!"

This time. Somehow it does not surprise me that Dr. Petermann is not an easy man to live with.

"What did Margaret Yang do?" I try again.

Petermann sighs like a petulant child. "Margaret Yang was just starting out as a research assistant years ago, when you and Max first came to CDD," he says. "She was brilliant. The most gifted student I had ever seen. And I was remiss to admit it at the time, but I couldn't keep up with her. She seemed to have a handle on more than just the brain, she understood the *mind.* She understood it in a way I could not. And it plagued me." Petermann looks into the distance for a moment, as though remembering past demons.

"I heard rumors that Margaret was carrying out some unorthodox practices at the lab, and I fired her from the program," he says. Then he notices the look his wife is giving him. "What, Virginia! What else is there to say?"

"Maybe something along the lines of, 'I'm sorry,'" she says, her tone softening as she rests a hand on his forearm.

Petermann grits his teeth for a moment, before inhaling. "Fine, I am sorry. I should have kept her, I should have asked her to stay on and work with me, but I was jealous. Selfish and competitive. And I suppose I still am. Otherwise I would have contacted her already."

At this, Petermann takes both my hands in his. "Alice, I'm sorry. When you came in that day, I found you and Max in the system and I saw you'd both been under Margaret's care. I knew she must've had something to do with your dreams, but instead of telling you how to find her, I wanted to fix it myself. I'm so sorry, Alice. I know all you ever wanted was answers."

It's taking me a moment to fully understand what I'm hearing. "You would've contacted her already because . . ."

Petermann is patient. "Because Margaret Yang is the woman who did this to you and Max, Alice. She's the reason you dream of each other. She has to be. And she's the only one who can fix it."

october 17th

I am thinking it's a huge mistake that the Public Garden doesn't offer more swan boat rides at night, because that's where I am now, cruising along the pond under the stars. The Boston skyline looks down at me like a family over a newborn baby, and it's pretty spectacular. Everywhere my gaze shifts, all around the edges of the pond, are cherry trees. Their blossoms are such a bright shade of pink they might as well be electric. That's when I realize they are electric. The trees themselves aren't growing petals at all, but hot-pink Christmas lights, casting us all in a rosy glow.

I turn to point this out to Oliver, but Oliver isn't there. Max is.

"Hi," is all he says, and he reaches out to take my hand. My whole body melts as I prepare for him to pull me to his chest, letting one hand rest at the base of my neck, tangled in my hair.

I want to wrap my arms around his waist and rest my head just under his chin. I've missed him so much.

But just before Max's hand touches mine, he pulls back.

"What?" I ask.

"Did you feel that?" he asks, staring at his hand like it doesn't belong to him.

"No?" I say, confused, and reach out to touch him. But this time I do feel it. It's like our bodies are two magnets that are repelling the other. I can't get close enough.

We let our hands drop to our sides and stare at each other, confused.

For the first time, I look ahead, and I see that this swan boat isn't like the one Oliver and I took the other day. It's being pedaled by an actual swan, a giant one with soft, luxurious feathers. I reach out and stroke its neck as if it were a pony.

At this, the swan turns around.

"Thank you," it says. "That feels nice."

"You're welcome," I say back. "You're a very polite swan."

"And you are a very skilled back scratcher," it says.

"Should we go and find her?" the swan asks.

"Find who?" I say.

"Margaret Yang, of course!" the swan explains, pausing for a moment to prune itself. "It's the only way to fix everything."

I look to Max, sitting way too far away, and he just nods. "Let's go and fix it," he says. His expression is dead serious.

"Tomorrow?" I ask.

"*First thing,*" *he replies.* "*Alice?*"

"*Yeah Max?*"

Once again he tries to reach out and touch me, and once again his hand can't break through. "*I don't like this,*" *he says.*

"*Me neither,*" *I say.*

"*Tomorrow,*" *he repeats.* "*I'll see you soon.*"

"*I'll see you soon,*" *I say.*

26

Rio de Janeiro, 22 miles

"WHAT ARE YOU doing?" my father asks, showing, uncharacteristically, that he is actually paying attention.

"Nothing," I say, looking at him blankly over the top of my coffee mug.

"Your knee is jiggling, and it's moving the entire table. I'm trying to do the crossword. What's wrong?"

"Nothing is wrong," I say. "I just have a few things on my mind." *Like will Max show up today? Did the plan we made in the swan dream hold true?* I think about texting him and just asking, but decide against it. I haven't heard from him in reality since our conversation in the library. Yes, there was something coming between us in the dream last night, too.

But what? I think as I stare off into space.

"You're doing it again," my dad says. "The leg thing. Why don't you take Jerry for a walk? He has an uncanny ability to fall asleep on my foot, and he really needs the exercise."

*

I do my best to steer Jerry away from the Public Garden, because it feels kind of funny going there right after I dreamed about it, but Jerry will have it no other way, pulling me through the gates like a furry Zamboni.

He immediately waddles straight for the pond and begins sniffing methodically around the exterior, as though he is tracking something. That duck, probably.

That's when I see it. A small swan, floating alone in the water about twenty feet away. And it's staring right into my eyes.

I stare back curiously. What it's actually probably doing is eyeing Jerry, the furry hunting beast by my side, having witnessed the duck fiasco in the very same pond a week ago.

But that's when the swan winks.

There is no mistaking it.

And I know it's a sign. I have to go to Maine to find Margaret Yang. With or without Max.

But Max's Volvo is double-parked in front of my house when Jerry and I return, and Max is waiting on the stoop, holding four coffees.

"I didn't know what kind you liked." He shrugs as we walk up. "So I just got like . . . all of them."

Despite myself, I can't help but smile from ear to ear.

"What?" he asks.

"Nothing." I shake my head. He did mean it. Agreeing to come. Which means he also meant it in the dream when he said he hated not being able to touch me. "How are we supposed to drink all those?"

"Well, we're apparently going to have help," he says.

"Hiiiiiiiiiii," Sophie squeals as she runs out of the house like a flying squirrel, nearly tackling me to the ground. Then she pulls away from me and looks at my surprised face.

"Oh my God, I knew it. I was just saying so to your dad. I was like, she completely forgot I was even coming this weekend. You did forget, didn't you?"

"Um," I start to say.

"Even if you did, just lie," she suggests.

"I did not forget?" I try.

Sophie lets out another squeal and hugs me again, jumping up and down and pausing to straighten her glasses when they nearly fall off her nose. She is all rosy cheeks and shiny straight brown hair. I forgot how much light she emits without even trying. "I met this one, by the way," she says, nodding to Max. Then she leans in and whispers, far too loudly, "Even hotter than you said."

I just hang my head in shame, and Max pretends not to hear and takes a sip of coffee to hide his smile.

"Oh, hello, Gerald," Sophie says then, glancing down at Jerry and looking away disdainfully.

"You know that's not his name," I chide her.

"Maybe I don't care," Sophie huffs.

I roll my eyes and turn to Max. "Sophie hates Jerry because he ate her favorite Barbie doll when we were little," I say. "And she's never forgiven him."

"Why would I forgive a slobbery beast with no self-control or sense of decency?" Sophie puts a hand on her hip. "One minute Barbie had a head and face; the next we were monitoring his bowel movements for signs of blond hair to make sure it had *passed*." She shudders.

"Watch what you say about Jer-Bear," I hear someone say, and I turned to find Oliver on the sidewalk, astride his Segway like a modern knight.

"And what is going on here exactly?" Sophie asks. "Seventeen going on seventy? My nana has one of those. Hers is hot pink. You guys could take them on your dates together."

"Don't knock it till you've tried it," Oliver says. "Which you will never get to do, because with that attitude you're never going to ride it."

Sophie gasps as though she has just been slapped with a glove, and I take the opportunity to interrupt.

"Okay, guys, Max and I actually had a plan today." I turn to him, suddenly nervous. "Just to confirm, that is why you're here, isn't it?" I ask. "The road trip?"

Max gets up and walks over to me, looking confused. "Of course that's why I'm here. I told you I would be, didn't I?"

I can't help but relax, breathing a sigh of relief, and Max squeezes my shoulder, which makes me the opposite of relaxed all over again.

"Road trip!" Oliver exclaims, rubbing his hands together. "Where are we going?"

"*We*," Max says, pointing from himself to Sophie to me, "are going to Maine. I have no idea where you are going."

I expect Oliver to reply with something witty, something to save face. But instead he does something I've never seen him do before. He lets his guard down, and he actually looks hurt as he turns back to remount his Segway. "Oh," he says. "Okay."

"You know what?" I announce. "I think we have room for one more."

"We do?" Max asks, raising his eyebrows in surprise.

"*We do*," I say, turning to give him a look.

"Whatever," Max mutters. "As long as I'm driving."

*

It turns out Max Wolfe is a big fan of Motown, and I'd be lying if I said it didn't take me by surprise. But as we cruise up I-95 toward Maine, I realize it makes a bit of sense. Like Max, Motown is classic. It's a little bit reserved, but it still knows how to have a good time.

"I didn't know you liked this kind of stuff," I say.

"It's fun to drive to," Max explains. He seems really relaxed today. We're about forty minutes outside the city, and the leaves are positively on fire. Lemon yellow, fire-engine red, and a color of orange reserved for only the cheapest orange soda you can find.

"I wish they stayed this way all year long," I say wistfully.

"Me too," Max agrees. "But then we wouldn't have snow . . . or summer."

"You're right," I say, and let my head fall back against the seat as I listen to Sophie and Oliver bickering behind us.

"I'm just saying, no offense, but I think I have a solid chance of replacing you as best friend by the end of the school year," Oliver says. "I mean, how long have you known Alice anyway?"

"Oh, only like, my entire *life*," Sophie replies. "But what's that compared to knowing her for not even two months?"

"I'm sensing quite a bit of hostility from you right now, Sophie, and I gotta tell you I'm sort of into it," Oliver says. "But I'm still going to need more evidence of friendship."

"Alice and I have an old inside joke where we pretend we have clones of each other that we hang out with when the other isn't around, because that's how much we miss each other when we aren't together. Can you beat that?" Sophie asks.

"Do you know that a woman in England just cloned her dachshund? It's true. I read about it," I call back to them.

"You would read something like that," Max pipes in. He was so intent on the road, I hadn't even realized he was listening.

"I'd like to clone *both* you ladies," Oliver calls out.

"In your *dreams*," Sophie shoots back. Then she pauses for a second, thinking. "I guess that phrase holds a little more meaning in this crowd."

"Well, I've known Alice longer than either of you, so beat that," Max says. And the car falls awkwardly silent.

"Yeah, but only in a weird parallel dream universe, so I'm not sure that counts," Sophie says.

"Speaking of parallel universe, did you just see that sign?" Max says quietly to me. "Rio de Janeiro, twenty-two miles."

"That's not possible," I say. "There's no Rio in Maine."

"I know," Max says, looking at me pointedly. "That's the point. We're probably going to get totally lost because our minds are dreaming up alternate road signs."

But I'm thinking about something else. "So that time in the cafeteria, when I asked you about the Amazon . . . you remembered that, right?"

"Of course I did," Max says. "You were so sad that week. You missed your dad like crazy. I was trying everything I could to make you happy. The fried plantains were the first thing that worked."

"I knew it," I say, a little drowsy.

"You're falling asleep, aren't you?" Max asks.

"Plains, trains, and automobiles," I manage to mumble. And just as my eyes are about to close, I see the weirdest thing I've seen so far, since my reality and dreams started bleeding. A

245

motorcycle has sped up next to the car, and Jerry is at the wheel, with a smaller bulldog riding shotgun. They're wearing tiny helmets and goggles. Jerry's black, and the smaller dog's hot pink. They turn and stare at me for a second before riding off again.

27

i *like* your alpacas

THE FIRST THING I do when I wake up in the passenger seat of Max's station wagon, besides notice how beautiful my surroundings are, all green farmland and stone walls and quaint shingled houses, is wonder why there is a camel wearing a fur hat staring at me through the window. The second thing I do is notice that I am totally alone.

"Alpacas have got to be one of the most ridiculous-looking animals on earth," I hear Sophie say as I step out of the car and join the rest of the group where they are leaning against a large wooden fence, peering into a field. "He needed a break," she adds, and points to Max, who is stretching.

Directly facing them and looking about half as curious is a small pack of alpacas, noiselessly chewing on grass. They do look a lot like llamas, except their fur is shorn so they appear to be wearing wide, fuzzy bellbottoms, and the tops of their heads carry chic bouffants of frizzy hair.

"They sort of look like eighties pop stars," Oliver observes.

"I don't think they like us," I say.

"That's probably because Sophie insulted them." Max smirks.

"Did Max Wolfe just make a joke?" Oliver waves his hands in front of Max's face and then says loudly, *"Max, are you in there? Can you hear us?* Or is this the beginning of some *Invasion of the Body Snatchers*-type horror flick?"

"Shut up," Max says playfully. Then in a deep scary voice that surprises all of us, he says. *"Or you'll be the first to die!"*

"Another joke!" Oliver cries. "Now this is just getting freaky." Oliver is still laughing when he falls flat on his face, and then Max is the one who is laughing.

"Dude, did you just trip me?" Oliver says from the ground, and he does not sound pleased.

"Relax," Max says. "I was just kidding around. I'll help you up." He reaches out a hand to Oliver, who moves to take it but instead pulls Max down onto the grass with him.

"What the hell?" Max yells.

And suddenly they are wrestling.

"Real mature, Healy!" I hear Max grunt.

"You're one to talk, Wolfe!" Oliver sneers back. "What, are you showing off?"

"Are they okay?" Sophie asks, walking up beside me.

"I think so?" I say. "I think they're just idiots. They have a history."

Then we hear a voice from behind us that makes even Oliver and Max lift their hands off the ground. "You boys better get your act together. You're scaring the kids," it says. We turn to find an older man with salt-and-pepper hair, a navy wool sweater, and high rubber boots strolling toward us. He's pointing toward the field, and that's when I realize *kids* refers to alpacas.

"Sorry, sir." Max and Oliver stand up immediately, wiping off their knees, like foot soldiers at the attention of their general, which is amusing since this man comes up no higher than their chins. But there's something about him, an undeniable presence. It makes you listen closely.

The only person who does not seem to be intimidated, of course, is Sophie. "Are you Alfred?" she asks, glancing at the sign that says ALFRED'S ALPACA FARM.

"I am," Alfred says.

"I like your alpacas." She smiles, as though complimenting his boots.

"Thank you, young lady." Alfred smiles back. "Would you be interested in a tour?"

Even though we were on a mission, not one of us says no.

*

It turns out alpacas are not just fun to look at, they are quite useful. We follow Alfred up over the rolling hill of his property, past his white-shingled farmhouse with a wide wraparound porch, and into a big red barn, while he shares with us the secrets of his trade. We learn that alpaca fiber is three times warmer than wool, and much more fine. We learn there are two types of alpacas—Suri, which come in a range of colors and have curlier locks, and Huacaya, which is the most common breed found in the United States. We all take a turn spinning fiber into yarn at the wheel.

"I made you this," I hear Oliver tell Sophie under the heavy beams of the barn, holding out a small piece of yarn he just spun. Sophie responds by giggling and walking away, but not before taking the useless piece of yarn with her, and I can't help but raise my eyebrows at this.

The best part is that we even get to pet an alpaca or two, and I am just bidding good-bye to a sweet one named Mildred when I glance over and see Max, practically nose to nose with another, whispering sweet nothings to it. He catches me smiling and clears his throat, giving it one last swift pat atop its head before walking my way.

"What? We had a connection," he says.

My heart can't help but swell at the sight of this Max. This is the Max I know and love. Open and relaxed and happy. I go to rest a hand on his back but pull it away almost instantly, unsure of what's okay anymore. Max gives me a look I can't decipher.

I wish things were simpler. That this was just a normal day

hanging out with friends at a normal alpaca farm. And Max was my normal boyfriend, who I didn't dream about. I wish Sophie lived here. I wish I hadn't seen my dog ride by me on a motorcycle today. I wish we weren't losing our grip on reality.

We find Alfred, Oliver, and Sophie standing on the porch. Sophie is holding a beautiful cream-colored sweater she just purchased, and Oliver is holding a box of sugar cookies shaped like alpacas.

"I'm sorry, Mildred!" Oliver cries, before biting off one of the alpaca cookie heads. "But you are delicious. What?" he asks between chews when he notices the way I'm looking at him.

"Nothing," I say, breaking off a sugar cookie alpaca leg as we turn back toward the main road. "I'm just happy. I wish it could stay this way."

"Why can't it?" Oliver looks genuinely confused.

"Because things are about to change," I answer.

"Not if we don't let them." Oliver shrugs like it's all so simple, and I wish it were.

*

"So, how far are we from the college?" I ask Max as we pile back into the car.

"Only about ten minutes," he replies, looking at Google Maps on his phone. "So we should have answers in no time." A feeling of sadness rises up in my throat. After we find Margaret, nothing is going to be the same.

But as we drive through the campus of Wells College, I start to relax. It's strikingly beautiful, an abundance of pathways weaving around pristine brick buildings and giant leafy trees, and all of it resting atop vast, well-manicured lawns. A perfect little academic haven.

At least, at first.

*

"I'm afraid I can't help you with that," Doreen McGinty says between gum snaps over the top of her desk at the faculty center. We already tried Margaret Yang's office in the biology wing, and it was locked, and now we are hoping Doreen can provide us with a home address. Doreen's hair is both very large and very permed, like it hasn't been changed since the late eighties.

"She kind of looks like an alpaca," Max says under his breath as Doreen chews her gum, and I put my hand over my mouth to stifle a giggle.

"No personal addresses are to be given out to students, academic policy. My sincerest apologies," Doreen explains. But she does not sound very sincere.

"But we aren't students!" Sophie pipes up, trying to be helpful, and the rest of us groan.

"Then I definitely can't give it to you," Doreen says.

"What about when she holds her office hours?" Max tries. "Can you tell us that?"

"That I could give to you if you *were* students, but not if you aren't," Doreen replies.

"Doreen," Oliver says, coming over and leaning one arm casually along the top of her desk. "Let me ask you two questions. One. Has anyone ever told you that you bear a striking resemblance to a young Princess Diana? Because you do, Doreen. And two, hypothetically, if you were a few students who weren't technically enrolled at the moment . . ." He makes little quotation marks with his hands.

"So not students," Doreen deadpans.

"Tomato-tomahto," Oliver says. "Anyway, if so . . . how would you go about finding a professor?"

"Sure, I can help you with that," Doreen says, shuffling in her desk for something.

"I knew you could, Doreen." Oliver bats his eyelashes.

Doreen thwacks a thick stack of pamphlets down on top of her desk. "Applications for enrollment," she states. "Fill these out, and I can answer your questions when you get in next year."

*

Fifteen minutes later, we're sitting on a bench outside the coffee shop in the center of Wells, feeling totally hopeless.

"My charms always work on Dean Hammer's assistant," Oliver says, stunned. "Reference an attractive public figure from the eighties or nineties, then slip in your request, boom."

"We aren't in Kansas anymore," I say. "We're in Maine."

"Maybe you should try actually working for what you want instead of playing games all the time," Max says. I give him a look that says, *Whoa*, and he just shrugs.

"Spare me, Wolfe," Oliver replies. "I don't see you doing anything to fix the situation."

"I'd love to do that, Healy, but you seem to always be getting in my way," Max says.

"How can I possibly be getting in your way when you spend most of the time pretending I don't exist?" Oliver almost-sneers, and Max is quiet.

"I don't pretend you don't exist," Max says finally. "We grew apart. Our lives are different than they used to be."

"You ditched me, dude," Oliver says. "Don't try and deny it. We wouldn't even be hanging out right now if it wasn't for Alice." In response, Max looks pained. I can tell he knows Oliver is sort of right.

"So what are we going to do?" I ask, breaking the tension.

"We can always try her office again tomorrow." Oliver shrugs. "Or hit up the dining hall at dinner and ask around?"

"But where will we stay tonight?" I ask.

"What about Alfred's?" Sophie says. "He has that big old house. I think it might be a bed-and-breakfast, too."

"Really?" Oliver looks skeptical.

"In Maine, everything is a bed-and-breakfast," Sophie says with certainty.

We pile back in the car in slightly better spirits, but find ourselves back at square one when the engine won't start.

I am about to make a suggestion about a tow truck when I

notice how rigid Max's posture has become, and I choose to remain quiet. Oliver unfortunately does not get the hint.

"That's what you get for driving this hunk of junk," he mutters in the backseat. "This car is older than we are."

Sophie is tapping away on her phone, and I am still watching Max, waiting for him to explode.

"It was supposed to be my sister's," Max says through gritted teeth.

Oliver rubs his forehead for a second and exhales. "I'm sorry, Max. I didn't know."

Max turns around in his seat. "I drive this hunk of junk because it was supposed to be Lila's. You remember my sister? She used to babysit us every day after school, until she died?"

Oliver's face doesn't flinch. He just sits there taking it. "I remember," is all he says.

"So, I'm sorry if I ditched you, *dude*," Max says. "But I had to move on with my life. Do something besides play video games with you all day and drop water balloons off the balcony of your bedroom. And I'm sorry you got left behind, but I'm also sorry you couldn't grow up."

I wait for Oliver to yell back, to start something, but he doesn't. He just nods. "You're right," he says. And then he says it again. "I'm sorry."

Max tries the key a few more times, begging it to turn on, and when it doesn't he just leans his head against the horn, groaning along with it. Reluctantly, I put a hand on his shoulder, and he doesn't shrug it off. He just lifts his head off the steering wheel a little, tipping it to the side so he can stare at me, his eyes pleading.

"It's okay," I say. "Everything is going to be okay." I've never seen him like this before.

"I just want to figure it out," he says. "I just want everything to be right again. In life, and . . . with us."

"I know," I say.

"Bartholomew Burns!" Sophie cries from the backseat. And all three of us turn and stare at her.

"Say what?" Oliver asks.

"How much do you all love me?" Sophie announces, wiggling her cell phone in the air like it's a golden ticket.

"That depends," I say. "Is Margaret Yang inside that phone?"

Sophie shakes her head. "Bartholomew Burns," she says again.

"Bartholomew Burns, your old Latin tutor?" I ask. "The guy who wore the cross with a detachable Jesus on it?"

"It's true, he did wear a necklace with a detachable Jesus," Sophie calmly explains. "Sometimes he liked to wear a cross with Jesus, sometimes without. But that was a phase, and anyway, he could more than stand me, if you get my drift." She raises her eyebrows up and down.

"What does this have to do with anything?" Max asks.

Sophie rolls her eyes. "Because I posted a selfie of me and

Mildred the alpaca at Alfred's today, and Bartholomew saw it, and it turns out he goes here!" Her eyes light up, like *ta-da*. "So he messaged me, and I told him what was up . . . well, part of it . . . the not-weird parts . . . and he said we can crash with him tonight if we want, at his dorm! Like half his floor is out of town."

The tension releases from the car like pressure evening out inside an airplane. "Nice work, Soph!" I say, giving her a high five. "That's a great idea."

"There's just one problem." She makes a face. "He says he's having a huge party tonight . . . he hopes we don't mind?"

At the word *party*, Oliver's eyes light up. "I suppose we could attend," he says.

As we get up to make our way toward Bartholomew's dorm, I notice Max is looking back at the car with an odd expression.

"What's wrong?" I ask.

"I could've sworn she just flashed her lights at me," Max says.

"You're just tired," I say.

"No." He frowns. "They flashed. Which would be weird, even if her battery wasn't dead." His tone is off. He sounds very far away.

Then, with no rational explanation and nobody behind the wheel, the car honks.

Max looks at me, helpless. "This is getting really weird, Alice. We have to make it stop."

I look at him, his hair out of place and a wild look in his eyes. What will happen if we can't make it stop? Will Max go full-on meltdown mode?

But also, what will happen if we do?

28

your dog is really lucky!

ACCORDING TO MY very basic knowledge of college social life, which I have gleaned entirely from gems of modern cinema such as *Animal House* and *Old School*, there seem to be a number of foolproof ways to throw a decent party. The list includes such things as a great band, scandalously clad coeds, limitless amounts of illegal substances, and a general lack of consideration for the well-being of oneself and others.

It is safe to say that Bartholomew Burns and his suitemates at Leeland Hall, a two-story white-shingled house on the edge of campus, were not aware of this list or these movies, or they chose to ignore all of it out of some vague hipster principle. Perhaps we—Max, Sophie, Oliver, and I—should have anticipated this, given the wall of Latin awards and the expansive insect collection that welcomed us upon arrival to the suite. But I guess we just assumed that in college, anyone could be cool.

We were wrong. Terribly, horribly wrong.

"I'm not kidding when I say my grandmother's retirement community is more fun than this," Sophie says as she stands in the doorway between a room where people are playing Monopoly and one where they are playing video games, clutching a raspberry wine cooler. "I'm so depressed I could scream." She takes a giant swig.

"Hi." A skinny redhead approaches me wearing thick hipster glasses, and leans casually on the edge of the fireplace. "I'm Wallace," he says with a wink. "How come I've never seen you around?"

"She doesn't go here," Sophie mentions between chugs.

"Oh." Wallace nods. "I just thought maybe I hadn't seen you since I'm generally in the art studio. You know . . . doing my art." He looks at me intently then, as though expecting me to gasp in awe.

"So you're an art major?" I ask politely as Sophie unapologetically rolls her eyes.

"Thinking about it," he says. "At the moment I'm really just creating, exploring the possibilities of my work."

"And what kind of work do you do?" I say.

"It's so refreshing to hear someone ask that question," he says, and leans in closely. "Currently I'm doing a series where

I take photographs of my dachshund, Arabella, in historical contexts, wearing period-appropriate outfits, and use it as a commentary on modernity and the general lack of culture in our present-day world," he says in complete seriousness. "For example, last week I built a small-scale rendering of the White House and dressed her up as George Washington. Next week I'm hoping to do Frida Kahlo."

I stare at him, using every muscle in my body to maintain composure, as Sophie just starts cackling so hard I think she might actually be crying.

"Uh-huh," is all I can manage to say.

"Do you wanna see a photo?" he asks.

"Hell yeah!" Sophie yells, and just starts laughing again. And then I just can't handle it any longer, and I start laughing, too.

"You guys are really rude," Wallace observes.

"Your dog is really lucky!" Sophie manages to whimper as she wipes her tears away.

"Okay, people!" We hear a familiar voice shout. Sophie and I peer around the corner and are mortified to find Oliver standing in the middle of the room, holding a beer. "You don't know me. My name is Oliver, and I don't go here. I won't tell you where I go because that would betray my age and I think there is a sixty percent chance of me kissing at least one girl at this party tonight. But you know how that's not going to happen?" He walks over to the stereo and plugs in his iPod, which he has pulled out of his pocket. "If this party keeps going the way it's going. So that's all about to change right . . . now." He hits a button and cranks up the volume.

Within seconds, the rhythmic synth of Prince's "Kiss" comes gyrating over the speakers, and it comes on loud. The whole room seems transfixed as Oliver begins to wiggle his shoulders to the music, complete with spins, pelvic thrusts, and lip-synching.

My mouth is hanging open—I can't help it—as he forms the words with passion. I look over at Sophie and can't tell if she looks totally horrified or kind of into it.

But then, like magic, the room starts to move. Everyone is dancing, and I mean everyone. Even Wallace. Oliver makes his way over to where I am standing, but just when I think he is about to take my hand, he sings the chorus in Sophie's ear. *Kuh-kuh-kuh-kuh-kuh-kiss*.

I wonder where Max is as I dance, and then spot him across the room, bopping his head and shuffling his feet. I'm about to dance my way over when the crowd clears and I see he's not alone. A dark-haired girl in tight black jeans is circling around him with flamboyant, check-out-my-body, disco-type moves. I'm still glaring at them when Oliver spins me, and I lose them for a moment.

The song turns slow as "Purple Rain" comes on and I am just about to escape to a bathroom to avoid watching Max slow dance with the brunette when suddenly he is there by my side, taking my hand. Sophie gives me a look as Max pulls me through the party, past the gyrating dancers and loud conversations and outside onto the chilly front lawn, where all is quiet.

"Do you see this?" Max asks, his finger pointing up toward the sky. I can see it. Above us is a beautiful starry night, but the stars are all the colors of the rainbow, and they're twinkling like glitter nail polish.

"I can see this," I tell him. "It's incredible."

"I guess not all the dream-melding moments are that bad," he observes. I look at him, and the ground where we are feels so dark by contrast to the sky. And the space between us feels so cold and so far. As if on cue, Max pulls me to him, keeping one hand in mine as the other encircles my back, and my face rests in the crook of his neck as "Purple Rain" keeps playing in our ears.

I don't know if it's Prince crooning or the raspberry wine coolers, but something feels different. It's sweet but also a little sad. Like we've come to this place together, but we know that we have to say good-bye. To a whole part of our lives, half our lives, where we go at night, and in some ways, to each other. There is a reason I don't like to tell Petermann about our dreams, why I hold my dream journal so close to my heart. Our dreams are the one thing we share that nobody else can touch. And now we're going to lose it, and I am terrified.

I look down and see we're floating again. Max sees it, too. But we aren't scared this time. I just hold on tight and think that if this were a dream, it would just go on forever.

29

he always shows up

"I NEED TO ask you something, and I don't want you to laugh at me," Sophie says. We're lying side by side on a hammock in the yard outside Leeland Hall, all bundled up in wool blankets we stole from the common room. Her eyes are half-open and her hair is sticking out in every direction possible from dancing so hard. It's pretty difficult to take her seriously right now.

"Okay, I'll try," I say.

"Why does Swiss cheese have so many holes in it?" Sophie asks. "Or for that matter, any holes at all?" And I don't even try to stop myself from erupting in laughter.

Sophie gives me a tiny punch in the arm. "I told you not

to laugh!" she cries. "Come on, you can't tell me you haven't wondered that before."

I stare at the sky, still full of multicolored twinkles, and am disappointed that Sophie isn't able to see it, too. Because she'd love it.

"Yes, Soph," I say, and glance at my watch. 11:59. Where was Max? He disappeared after our dance, and I haven't seen him since. "I think about cheese fungus all the time." Then I start laughing again.

"Mmm, *fungus*," Sophie says between giggles, and we laugh even harder. "I love you, Al," Sophie says once we've settled down, and leans her head on my shoulder.

"I love you, too, Soph," I say, standing up and giving her head a little pat.

"Do you know who else I like?" she asks.

"I have an idea," I say, rolling my eyes.

"Max."

"No kidding," I say.

"I get it now," she says. "And I see the way he looks at you, and I love that."

"Then why is he always disappearing? Like, where is he now?" I say, throwing my hands up in the air with a sigh. "I'm going to go to bed, all right? Will you be okay?"

"Okay, you go to bed," she says with a big smile.

"Sure you don't wanna come?" I ask.

Sophie just shakes her head. "I'm good. I'm gonna stay out here a little longer and see if I can make these stars change color like they do for you."

I smile. "Holler if you need me."

"I will," she says, snuggling up more in the blankets. "And Al?" she calls.

"Yeah, Soph?" I wait.

"I know he's always disappearing. But do you know what?"

"What?" I ask.

Sophie turns her head practically upside down so she can say this last part while looking back at me. "He always shows up. At CDD that night you broke in, on your front stoop with coffee . . . even in your dreams. He shows up."

*

Bartholomew Burns told me there was a spare room open on his floor, lived in by a girl who was away on a trip with her a cappella group, which sounded pretty normal to me. Perhaps I'd have to deal with a few too many Taylor Swift posters, but I could live with that. Besides, I like Taylor Swift. I just don't announce it publicly. But when I open the door to 201, there is no Taylor Swift, no pink beanbag chairs, no shabby chic vanity mirror.

There are ponies. Ponies, and only ponies, everywhere.

Pony posters on the walls. Riding ribbons spanning an entire bulletin board, pony sheets, and photographs of a dark brown horse with a white spot between its eyes on every possible surface.

"Valerie is a riding champion," Bartholomew Burns says when he walks by and catches me still standing in the doorway, gaping in awe. "Did I forget to mention that?"

"What's the horse's name?" is all I can think to ask.

"Theodore," he answers, before trotting down the stairs.

I brush my teeth and pick out a copy of *Horse and Hound* magazine off her desk to read myself to sleep, trying not to make eye contact with Theodore in his many incarnations. I've just dozed off with the magazine across my chest when I hear someone come into the room.

I open my eyes with a start, fully expecting to have to apologize to Valerie, who surely will have somehow returned early from her trip and is wondering who the heck is in her pony bed, and I am stunned to see Max instead.

"Hi," is all he says. He stands there, one hand in his pocket, one hand still on the door, his eyes wide.

"Hi," I say, sitting up on my elbows, my eyes a little fuzzy, as Max takes a seat at the end of the bed. "Is everything okay? Did Oliver finally blow the speakers downstairs?"

"No." Max chuckles. "Not yet anyway." He's facing away from me, and his posture is rigid, his hands clutching the sides of the mattress. "So."

And suddenly I think I know what's happening. "Wait," I say.

"What?" He turns and looks at me, confused.

"I don't think you should be in here." The words come out a little desperate before I even have a chance to decide if I want to say them or not. He is just too close, and he looks so good. And if he's still not sure what he wants, or if he's just going to choose Celeste after everything, I really need him to leave.

Max looks at me now, straight into my eyes. And then he just says, "Why?" And my heart starts to pound a million miles a minute, because him asking why he shouldn't be here is like an acknowledgment of everything that is happening.

I swallow. "I thought you wanted to be alone," is all I can manage to say.

"I did say that," Max says now, his eyes not leaving mine. "So," he tries again. "I don't know what to do. I've been walking around campus, wracking my brain, trying to figure out what to do. Because I want to get better, really. I know we have to get better. I know the dreams have to stop. But I also don't want to lose you."

You could hear a spider sneeze in the room right now, it has gone so quiet. No party music, no footsteps on dorm stairways, no shouts of revelry. Just silence, and my eyes and Max's eyes and Max's perfect mouth and the feeling that is welling up from the bottom of my stomach up through my chest and neck to the tops of my ears.

"I can't lose you, Alice," he says again. And then before I can help myself, I have leaped across the bed to kiss him and fall into his arms, my legs circling his waist. And he accepts me, his arms coming up around to support my back while his hands grip the base of my head, under my hair.

"I can't lose you," he says for a third time, in a whisper. And I take his face in my hands and push his hair behind his ears, as I stroke his jaw with my fingers.

"You will never lose me," I say. "I'm right here." And I kiss him again.

OCTOBER 18TH

"Here's a good one," I say, leaning over to hold the slide viewer in front of Max's eyeball. We're back on the crew docks at school and it's twilight, the most perfect time of day. In front of us the Charles River rolls by, bright turquoise. I've got a pile of slides in my lap and am sifting through them, placing them one at a time into the antique wooden viewer and holding it up to my face, before passing it on to Max, who is lying on his back, holding a book over his face with one arm, while the other rests behind his head.

He closes his other eye, dramatically scrunching up his entire face as though it helps him see better. I know he isn't that interested; he'd rather be reading. He's just doing it to make me happy.

"Ooooh, that is a good one." Max nods in agreement. "Put it in the keep pile."

To the right of my knee is a neat stack of slides, the ones we have decided to save. For what reason, I'm not sure.

I lift another slide up to my eye, making a face of my own at what appears to be a professional portrait of someone's obese cat, and then replace it with another. The next one is a succulent wall, looking green and glossy and very much alive, but I don't show that one to Max because it reminds me of Celeste. And then I get to a yurt made of sunset red canvas, on the edge of a snowy ledge, facing what looks like the Alps. Two sets of skis are stuck into the snow, and you can just make out a fire glowing from behind the flaps.

"This," I say, holding it up for Max, "is absolutely perfect."

"I'll be the judge of that," Max says, holding his book aside and readying himself for the slide viewer again. As he examines the photo, I examine his face. The crease between his eyebrows when he's really focusing on something, the curve of his jaw, the slight dimple in his right cheek. Then I watch his eyebrows rise. "Wow," is all Max says. Then he moves the viewer away from his eyes so he can look directly into mine.

When I finally look away, I see we're no longer on the dock. We're in the snow. I have a puffer jacket on and hot-purple ski pants, and Max has the same, but his parka and pants are shades of blue. About twenty feet away and glowing with light is our sunset yurt.

Max is giving me a look I know well. A look that makes me say, "Please don't." But he keeps smiling mischievously. "Please don't," I try again, this time louder, but he doesn't listen. He throws a snowball right at my face.

I glare at him. "What are you, five?" I ask.

"Yup," he says with a grin. And then he leaps up and tackles me to the ground. The snow is incredibly soft, cushioning me as I fall backward.

Max wipes at some of the snow on my cheek, but leaves a little bit. "How could I have done such a horrible thing?" he says dramatically. "Here, let me help." He leans in and slowly kisses my bottom lip, taking some snow with him. Then his eyes go wide.

"I know, I know. I'm a really good kisser," I say.

Max rolls his eyes. "Here. Open wide." He picks up a bit of snow and sprinkles it in my mouth. It tastes like lemon shave ice.

"Yum," I say, and bite my lip.

"Yum," Max says, and kisses me again.

30

the fuzzy fish

DON'T MOVE.

That is the first thing I think when I open my eyes. Because there is a heavy arm draped over my waist, a Max arm, and I am terrified of it sliding away. His other arm is scooped beneath the pillow below my head, and the fingertips are peeking out on the other side, past my face.

Don't move.

Because really, Max is the fuzzy fish, the species we discovered deep in the Amazon in our dream when we were kids, never before seen by the world. We had to tread lightly as we approached it, so it wouldn't get scared and swim away.

Max is definitely the fish. But then Max moves. Just a little bit, just a stir. I hear his breath intake slowly from behind me, and my throat catches. I don't know why I expect him to leap from the bed and go running out the door, never to return, but I just do. I can't help it.

Slowly, I roll over to face him. The sight of his eyes so close, open and looking back at me, turns my stomach inside out and my bones to jelly.

Max doesn't say anything. He just watches me intently, his eyes a little sleepy. I wonder if I didn't just dream about the slides and the yurt—maybe I dreamed it all. The whole thing with Max last night. Maybe I started earlier in this room. Maybe nothing even happened. It's all so unclear these days.

Then Max swallows, and as if it's the most casual thing in the world, he uses both arms to pull me to him, kissing me as my whole body melts into his.

I don't know if we're kissing, or just breathing each other in, but the point is that I cannot get enough Max.

"I was afraid you would swim away." I pull away just long enough to tell him.

"What?" he mutters between kisses.

"I was afraid you would swim away like the fuzzy fish."

"Less talking, more kissing," Max demands, and I giggle and oblige. Until I catch sight of something over the top of his shoulder. Outside the window giant fluffy snowflakes are falling.

"Snow?" I jump out of bed and run to the glass. But outside there's no snow at all. Of course there isn't.

"Could you come back here, please?" Max calls. "Lying here was much more enjoyable about thirty seconds ago."

"I swear I just saw snowflakes out the window, but when I looked, there was nothing there . . ." I explain as I climb back in beside Max and tuck my back into his chest. Soon enough Max's arms are fully wrapped around my body again and my head is in the crook of his neck.

"You have cocooned me," I declare.

Max's voice comes out in his *Invasion of the Body Snatchers* voice again, deep and robotic. "She-has-been-cocooned," he says. And after a brief moment of silence, I start giggling hysterically.

"*God*, you are weird," I say. But I keep laughing.

That's when Oliver bursts in and cries, "Sophie and I are getting married!"

"Excuse me?" I say, sitting up. Max just buries his head under a pillow.

"You heard me," Oliver says. "Sophie and I are getting married, and you are all invited."

Sophie saunters in behind Max, wearing big sunglasses and looking a little worse for wear. "Actually, we made out when I was drunk," she mutters. "And also, we found Margaret Yang."

31

teddy bears

I GUESS IF I'm being truly honest, I had pictured Margaret Yang as looking like she walked out of a Marvel action movie, wearing some slick suit and a pair of five-inch stiletto heels. She'd pop open a briefcase and punch in a bunch of numbers, then zap us between the eyes with a minuscule metal stun gun, and we'd be all fixed and ready to roll.

Instead, the Margaret Yang we find seated at the Blue Cow diner on the corner of Main and Milk Streets, just off the Wells campus, is clad in a thick gray cable-knit sweater and Crocs with wool socks, her hair pinned in a loose bun at the back of her head.

"Professor Yang?" I say quietly as I stand over her booth, on top of which she has spread out about six different newspapers, coffee, waffles, eggs, and bacon. So much food for such a small woman. She's clearly been here for hours, because she was here earlier when Sophie and Oliver came to get coffee and overheard her talking to a student.

In response, Margaret Yang silently holds her left hand up to my face, while her right hand skims the last lines of an article she is reading. I am tempted to order a coffee while we wait, and Max is definitely eyeing her bacon like he hasn't eaten in days.

"Done," she says, still not looking up, and instead pausing to take a sip of coffee. "You may sit."

Carefully, Max and I take a seat across the booth from her.

"You may present your topic," Margaret starts to say as she pours some more cream in her mug. But then she looks at us for the first time. "Oh," is all she says.

"Hi," I say, with a small hand wave.

"You aren't in my Neuro 260 class," she observes.

Max and I shake our heads.

"So you are not here to present your research topics for next semester," she says.

We shake our heads again.

Margaret Yang stares at us as she slowly stirs her coffee. "So, tell me, then," she says as she looks down to set her spoon on her plate, her face breaking into a warm smile. "How is Jerry the dog?"

*

"So, let me make sure I've got this right," Margaret says, now on her third cup. I am gratefully clutching my own mug and have nearly matched her in refills, while Max is chowing down on a fruit-covered waffle. We've told her everything. About the dreams, and finding each other again. About our work with Petermann and his arrest and the road trip. "You are seeing odd things pop up in your reality that you know shouldn't be."

"Yesterday I saw my dog drive by on a motorcycle," is all I can think to say in response.

"And Petermann told you he believes it's dream bleeding," Margaret says.

"Do you think he could be wrong?" I say, sitting up a bit straighter, and I notice Max stops chewing. *Please let him be wrong*, I want to say.

"It is certainly a first, but in this case, unfortunately, I believe he's right," Margaret says, signaling for the check. "Are you aware of what a transitional object is?"

I recall a lecture we had with Levy a month or so ago, after discussing attachment theory in children.

"It's basically a teddy bear, right?" I say.

"Very impressive," Margaret says. "That's right. Transitional objects are given to young children as something they can attach themselves to, besides the caregiver, to make them feel safer when they are exploring the world, or when they sleep at night."

I think back to my mother leaving, to what brought us to CDD in the first place. "I don't think I had one of those," I say.

"Yes, you did." Margaret Yang gives a confident nod.

"What was it, then?" I ask. "Jerry?"

In response, Margaret just looks pointedly at Max.

"I don't get it." I frown.

"Me?" Max says.

"Yes." Margaret places her hands on the table, one on top of the other. "You have to understand, when I met the two of you, my heart broke. I was young, just starting out. At that point in my treatment I'd run into a few adults with insomnia, some stressed-out college kids at most. I'd never seen children your age before. You'd both suffered these unbelievably hard experiences, death and desertion, and you were so small and so alone. You needed something to make you feel safe, and nothing was doing the trick. That's when it hit me. You could have each other."

Max and I share another look, but this time we hold it. I think about the story he told me with the chocolate Legos. "I never really expected it to work," Margaret says. "But I was adventurous and trying to make a name for myself. And somehow, you connected. You found each other. I expected that, like all kids do with their blankies and teddy bears, you would simply outgrow it. But apparently you never did."

I finally look away from Max to Margaret. It all makes so

much sense. "Then maybe we never need to?" I say hopefully.

"I wish that were the case, Alice. But I think we have enough evidence to the contrary, now that you've met in real life. Not if you want to tell the difference between sleeping and waking. We have to get you out of each other's dreams as soon as possible."

Max and I are listening to Margaret Yang when I feel his hand grip mine under the table.

"Are you sure?" I ask. "There's no other way?"

Margaret Yang simply shakes her head.

*

Half an hour later Max and I are still holding hands as we lie on Margaret Yang's bed back at her faculty apartment, where she places EEG caps on our heads and then a small metal object the size of a cell phone battery at the base of our necks.

"We're going to be okay, Alice," Max says as our eyes begin to close. "No matter what, we have each other."

I have never been so scared in my entire life, but I put on a brave face. If I can make Max think I believe him, maybe I actually will. "Would you like me to tell you a story?" I ask.

"Yes, please," Max says.

"Okay," I say. "One day a nine-year-old girl is walking around the Museum of Modern Art. It's totally empty. There aren't even any guards. But she doesn't really mind, because it gives her more time to look around." I rub my thumb along the knuckle of his forefinger, and I can feel him start to relax. "Then suddenly, all the paintings started to disappear. Or rather, the images on the paintings, and eventually the canvases are all white. She hears a noise and realizes she isn't alone in the gallery after all. There's a boy there, and he's holding out a giant box of felt tip markers, in every shade." I chuckle out loud, thinking of the memory. "And they spend the rest of the day coloring in the paintings with whatever they want, and then they fall asleep on the roof in the sunshine. And even though when she wakes up he's gone, and she's back in her apartment, she somehow feels better. Stronger. Like someone was there to save her."

"Was that the first dream you remember having about me?" Max asks softly, and I nod in reply. "I remember it, too," Max says. "It was such a great day."

"I'll see you soon, Max," I say, squeezing his hand tight.

"I'll see you soon," Max whispers.

October 18th

Max and I are curled up back on the dock at the Charles River, this time on a bundle of pillows, and I am dangling the slide viewer in front of our faces again.

"None of these are good enough," I say impatiently, looking at an image of a vegetable garden. But then I replace it with another and stop. "Wait. I found one."

It's a photo of some beautiful cliffs in Ireland. I pass the viewer to Max and he just says, "Sold." And suddenly I am there, walking among the thick grass as it ruffles in a heavy wind. Max is up ahead, holding a sweet-looking Shetland pony wearing a Shetland sweater, and I start to run to meet them. But I trip and fall on the uneven field, and when I get up again, the pony is there, but Max isn't, and the rope he was holding just dangles in the wind.

"Max?" I yell. "Where are you?" I am spinning around and around, but all I see is green, and this time he doesn't pop up like he did between the foam Jenga blocks.

"This isn't going to work," I say to myself, and I start running back down the hill where I came from, before I trip and fall again.

When I land, I'm back on the dock, but Max isn't there, either, so I quickly pick up another slide. It's of the Golden Gate Bridge.

"This'll do," I say, because it could be a photo of Siberia and I'd still take it if it got me to Max. And suddenly I'm at the top of a steep San Francisco hill, in one of the little yellow cars they rent to tourists, and Max is up ahead, laughing in his stupid helmet.

"You look ridiculous," I call out.

"Safety first!" Max cries. "Race you to the bridge!" And he's off. I follow him through the city, racing around trolleys until we are cruising over the Golden Gate. But as we come to the end, he turns abruptly off the road, and when I finally get there, a dusty spot overlooking the bay, he's gone again. I sigh and gently rest my head on the little steering wheel. No. No-no-no-no-no. When I lift my head, I see a chocolate Lego on the dashboard. I pop it in my mouth and desperately chew.

Back to the dock I go, and this time I'm more specific. I toss the slides aside, one by one, until I find an image of a beautiful, clean wooden raft, resting atop calm ocean water with a pair of thick striped beach towels laid out on top.

"How far can you run from me here?" I say, and just like that I am there, lying on the towel, feeling warm and happy in the sun.

I take a deep breath, and next thing I know there is water drip-ping all over me.

"What kind of dive should I do?" Max asks with a mischievous grin, soaking wet as he shakes his wet hair over my body, and I squeal.

"Don't dive!" I try to suggest as casually as possible. "Just lie down here with me for a minute."

"I'll be right back, Alice," he says.

"No, you won't," I say. "You won't be right back. Please just stay here with me."

"Alice." Max looks at me like I'm nuts. "Where could I go?" He motions around us and he seems to have a point, because we're in the middle of the ocean, with nothing around for miles and miles. But it doesn't make me feel any better.

"Max, don't." My voice begins to come more frantic.

"Cannonnnnballlllll," Max calls, flying out over the water, and before I can stop myself, I have leaped in after him.

The water is so blue it's practically neon, and I can't tell if I can see miles ahead or not at all because there is nothing to see. There is no Max. Then suddenly a foot kicks out in front of me out of nowhere and I try and grab onto it, hoping he'll drag me wherever he goes. But the foot escapes my fingers and is gone as quickly as it came.

But then it appears again, this time a little farther away. I swim and swim and swim, pulling my arms and kicking my legs over and over until a short stepladder comes into view underwater, and I take it. Despite all the swimming I'm still not tired. I'm just desperate for anything that might lead me to him.

When I pull my body over the edge, though, I'm not back on the raft, I'm back on the dock at school again, and this time I scream in frustration. My hand shaking, I snatch another slide off the wood and stuff it in the viewer once more, not even bothering to look at what it is until I'm suddenly there, among the shelves of a vast library.

I am just about to cry his name when I hear him call out first. "Alice?" He sounds just as scared as I do.

"Max?" I cry.

"Where are you?" he asks. "Why can't I get there?"

"I'm right here!" I cry. But this time there's no response. "Max?" I try again, and nothing. I want to push over all the stacks to see around them, but I don't want to risk hurting him. So I just start shoving books off the shelves, trying to see through to the other side. I call his name over and over and over, waiting to hear him call out to me again.

But he doesn't.

He is gone.

32

it's not the same

ONCE, WHEN WE were living in New York, my school took a field trip to Mystic Seaport, three hours away in Connecticut. The bus left at six a.m., so I woke at five, let myself out, and headed for the subway. As I walked, the sun barely rising above the city streets, I thought to myself how lovely it was. The whole city was dreaming. All was quiet on the street, but up there in people's beds, the possibilities were endless. Maybe there was even someone else out there like me, lucky enough to dream of their soul mate.

"It's over," Margaret Yang says gently when we open our eyes, the room as quiet as the city streets that morning in New York, and the memory of it makes me want to burst into tears. "But you put up a good fight." She looks from me to Max, who has dropped my hand and is just staring at the ceiling, motionless. "You both did."

*

One of the nice things about having people like Sophie and Oliver as friends is that when you don't feel like talking, they do it for you. It turns out that Max and I had missed quite a lot of action at Bartholomew Burns's dorm party the night before. Apparently some guy got so amped about his Monopoly win that he chugged a wine cooler, ripped off all his clothing, and went running through the campus naked . . . to be followed enthusiastically by everyone else. And upon returning to the house, one of those naked people walked back in and chose to profess his adoration for a girl, and got punched in the face by some drunk art major who was trying to impress her. That naked guy was also the guy who won Monopoly and started the whole naked run, and, yup, that guy who won Monopoly was Oliver, the drunk art major was Wallace, and the damsel in distress was, of all people, Sophie.

"I saved you," Oliver says with a big stupid smile as he wraps an arm around Sophie's shoulders in the back of the car. Campus security was kind enough to jump-start us, free of charge, and it turns out that was all Max's station wagon needed, because she's a tough old lady. We're headed back to Boston, cows and sheep speeding by in a blur outside the windows. Then Oliver pulls Sophie's head to his chest. "Shh, my child," he says. "Everything is all right. I'm here now."

"My hero," Sophie mutters, rolling her eyes. But since we've been friends as long as we have, I know something Sophie doesn't know yet. I know that she likes it, and she likes Oliver, too.

They try to ask us about Margaret and about what happened. I think they can tell something is off. We answer their questions to the best of our ability, but I mostly tune out. The whole world just seems so flat. So gray. The coffee we drink is less delicious, the leaves less electric, even though I know nothing should have changed. I sleep a lot, letting my eyes flutter closed, my consciousness drifting in and out, but I don't dream, and have trouble figuring out if I've slept at all. The only thing that helps me tell I did is waking up to see how many more miles we've traveled, and all the while Max is just sitting there silently staring at the road, turning the Motown up full blast.

*

I can't put my finger on it, but as we pull into town, despite there not being a cloud in the sky, it feels like there's no sun either. Over the past couple weeks the air has smelled like flowers, like every tree was sprinkling me with fragrance as I walked beneath it, but it doesn't smell that way anymore. Even the bricks of the houses seem less red. At a stoplight I stare hopelessly at an outdoor café, waiting for something strange to happen—for the waiter to start singing or the little dog in the sweater to start reading a book, or for someone to begin an incredible food fight. But nobody does. It's not that such a thing definitely would've happened before; it's just that now there is no possibility it ever will again. I feel as if I've lost one of my senses altogether.

We drop Sophie and Oliver off at the Taj, because Sophie has a few hours to kill before her train and Oliver wants to give her a tour of the city. I know this is something I should be doing with her. She's my best friend. But I can't muster the energy, and she seems to understand.

"I'm still not sure I get what happened," she says, standing on the sidewalk as I pull her scarf out of the backseat of the car and wrap it carefully around her neck. "But I know it's going to be okay. Whatever you are going through right now, I'm happy you have friends here. And you have Max. He'd never let anything bad happen to you."

"I know," I say, nodding. I want to give her a smile of reassurance. Sometimes you do that for the people you love. But I can't seem to find any smiles inside my mouth at the moment. "Hey, Soph?" I ask.

"Yes, Al?" she says, zipping my coat up a bit tighter.

"Thank you for coming. I miss you already," I say.

"I miss you, too," she says. "But I think we've proven we aren't going to let a little distance get between us. Besides . . . maybe I'll be back sooner than we think?"

She glances in the direction of the street, and I turn back to where Oliver and Max are standing by the car, shifting their feet and absently checking their cell phones.

"The new Helix 300 just came out today," Max says, shoving his phone back into his pocket and not looking at Oliver.

"I saw," Oliver says with a nod, looking at the windows of the Taj like they're HD television screens. "I'm still on the email distro, too."

"Well, I'm dying to play . . ." Max says.

Oliver's face lights up, almost despite himself, and then he takes a wary glance at Max.

"If you . . . might wanna join sometimes . . . I dunno," Max finishes, unsure.

Oliver shuffles his feet. "I'm not sure . . ." he says dismissively. But then he smirks. "I've picked up some new techniques since the ninth grade. You think you can take it?"

Then Max throws his head back a little and laughs. "Try me," he says. And they shake hands as Sophie and I share a knowing look.

"So, are you guys gonna make out now?" Sophie asks, and Oliver chases her around the car, squealing.

*

Max tries to make conversation as we drive to my house. I can tell he's happy. He and Oliver are going to be friends again. Max and I aren't going to go insane. All the drama is over. Why can't I be happy, too? Why can't I shake this hopeless feeling inside of me?

"Do you feel it?" I ask him, when we're standing outside my house. He leans up against the car's side door, his arms crossed. A few schoolgirls walk by, turn back to glance at him, and start giggling. Max is oblivious to the fact that they are even there or that he looks like an LL Bean boyfriend.

"Feel what?" Max asks, but he sounds wary.

"I know this sounds stupid, but it's just . . . not the same," I try to explain.

"What's not the same, Alice?" Max asks. There's a warning in his voice. "We should be happy about this . . . We've fixed it like we wanted to, and you and I are going to be okay."

"But it's not the same," I insist, unintentionally tapping my fingers against my leg.

"*What's* not the same?" Max asks again, sounding a little impatient.

"Everything!" I practically yell, throwing my hands in the air. I feel like I'm going to start crying.

At this, Max clenches his teeth, and looks away from me. "I'm the same."

I sigh, not sure of what to say.

"Alice," Max tries again, slower this time, trying to calm me down. "I know we lost the dreams. But we were afraid of that because we didn't want to lose each other. And I know we won't. Nothing's going back to normal, because nothing was ever normal to start with. This is our new beginning, Alice, and it's going to be better than it was." He reaches to pull me to him, but I step away, clutching my hands inside my coat pockets.

"But that's just it," I say. "Nothing was ever normal. It was magic, Max. Don't you remember? Before the dream bleeding, before everything went off track. And now the magic is gone. There's no going to bed anymore knowing that something amazing is going to happen."

"But, Alice, it wasn't real," Max says.

"It was real for me."

"And what about me?" Max says. "Things may have changed, but I'm still here, and you being like this, you're basically telling me that's not good enough. That the real me isn't good enough."

I don't know how to tell him that he's wrong. That I love him. But I also loved the boy who thought everything was an adventure. Who pushed me down a staircase on a foam boogie board and chased me through the hallways of the Met throwing Oreo cake at my face. "I know, you're here now," I say instead. "But for how long?"

Max shakes his head, blinking. "What does that mean?"

"You've done it before!" I say. "One day you're my dream boyfriend, the next day you're with Celeste. One day you're my friend, the next you're not. One day you're kissing me at the Gardner, and the next you're saying it didn't mean anything. What about the next time that happens? Except this time, I won't have a dream to go back to. I'll be alone."

Max stares at me in shock. "I love you, Alice," he says. "I can't believe that's how you feel about me, after everything we've just been through." Then he walks back around to the driver's side. "I don't want to fight about this anymore. Let me know when you're ready to live in the real world. With me."

Max slams the door and drives off.

33

patio lights

"SO, TELL ME, how are you?" Delilah Weatherbee says to me as she exhales some hookah smoke into the middle of her office.

"Are you sure we should be doing this?" I say skeptically. "You are technically an authority figure."

"It's all natural and non-addictive," she states. Then she adds, "Besides, you look like you could use it, and nobody comes up here anyway." On the second point, she might be right. In all the times I have come to visit her, I have never noticed a single other person around. And on the first point, she is definitely right. It's almost a week after my fight with Max and I am in a "whatever gets you through the day" kind of place. Sometimes it's frozen yogurt, other times it's punk music, and sometimes it's just lying hopelessly on the sofa spooning Jerry as I stare into the fireplace. And on this occasion it is smoking hookah with my college counselor. Anything to provide temporary relief from the unimaginable agony coursing through my heart.

He still isn't speaking to me. No snide remarks in psych or looks in the hallway. He carries on for the most part like I'm not even there, except to pick up a pencil I dropped in class one time, and set my phone gently next to my tray in the dining hall two days ago, when I'd left it in the food line. But in each instance, he turned away without a word, all proud shoulders and head slightly upturned. To the majority of the school, nothing has changed. Nobody else knows about Maine. But they know he broke up with Celeste, and they know he isn't talking to me.

It's on me. He put himself out there, and I still can't wrap my head around it. The idea of this new beginning, as he said. The uncertainty of what it means for us. It's one thing to withstand this new, dreamless world alone, but it's another thing entirely to try and do it with Max. It hurts too much.

Celeste, meanwhile, is fine. Better than fine. She's already started dating some architecture major at one of the local colleges and is hardly around anymore. But when she is, we are starting to talk again. Still, I would be all alone were it not for Oliver, who is my eternal savior, eating with me in the dining hall, Segwaying next to me as I walk to class. And now that he's fallen for Sophie, our friendship can proceed without any more complications.

I sigh and put the metal mouthpiece to my lips and inhale. At least one thing in my life isn't complicated.

"I can't help but feel you're dodging my question," Delilah observes as she watches my long, drawn-out exhalation. And she's right again.

"I'm fine," I say.

"You don't seem fine," she says. "Have you given any more thought to the questions I asked you at your last visit? How you are choosing to define yourself at this time in your life?"

"I guess I just don't understand why everyone is so desperate for me to know everything. Who I am, what I want to do. I'm only sixteen. Why should I?" I say. "Since when is a sixteen-year-old supposed to hold the keys to the future?"

"Nobody is asking you to know that," Delilah says. "All anyone is asking is for you to start trying to figure it out. And there's nothing very scary about that, is there?" she asks.

"No." I shake my head. "That actually doesn't sound very scary at all." I understand what she means now. We have to try to move forward. Otherwise, how do we expect to get anywhere?

When Max drove off that day, I just stood on the empty sidewalk, watching the lights flash from green to yellow to red and back again, wondering what had happened. How did it all go from wrong to right to worse than it had ever been? How could Max accuse me of not actually loving him, when he's the only one I ever wanted?

What he doesn't seem to understand is that it's not about him. It's about the dreams. The dreams were what I could count on. Where I could go when nothing else was going right. Back in New York I wasn't allowed to paint my bedroom a color other than ugly eggshell white, so I hung up twinkle lights. That's what the dreams did for my life. I covered it in patio lights so none of it seemed as bad. The dreams were where I could always count on being happy . . . where I could always count on *him*.

Max said I don't know how to live in reality, and maybe he's right. Maybe I need to take down the lights and stare the eggshell in the face.

*

When I walk into the house after school that day, the first thing I see are my father's legs sticking out from beneath the sofa, as Jerry looks on with a concerned expression. Things keep getting weirder and weirder around this place. Last week when I came home he was rigging a giant basket to a rope that extended all the way to the top of the staircase, so he could hoist Jerry up and down.

"For his knees," he explained, as though it was perfectly normal, as Jerry stood off to the side, eyeing the contraption warily. "He's not getting any younger. This way he can go where we go with ease."

The man needs friends.

"Dad?" I call out now. "Are you okay?"

At the sound of my voice my father wiggles his body backward and pops his head out, clutching Jerry's tennis ball in one hand.

"He lost it again," he explains, before handing the ball to a patiently waiting Jerry, who takes it and drops it, bouncing it to himself for a moment before losing it under the sofa again. My father's shoulders slump. I start tapping my fingers against the side of my leg to a made-up rhythm as I psych myself up for the question I need to ask.

"Hey, Dad, did you happen to hear back from Madeleine as to whether we'll be seeing her on this trip?"

"Great question," my dad says, getting back down on the floor and searching under the sofa again. "Not entirely sure on that yet."

"What does that mean?" I ask.

"I'm just not sure if she's going to have time between the conference and all the travel," he starts to ramble, but the end of it gets cut off, muffled by the sofa.

My father, a grown man, is actually hiding from me. I tap my fingers faster. This is harder than I thought it would be.

Let me know when you're ready to live in the real world, I hear Max say.

Screw it, I think, and I lie down on the ground, too, so both my father and I are on our stomachs with our heads stuck under the sofa. Behind us I hear Jerry make an anxious whinnying noise.

"Alice, what are you doing?" my father asks.

"Dad," I say. "Look at me. The conference is in five days. Have you heard from Madeleine at all?" I ask. "Did you even reach out to her?"

"I wish you would call her *Mom*," he tells me again.

"I would be able to do that if she'd been one," I say. And he closes his eyes for a moment, as if I have pained him. "Dad," I say, "Mom left us. She left us for monkeys, and she's not coming back. We have to accept it, and we have to talk about it." As I peer at my father in the dim light under the sofa, I consider that perhaps, for us, this is our womb. The place we feel covered enough to share how we really feel. Like a person going into a fetal position, or Jerry taking his treats under the dining room table to eat them in peace.

Eventually, my father nods. "That sounds like an excellent idea, Alice. How about we do it over some cake?"

"That depends," I say. "Is it edible?"

*

"I always knew she wasn't coming back," my dad says as he digs his fork into a surprisingly moist piece of red velvet. "But it was so much easier to deny it than to come to terms with the kind of person she truly was. The kind who could desert her family, her husband, and most of all, her daughter." He pauses. "It was easier to ignore that fact than to confront the idea that I never really knew her at all."

"That must have been hard," I say, taking a sip of coffee.

"It must have been hard for *you*," he says, placing a hand on mine, and this time he's not so quick to remove it. "You were so young. I know I failed you in this, Alice. I know she caused the nightmares, but I should've been able to stop them. I should've been able to make you feel safe. But I didn't want to talk about it, and you were alone. And I'm sorry."

I tell him it's okay and take another bite of cake, chewing slowly. He managed to get the texture right this time, but he also seems to have added twice the salt and half the sugar. This conversation makes me feel so much better, but it still doesn't make me feel totally right. There's still one apology I'm missing.

"It means a lot to hear this from you, Dad. I just wish I could hear it from her," I admit.

"Well, maybe *you* should email her," he suggests. "At this point, what's stopping you?"

I get up and start clearing our plates without thinking. No way was I going to email Madeleine. She was the mother. That was her job. But then, for what must be the fortieth time today, I think about Max.

Slowly I set the plates down in the sink, grab my bag, and head for the kitchen door.

"Where are you going?" my dad asks. "Was the cake that bad?"

"It was the opposite of bad," I lie. "It was delicious. But now I have an email to write." I pause in the doorway, then walk back to give him a kiss on the cheek. "That was a good talk, Dad. We should have them more often."

In response, my father smiles widely, adjusting his glasses a little bit. "I'd like that very much," he says.

It's time to take down the patio lights.

34

all we have

FROM AN EMOTIONAL standpoint, there is really never a good time to cause your imaginary dream boyfriend to break up with you. I have been well aware of this every day for the past week, since we got back from Maine. But from a practical standpoint, as I approached the new science center, balancing my succulent trays atop my bike basket, I could have really benefited from the use of my imaginary dream ex-boyfriend's station wagon.

"Alice." Parker walks up, arms outstretched toward my succulent trays. "This is a sight to behold! You've come a long way since that first day in Terrarium Club!"

"Thanks!" I say. "I've had some time on my hands." By that I mean the time I would have usually spent sleeping. But since

I'm too afraid to go to sleep and not dream of Max, instead I've been doing my homework and tending to my succulents. The other night my dad heard me in the yard at two a.m. and came out wielding a baseball bat.

"Well, set them down over there by Celeste, and then if you want you can help Jeremiah measure out where the installations are going to hang, that would be excellent."

I glance over to where Jeremiah and Celeste are standing on two ladders next to each other. Jeremiah gives a small wave and brandishes some measuring tape.

"Did you ever build your vacation home for Socrates?" I ask as I extend some tape and Jeremiah makes small lines on the wall with the tip of a pencil.

He seems genuinely shocked. "I can't believe you remembered his name. He'll be so honored," Jeremiah says.

"Well, please let him know," I say with a smile.

"I don't have to. He heard it himself." Jeremiah winks.

The measuring tape rolls back into its cage with a snap. "What does that mean?" I ask nervously.

Jeremiah slowly makes sure the coast is clear before unzipping the fanny pack he is wearing at his waist, and out pops the head of a small green lizard.

"Say hello, Socrates," Jeremiah says.

Socrates just blinks, and Jeremiah looks at me expectantly.

"Oh!" I exclaim. "Hello, Socrates!" I say, a little too loudly to compensate for my insincerity.

But Jeremiah gives me a disgusted look. "Not so loud!" he hisses. "Do you want us to get suspended?"

"Sorry," I whisper, shaking my head.

And when I do, I see Max is walking across the quad, a stack of books tucked under his arm, heading in the direction of the gym. I watch his slow gait wistfully. He always knows where he's going, what's next. I wonder if I will ever manage to get over him, or if years down the line I'll be in therapy, still talking about a guy I barely even knew when I was conscious. My swan. My African parrot. My fuzzy fish.

Just then, an email pops up on my phone. I see who it's from. My hand starts to shake a bit, and I waste no time opening it immediately.

"Actually, will you hold Socrates for a second?" Jeremiah asks. "I really have to go to the bathroom, but Socrates is afraid of the sound of the toilet flushing."

"Sure," I say, not paying attention, as I hold out my hand that's not clutching my phone. I feel something scaly and squirmy land in my palm as I eagerly read the message.

My Dear Alice,

Thank you for your email. I'm not sure I've been made aware yet of these Google Alerts you mention—we hardly have internet here!—but as always, I'm impressed with how intelligent you are and how industrious you've become.

To your first question, in terms of my visit to

Washington DC, I will unfortunately not be able to extend my visit to Boston, as my flight is a direct round trip from Casablanca. But my heart is warmed to hear how you are enjoying Nan's house, particularly that old bike. I got a lot of use out of that thing many years ago.

On to your second point. You asked if I would not be stopping by after DC, when could you expect me? And I am sorry to say I'm not so sure. Research here in Madagascar has really picked up, and I have been invited to speak in Paris in two months, and New Zealand three months after that, which frankly puts me at capacity for international travel for the rest of the year.

To your last point, I would like to keep the discussion ongoing on the topic of you coming here to visit. As you can see, my schedule is inflexible and complicated. But I am charmed by your interest in our work.

Give your father a hug for me, and Jerry a sweet pat. I miss them both, and you. Keep working hard in school, you'll need it. And above all else, don't be afraid to follow your dreams, Alice. After all, they're all we have. What are we without them?

Love,

Mom

I stare at the last two sentences, letting the hand holding the phone drop to my side. Dreams are all we have? I frown. No, *Mom*, they are not all we have. We have so much more than that. We have friends and loved ones and real life. We have people that matter, real people, and what we do matters to them in return. They rely on us.

At least I do.

I look back up just in time to see Max entering the gym, and I swallow. I am an idiot.

"You know," I hear a voice say, and look down to see Celeste leaning on my ladder, holding the measuring tape that just fell off one of the steps. She glances in the direction of the gym. "I've seen him sleep a few times." She hands the tape back to me gently. "He never looked happier than when he dreamed."

*

The door to the gym elevator is just about to shut behind Max when I wedge myself in it and, after the doors close and before I can psych myself out, press the Stop button.

"Alice, are you crazy?" Max says.

"Do you really need me to answer that question?" I reply.

"Do I need to remind you that you are terrified of small confined spaces?" he asks.

"Nope, no need for that," I mutter, glancing around the tiny torture chamber. "I am well aware."

"What are you doing with Socrates?" Max asks then, and I

look down to see the lizard dangling helplessly from my hand, no doubt certain that death is imminent.

"Does everyone in this whole school know Socrates?" I ask.

"He was our class pet in elementary school, and Jeremiah adopted him," Max says. "So, yes."

"Well, that explains it," I say, holding Socrates up and looking him in the eye. He responds by blinking at me several times, and it occurs to me that when Jeremiah gets back from the bathroom, he is absolutely going to be out for my blood.

"Alice," Max says, gently bringing me back to reality. "How about we allow the elevator to move again, before you have a breakdown?"

But I brush the idea out of my head. I have other things on my mind. "I'm sorry," I say.

"It's okay," Max says, not getting it. "Let's just press the button . . ."

"No," I say, "not about that. About what I said. About how I felt. I'm sorry that I made you feel like you weren't enough, Max, because you are. I was afraid. For my whole life, the dreams were all I had. They were the only thing that made me feel less alone. And you were part of that. And you got over it, you learned how to function, but I didn't. And I didn't understand that when I lost the dreams, I wouldn't lose you, too."

Max isn't saying anything, he's just staring at the floor, so

I keep going. "And you were right! I do need to live in reality. And I'm trying. I know I can't just escape my problems. I mean, I'm standing in an elevator! And I even talked to my dad about my mom."

At this, Max meets my eyes with a sad smile. "That's really great, Alice," he says. "I'm glad to hear it."

But I keep talking. "So I'm saying, everything is fine!" I try again, because this isn't the response I wanted. "I mean, look at me! I'm literally standing here in an elevator, confronting my fears, because of you. It doesn't get any more real than this, Max. I don't need the dreams if I've got you." The hand that's not holding Socrates is feverishly tapping rhythms against its own palm, and my body is starting to feel a little hot. Is there no air in here?

Max just keeps giving me that sad smile.

"Max?" I ask. "Say something."

"I don't know, Alice." He shakes his head. "Maybe we're just too different."

"What do you mean?" I ask, the blood draining from my face as Socrates squirms between my fingers. Now it doesn't matter if I'm in an elevator or not. I could be buried six feet beneath the ground and I'm not sure I would notice.

Max keeps talking. "I've been thinking about it all, too, about what I said. The thing is, you've always lived in the dreamworld. And it's one of the most incredible things about you. I don't want to take that away from you, but it seems like

I do. Maybe we worked in the dreams, but in reality . . . maybe it's just not meant to be."

I stand there for a moment, frozen. "But I fixed it," I try again. "I'm in an elevator."

"I know," Max says. "And right now we need to get you out of one, before you lose it."

Slowly, he presses the Stop button again, and when the doors open this time, we find Jeremiah, Celeste, and Dean Hammer waiting for us.

"We had to call security," Dean Hammer fumes. "Are you two all right? And who is responsible for this reptile?"

Without a word, I hand Socrates to Jeremiah and leave Max to explain while tears begin to slide down my cheeks.

NOVEMBER 1ST

Somewhere out there, it sounds like Darth Vader is chuck-ling. *This makes zero sense, since he was arguably the most serious man in the entire solar system, in the history of time. But there it is again, deep and sinister: Ho-ho-ho.*

"What is that terrible noise?" I ask, sticking my head out of the safari tent and rubbing my eyes.

"Hippos." Max looks up from his reading at the breakfast table. He gives a nod to the left. "We're camped next to the river, and they seem to have a lot to say this morning."

"I can't tell if they are laughing at us or plotting our demise," I say, grimacing as the strange bellows echo over the camp. "What?" I ask Max, who is giving me a look.

"Nothing!" He shrugs his shoulders good-naturedly. "You've just never been a morning person."

I shuffle over to the folding camp table and take a grateful sip of coffee from his mug as I sit down.

"Get your own," he protests. But he knows I won't, so he pours himself a new cup. "Come on," he says then, standing up and extending a hand to me. "Time to go and see the lions." His brown hair falls softly in his eyes, and the sun shines from behind his face, making him look almost otherworldly.

"Are there baby ones?" I ask hopefully.

"Of course," he answers.

"How will we get there?" I ask.

"Did you sleep okay?" Max looks concerned. "The answer is hot air balloon, like always."

Before I know it, the balloon is touching down among the lion pride, who watch us carefully from where they lie in the long grass, and my fingers go a little numb. But Max pulls a fluffy green tennis ball the size of a grapefruit from his back pocket.

"Ready? Ready?" he shouts, "Go get it!" and hurls the ball across the plains. The mother lion runs and grabs it like a giant golden retriever, then drops it panting at our feet and purrs as we scratch behind her ears.

"Looks like we're in." Max laughs.

I want to laugh, too, except I am struck by one terrible thought: This isn't Max.

He looks like Max and he smiles like Max, he's sweet and kind like Max. But he's not my Max. He's like a Max decoy. A stand-in. He isn't him, and we aren't us. This isn't something we will each wake up in our beds tomorrow and share, one moment in time the rest of the world will never know about except Max and me. This is just a regular dream. I can't explain it. I just know.

"Can we go now?" I ask Fake Dream Max.

"But we just got here!" Max cries.

"I really wanna go home," I say, a little frantically now.

Fake Dream Max looks at me, confused, tilting his head to one side. "Okay, Alice," he says with a nod. "We can go home now."

35

sparkly

I CAN'T HELP but feel that it's rather rude of Jerry to keep barking incessantly in the front hall when some of us have better things to do, like lie in our beds hating everything.

That isn't true, though, and I know it. Anytime I'm upset, my father will always ask me to think about everything good I have going on. I'm doing well in school, and I joined a few more clubs—BARA, the Bennett Animal Rescue Association, and the Photography Club, and I started my own weekly music podcast. I've even begun picking out potential schools I'd like to go to after Bennett. Now that we've talked about my mom, my dad and I are better than ever. I have a lot to be happy about.

I just don't have Max.

Jerry barks again and I storm over to the intercom, pressing the button for the kitchen. "Dad?" I call. "Will you please let Jerry out? I'm sleeping." It's only when he doesn't answer that I remember he left early this morning for a conference in St. Louis. I am alone, and Jerry needs to go to the bathroom.

I pull on a sweater and some boots and jog down the stairs, throwing on a gray wool coat.

"Jer?" I call. "Where are you?"

When I hear his bark from outside, I throw the door open, annoyed. "How on earth did you get out here?" I ask before noticing that something is very different, and I wonder if I haven't actually woken up yet.

As usual, the front walk is covered in fallen leaves. But instead of reds and blues and browns, the leaves are neon pink.

And standing a few paces down, among the leaves, wearing a tuxedo, is Max.

And standing next to him, in a much tinier tuxedo, is Jerry.

And Max is holding a pizza box.

"What is this?" I barely manage to ask, slowly taking a few steps toward him.

"Here," Max says, grinning, his eyes a little glassy. "Open it."

I open the top of the box, feeling like Julia Roberts in *Pretty Woman*, and am stunned to see not a pizza, but a giant Oreo cookie cake.

"Am I dreaming?" I ask in all seriousness, looking around and rubbing my eyes.

"No, you're not." Max laughs, but his voice comes out a little choked. "And that's exactly the point I'm trying to make."

I tuck my hands inside the sleeves of my sweater and bite my lip. "I'm confused," I say. "That day in the elevator . . ."

Max tips his head to the side. "I know. I know I said that we are just too different. But then I thought about it . . ." He chuckles again. He's honestly acting a little manic, back and forth between giggles and almost-tears. "Getting in the elevator. Just to tell me how you felt. You are totally insane, Alice, and you do live in a dreamworld sometimes. You prefer things when they are stranger and prettier than everyday life. But that means you also make every moment of *my* life dreamier. More exciting and unexpected. When you are around, my life is *always* sparkly. And I don't want to change you. I don't want to run from it, either. I want to make you feel the way you make me feel. I want to make you happy."

I'm so happy I can barely speak. I never thought I'd hear him say these words. I want to grab him by the lapels and hold him tight. So, after carefully taking the pizza box from him and setting it on the ground, that's exactly what I do.

"You do make me happy," I say, my cheek pressed against his chest. "Dream Max and Real Max. The one who knows how to push the limits, and the one who grounds me and brings me back to earth. I can't imagine going back to the way things were, when all I knew was Dream Max, and Real Max didn't exist. It would be like reading alternating chapters of my favorite book, or listening to a skipping record. And I feel like I've ruined it, and we can't go back."

"But that's the thing, Alice," Max says, running a hand up and down my back and resting his head on top of mine. "We don't have to go back. We have each other. No matter how different we are or how many dumb things we do, we make each other better. And what we have is better than what the dreams could ever give us. It's real."

As Max pulls away from me, my heart feels like it's doing rhythmic gymnastics. Then he kisses me, and it's the best kiss yet, because it means more than all the others before it. And I'm not afraid anymore. Of losing the dreams or losing him. I have him. My swan. My African parrot. My fuzzy fish.

I kiss him back, the world around us disappearing completely. When we break apart, Max reaches into his pocket to retrieve something while I reach down to the Oreo cake and pick up a piece.

"One more thing," he says, handing me a cell phone case with Jerry's face on it.

I stare down at the phone. Even when he's being the most romantic person on Earth, he's still the most practical. Still looking out for me.

"You know you need it," he says. Then he looks worried. "Did I ruin the moment?"

I shake my head. "No," I say, looking up into his eyes. "It's perfect." And then, without warning, I smush a giant piece of Oreo cake across his cheek.

"Oh, really?" Max cries. "You thought that was the right move for this moment?"

I start to back up slowly, inch by inch, grinning wildly. "Maybe?" I say, shrugging.

"You should probably run now," Max replies, pieces of Oreo falling from his face. And then I take off shrieking into the house, Max on my tail, Jerry nipping at our heels.

36

see you soon

ONE MONTH LATER, I sit at my windowsill, marveling at how beautiful Boston looks under a blanket of snow. The cars nearly disappear beneath it, so all you see are gas streetlamps and the orange light of people's windows. The snow seems to muffle sound, too, especially at night, and I feel like I'm living in a different time.

"Bug," my dad says over the intercom, "sorry to interrupt, but we were just wondering, did you feed Jerry tonight? Or should we do it?"

Before I even open my mouth to answer, the unnerving sound of his boyish giggle comes over the line, too, and I make a face instead.

"Margaret," my dad says. "Stop it. Alice will hear you."

"I fed him, Dad," I call out. "And I'm on the phone."

"Tell Max I say hello," he says, and the intercom clicks off amid laughter.

"Did I just hear your father . . . giggle?" Max asks. His voice is deep and crackly and I can tell he's in bed.

"Margaret is here," I explain.

"Again?" he asks.

"Again," I say. Once I told my dad everything that had happened, he wanted to be connected with Margaret immediately to make sure I was okay. She was in town for a conference and it was like they'd known each other their whole lives. Like her Crocs and his worn penny loafers were meant to sit across from each other beneath the kitchen table, perusing their various academic periodicals. Not to mention they both owned the same color corduroys. I shudder. "It's honestly a little gross, how gooey they are for each other. But I've never seen him this happy in my life." I pause. "They've been . . . cooking. She's totally patient with his culinary inadequacies. I think it's making me fat." I stand in front of my floor-length mirror and stick my tummy out intentionally. "Too much cake."

"You're gorgeous," Max says, almost defensively.

"Even if I blow up like that little blueberry girl from *Charlie and the Chocolate Factory*?" I ask.

"Violet Beauregarde," Max says. "And yes, even then."

"You really do know everything," I say, getting under the covers.

"So do you. You just don't always bother with the details," he says.

"Wanna come over?" I ask. It's an inside joke. I know he won't, but it doesn't mean I'm not serious.

Max lets out a low laugh. "We both know I'd like that, but my mom's on my case now that she knows we're dating. She likes you," he clarifies. "She just doesn't like how close you live. I guarantee she knocks on my door any minute to check up on me."

"Fine," I grumble. "Maybe I'll just go downstairs and ask Margaret to reverse the procedure so I get you back in my dreams again."

"Not unless you wanna see your dad and Margaret Yang making out," Max warns. I squeal and we both erupt into laughter. "Besides," he says, "we both know you still dream about me anyway. And I dream about you. We just don't dream together."

In the pause, I just listen to the sound of his breathing for a little while. It's so comforting. I don't have any trouble sleeping anymore. This is the only noise machine I need.

"What?" I say after a few seconds when I hear Max laughing softly on the other end of the line.

"I just can't believe there was ever a time before this," he says.

"Go on," I say, blushing. "I like where this is going."

"I just mean, there was basically always a dream you, of course. But to think that only a few months ago you didn't really exist. You were just this person I looked forward to seeing every night and hated saying good-bye to. You were my secret. My dream girl."

"Say that last part again?" I ask.

"I've said it a million times before," Max mumbles. "I should record it for you on your phone."

"That's actually a great idea," I say. "It could be my ringtone!"

"Alice, I was kidding."

"I'm still waiting for you to say it again," I say.

Max sighs, but it's a happy sigh. "Alice Rowe, you are my dream girl."

I smile quietly.

"But now I have to go to bed," Max says.

"No!" I command.

"Yes," he says. I'll see you in . . ."—he pauses—"six and a half hours? I've gotta go. I'll see you soon." After everything, he is still just as serious as ever.

"See you soon," I say. But I don't put down the phone. "Max?" I say after a few minutes. "Are you still there?"

Max's voice comes out soft, as he drifts off into sleep, just the way he does every night when we do this. "You know I am, Alice. I'm always here."

I smile to myself, a sense of calm coming over me as my

whole body relaxes into the mattress, Max's breath creating a rhythm on the other end of the line.

The sooner I go to sleep, the sooner I get to wake up and see my dream boy again.

"Would you please stop somersaulting?
Because I don't like it,
and neither does the person sitting next to me."

—Lucy Keating, talking in her sleep, 2001

acknowledgments

THE DREAM TEAM: To Sara Shandler, the truly delightful human, who along with Josh Bank, always makes me feel like I have something to say that is worth hearing, and always knows the very best way for me to say it. Les Morgenstein for not hesitating to say "sure" when I walked into his office and clumsily announced I had something I'd like him to read. Joelle Hobeika for getting the proposal out the damn door, without which none of these acknowledgments could ever be written. Jocelyn Davies for immediately sharing my vision of what this book could be, and working patiently with me to make it so. Hayley Wagreich for fixing some of my toughest notes before I even had a chance to process them, and for putting Emperor Fluffbottom on her bulletin board. Natalie Sousa for creating the cover of my dreams (see what I did there). And of course: Romy Golan, Heather David, Matt Bloomgarden, Stephanie Abrams, Lori Paximadis for handling all the rest.

The VIP Read Team: Sarah Carden, Annie Martyr, Jennifer Graham, Marty Keating. For approaching the drafts I sent and questions I asked with dedication and, most of all, enthusiasm, fuel that kept me running until the end.

My Family: Mom, Dad, Mike, Andy, Shannon, and Laura, for their incredible encouragement, for always telling me I was funny, for always telling me to "write it down," and for being the lovable weirdos who gave me some of my best material.

Like Family: Nyssa Liebermann, Ghazal Moshfegh, Erin La Rosa, Cayley Lambur, Alexandra Jamali, Justine Wardrop, Kate Perry, Carly Holden, Kyle Blasman, Anthony Pucillo, Anna Carey, Nick Greer, Ben Shattuck, Nate Sherman, Pedro Noyola, Aaron Bergman, Liz Parker, Hopie Stockman, Susie Cooley, Alexis Deane, Rebecca Welsh, Matti Sloman, Susan Birkett, John Spooner. Some of you read, some of you spent entire dinners or walks or car rides discussing a bunch of teenagers I made up, and some of you just listened . . . which was often all I needed.

My Professors: Lisa Corrin for kindly and without judgment pointing out in an Art History paper that I cared more about the stories of the artists than the work they created. Jim Shepard and his amazing fiction seminars, for giving me purpose then and now.

The Ghosts of My Alloy Past: Lanie Davis, Katie Schwartz, Rachel Tobias, Liz Dresner, Theodora Guliadis, Beth Clarke, Emilia Rhodes, Stacey Silverman, Gina Girolamo, Maggie Cahill, Tripp Reed, Cheryl Dolins, Amanda Bowman, Ashley Williams, and Monsieur Socktopus, all of whom helped me along this journey from assistant . . . to assistant . . . to eventual author.

J. Allan Hobson, for his wonderful book *The Dreaming Brain*.

And of course, Ernie The Dog, who always keeps me laughing.

SOMETIMES YOU HAVE TO
READ BETWEEN THE LINES . . .

Keep reading for a sneak peek at Lucy Keating's new novel *Literally*,
a book about a book about falling in love:

Instinctual Response

IT'S 3:02 P.M. on Sunday afternoon, and I should be cleaning my room. Not because it's particularly dirty—it never is. Not because my parents told me to—they never would. Because my calendar says so—in yellow. Errands and necessary "upkeep" are yellow; homework blue; exercise (running on the Boardwalk, surfing with my dad) purple; appointments (teeth cleaning, haircut at The Hive) are in hot pink; and events like dinner with Ava at Papa's Poke Shop or Nisha's birthday party in Malibu are a bright teal. I call that one my "Friends/Fun" section. There are other categories for other things, but I won't bore you with the details. I'm a very visual person. I get that from my mother. I am also highly organized. I get that from absolutely nobody in my family.

The problem with it being three P.M., when I should be cleaning my room, is that I am not. Instead I am lying on my stomach on the living room floor, staring into the eyes of Napoleon, who, from his place under the wheat-colored sofa, stares back at me with challenging eyes, a lone pair of my underpants hanging out of his mouth.

"Don't do it, Napoleon," I warn.

Napoleon growls.

Ava told me the other day, after Napoleon growled at her, too, that she wasn't offended, because it was an instinctual response. "Sometimes the body reacts in ways we can't help, as a way of letting us know how we're really feeling," she told me. "Like how Nisha turns beet red whenever Ray Woods utters even a partial sentence to her. Or you always sweat in your armpits during exams. Or how I've barfed before almost every flight I've ever taken."

"My armpits don't sweat during exams," I protested, and Ava just smiled. It is very like Ava to say something like that. To dwell, not so much on the fact that something is happening, but rather why it is happening in the first place. She is good at trying to see the other side. For me, it's not so complicated. Things happen or they don't. You make them happen or not. And I consider an unexpected, instinctual response—blushing and sweating and growling—highly inconvenient.

Slowly, I reach a hand toward Napoleon's sofa cave, and his growl becomes a snarl. I withdraw my hand with an eye roll that I like to believe he can understand.

Napoleon is my father's dog. He is also my mortal enemy. It's not that I don't like dogs. Those golden retrievers you see lying by the fire in a soup commercial, for example, doing nothing but wagging their tails. Or that bulldog who rides a skateboard, wearing sunglasses, his tongue flapping in the wind. But Napoleon is different. My father found Napoleon in an alley with a dead rat when he was only a few months old. "Poor guy," he said. "Living in conditions like that." But I know the truth. I know that Napoleon challenged that rat to a fight to the death, and Napoleon won.

The back door to the kitchen opens and in wanders my mother, iPad directly in front of her face as she walks, her bob of straight blond hair swinging along with her, followed by Jae, her new design intern. At least I assume it's Jae. I can't see his face behind the giant stack of rolled-up pieces of vellum paper, probably displaying the plans for another one of her beautiful Southern California homes. Mom's specialty is remodeling old bungalows. She has a reputation for simplifying a house's design, modernizing it just enough, but without losing the character of the place. With deep oak floors and heavy beams balanced by bright white walls and mid-century furniture, our house is one of her best advertisements. One of the exotic pillows she sourced from India is currently wedged under my elbows.

"What are you doing on the floor?" my mom asks, still staring at her iPad as she sets down her bag and motions Jae to drop the plans on the counter. Then she grabs two seltzers from the fridge and hands one to him.

"Napoleon has my underpants," I explain.

"What a little pervert," she replies.

Jae just smiles politely. "Hi, Annabelle."

"Hey, Jae," I say, and then I sigh. I want to ask my mother if she could maybe refrain from calling our dog a pervert in front of her intern to whom I have never spoken more than four words on one individual occasion, but I know there's no use. My mother is unconcerned with formalities.

"How do you plan to get them back?" she asks now, finally setting the iPad down and looking over at me.

"Murder him," I say definitively, and she snorts. I glance back at Napoleon. He has not moved a muscle.

"You're a monster," I whisper.

"I'll pretend I didn't hear that," my father says as he strolls into the kitchen, his salt-and-pepper hair in its usual bed-head state, his jeans rolled round the ankles. Nobody ever hears him coming because he is consistently barefoot. "That's the beauty of working from home," he'll say if you point this out.

There's a joke in there, if you know where to look. The joke is that my dad hasn't "worked" in years. He was a TV writer in the late 1990s before selling a big ensemble comedy to a major network, and, after the finale in 2006, hasn't been to an office since. He spends most mornings surfing, which he took up after retirement, and reading, which he's always done. There's a smaller guest house behind our house that my dad refers to as his "lair," where he reads, screens movies, and takes an occasional meeting. Lately, he's been spending more time out there than usual, and occasionally, I've noticed him coming out early in the morning. He must be onto a new idea.

"Should we take a drive?" he asks the room. I notice how wrinkly his T-shirt is. "Head up to Topanga State Beach, maybe grab an early dinner and watch the sunset? What do you say, *you*?"

The *you* is always directed to *me*. I know it's kind of weird, like my own father can't remember my name, but it's actually the opposite. Something about the way he says it makes me feel like I am the only *you* there is. And that makes me feel good.

"I have plans," I explain. "Is that the T-shirt you were wearing yesterday?"

"Forgive me!" my father exclaims, ignoring my question. "What's on deck?"

I steel myself for a moment, considering that maybe if I talk really fast, they won't make fun of me, and we can be done with this conversation. "Well, I have to clean my room and then I have to take a run and—"

My father shoots a glance at my mother, like *How did we create this?* "Maybe you should shake things up a little bit? Prove to yourself that the world isn't going to end if you don't clean your room this afternoon?"

I frown, contemplating his suggestion.

"What are you doing on the floor?" my brother, Sam, says as he bustles into the kitchen, grabbing an apple and taking a giant bite. "Did Napoleon steal your socks again?" he manages through muffled chews.

"Underpants," my mother explains.

"You wanna go for a drive?" my father asks Sam. "Make a day of it? The whole family is coming."

"I'm not available," I say loudly. Why is it so hard for them to understand that even though they prefer to thwart general structure in their own lives, that's not the way I choose to live?

"Right." Sam rolls his eyes. "Maybe in between cleaning your room and taking a run you could find time to remove the giant stick from your–"

"Sam," my father warns. But you can tell he finds it funny.

I am just about to lose my temper when Napoleon makes a break for it, his scraggly body darting out from under the couch and through the kitchen door, which Sam just left wide open.

"Catch him!" I cry, but nobody even pretends to move. I scramble out after Napoleon and into the yard, but I've lost his trail. I am just kneeling down to look under a hydrangea bush, insincerely cooing his name, when I hear it.

"Looking for these?" a voice says, all crackly with just a hint of smirk. I cringe, knowing to whom the voice belongs, then turn slowly to find Elliot Apfel standing in the middle of my lawn, a paper-thin T-shirt falling over his sinewy shoulders, an unreadable expression on his lightly freckled face, my thankfully clean underpants dangling between the thumb and forefinger of his right hand. In his left, squirming like a mutant piglet, is Napoleon.

"Yes," I mutter, feeling myself blush as I snatch them away, and getting more frustrated when I remember what Ava said. Then I think, if there was literally one person on this entire planet I would hope to never be standing on my front lawn holding my underpants, it's Elliot. He will never let me live this down.

"Hot pink?" I hear him say behind me as I turn back to the house.

"Must you comment?" I call out without stopping.

"Did you really expect me not to?" I hear him call back.

Elliot is my brother's best friend. He used to be mine, too, back when we were little. We're the same age. Our moms went to art school together, before they diverged into photography and architecture. But then Elliot hit puberty and started acting weird and also, frankly, rude. And then he got a girlfriend and then another . . . and then another. Elliot has had more girlfriends than I have organizational colors on my calendar, which has always totally boggled my mind, since I don't think he's ever even heard of shampoo.

Now he has Clara, and she has lasted longer than most. Clara is the lead singer of Look at Me, Look at Me, the band that Elliot and Sam started together, the reason Sam states for why he decided to postpone college. I'm nearly one hundred percent certain the real reason is surfing, and I wonder if my parents know this, too. I wonder if, like me, they know it's unlikely that Sam will go to college at all.

Back in the kitchen, my family is still standing around chatting, more like roommates than humans who share genes.

"Elliot!" My dad points a finger enthusiastically. "I bet *you* wanna go for a drive."

"We can't actually, Dad," Sam cuts in. "We have rehearsal. I totally forgot." He turns to Elliot. "Sorry."

Elliot shoves his hands in his pockets. "We're gonna have to postpone rehearsal for a while, actually . . . considering Clara quit the band this afternoon." He purses his lips.

To know Clara Bernard is to know her Instagram. The entirety of my knowledge of her I've gleaned from there. Since she's usually taking selfies or keeping her lips suctioned to Elliot's face, it's difficult to glean her true essence. But her Instagram is well curated. Lots of well-lit, California-girl pictures of her on the beach, or leaning against one of the vintage cars at Elliot's dad's shop, her dark brown hair falling out of some floppy brimmed hat, or writing lyrics moodily in a notebook. The only thing Clara loves more than her Instagram is her boyfriend. At least that's what I always thought.

"She quit?" Sam asks, his eyes wide.

Elliot shrugs. "Apparently, the girl half of He/She got laryngitis and they asked her to fill in."

"Well, she'll be back," Sam says a little frantically, running a hand through his thick hair. Sam has my dad's hair, dark brown and prone to sticking out in wild directions, and I have my mom's. So blonde it's not even California; it's more like snow queen. "I mean, we're all in this together." Sam's voice is slowly increasing in tone and volume as he waits for Elliot to reply. "That's the plan. And she has *you*." He motions to Elliot, and the *you* is an actual squeak. "She'd never give up on you."

For a split second, a shadow flashes across Elliot's unreadable expression. Then he swallows. "Clara and I broke up," he says.

Nobody seems to know how to respond to this statement. Everyone just watches Elliot as he nods his head repeatedly, as it to say *Yes, it's true* to our unspoken questions. Even if I can't stand him, even if he did knock a glass of water onto my laptop while skateboarding through our house a month ago, and call me an embarrassing nickname in front of the captain of the water polo team last Thursday, I have to admit I feel the tiniest bit bad for him. He may never wash his T-shirts and Clara may have the depth of a wading pool, but somehow they worked. Not to mention they're an unnervingly good-looking couple. Were. Past tense.

Elliot exhales then, and I look down, realizing I'm still holding my underpants.

Also by Lucy Keating

Lucy Keating

LITERALLY

a book **about a book** about falling in love

HARPER TEEN

An Imprint of HarperCollins*Publishers*

www.epicreads.com

JOIN THE

Epic Reads
COMMUNITY

THE ULTIMATE YA DESTINATION

◄ **DISCOVER** ►
your next favorite read

◄ **MEET** ►
new authors to love

◄ **WIN** ►
free books

◄ **SHARE** ►
infographics, playlists, quizzes, and more

◄ **WATCH** ►
the latest videos